International acclaim for Susan Swan's
The Wives of Bath

Also by Susan Swan

The Biggest Modern Woman in the World
The Last of the Golden Girls
Unfit for Paradise
Stupid Boys Are Good to Relax With

The Wives of Bath

VINTAGE CANADA

A Division of Random House of Canada Limited

For Patrick, who was there

———

VINTAGE CANADA EDITION, 1994

Copyright © 1993 by Susan Swan
Preface copyright © 2001 by Susan Swan

All rights reserved under International and Pan-American
Copyright Conventions. Published in Canada in 1994
by Vintage Books Canada, a division of Random House of
Canada Limited, Toronto. First published in Canada in 1993
by Alfred A. Knopf Canada, Toronto. Distributed by
Random House of Canada Limited, Toronto.

Canadian Cataloguing in Publication Data

Susan Swan
The wives of Bath

ISBN 0-676-97454-6

I. Title.

PS8587.W345W58 1994   C813'.54   C94-931877-9
PR9199.3.S83W58 1994

Printed and bound in The United States of America

Preface: A Novel's Journey into Film

Writers often dream of their novel being made into a successful film. But a sad, little sinking feeling overcame me the moment I heard the screenwriter wanted to set the film version of *The Wives of Bath* in the present. This would mean jettisoning the time period of my novel about a murder at a girls' boarding school. Its tale of a friendship triangle between three girls reflects some aspects of my own experience as a boarder at Havergal College in Toronto in the early 1960s, so this period was nostalgic for me. It was a transition era before the protest generation—dominated by President Kennedy and the Peace Corps, lingering sexual taboos and rigid definitions of what it meant to be male and female. The ideas associated with this period were central to the novel. Hence my sense of loss. Could I bear to let someone else change my story? But the screenwriter, Judith Thompson, one of Canada's best-known playwrights, thought these ideas could carry over into the present. She didn't grow up in the 1960s and preferred to use a contemporary idiom.

My background in theatre meant I already knew that adaptations of novels were not adaptations at all, but translations, and with a very few exceptions, most theatre performances and films will suffer if the director tries to duplicate the book. Likely all of us have gone through the experience of going to the film of a well-loved book and coming away disappointed. Surprisingly, these films are often the result of a director trying to stay slavishly true to the novelist's vision. Directors risk turning a novel into a lifeless film unless they are free to create their own interpretation of a book. I'd learned this in the 1970s collaborating on theatre pieces with Toronto choreographers. Time after time, I was told my word-based notions wouldn't read on the stage. Time after time, the choreographers were right, and I learned to trust those with theatre experience.

Using language skilfully is not only the novelist's most powerful tool, it's the central tool and the matrix of the story. Novelists have to create the effects, including making a character, through dialogue and descriptive passages. Plays depend, in part, on verbal play for their dramatic impact while films are not a linguistic medium at all. Dialogue aside, language in screenplays is used to point to the right kind of imagery. This is humbling, but essential for a novelist to understand! So I uttered a bittersweet sigh and gave Judith the go-ahead with the modern setting.

Later, reading Judith's original screenplay, I was delighted by her interpretation of the boarding school triangle although superficially her script looked vastly different from my novel. For one thing, Judith's characters now spoke modern slang. And there were other changes. One of the girls' cultish worship of King Kong as a symbol of masculine power had been exchanged for the love of a falcon, kept secretly on the school grounds; the boarding school of Bath Ladies College was now liberal; and Mouse, the narrator, had lost the hump that might have made her look a little grotesque on the big screen.

Still, I was pleased to see how closely Judith kept to the emotional ground of the story and to its three characters. Intact were Paulie Sykes, the boarding school rebel who wants to pass as a boy; the kind and beautiful Tory Quinn, who struggles with Paulie's idealizing love; and Mouse Bradford, the timid new boarder. She'd made Paulie, Tory and Mouse come alive through believable screen dialogue and skilful interpretations of the emotionally important scenes in the novel.

For instance, in the novel, Mouse has a dream in which she is unable to help her dead mother when one of the vengeful boarding school matrons shears off her mother's golden hair in a tower room and pours oil on her mother's frilled blouse. In the screenplay, the three girls read, out loud to one other, letters that they've each written to their mothers. Tory confesses she's as addicted to her mother's love as she is to chocolate; Mouse worries she can't remember her mother's face now that she's dead; and Paulie asks her mother—a teen prostitute who gave her up for adoption—to meet her for a beer on the same street where, Paulie writes, "you sell your ass." This is a funny and profound scene because the audience sees not only Mouse's vulnerability but the vulnerability of the other two and the way all their fates are inextricably affected by their mothers' personalities and expectations.

A mother is, for better or worse, a girl's first role model. And for me, the core of the novel revolves around the struggle of the three girls to come to terms with what they feel is an unheroic identity, namely, growing up female. In the novel, Mouse is confused by the two female choices in the early 1960s. On the one hand, Mouse sees the mothers of the boarders who meet the feminine standards of the day, but lack real power or authority. On the other, she encounters the teachers and matrons of the boarding school who remind her of Chaucer's Wife of Bath because they are the only women she has met who live by their own rules. Yet even their power is limited, and Mouse concludes near the end of the novel: "We were all Wives of Bath—from the teachers who terrorized us with their bells and gatings… But no matter how hard any of us struggled. . . Bath Ladies College was only a fiefdom in the kingdom of men."

In Judith's script, set in the 1990s, the teachers and matrons are kinder and less marginalized than their counterparts in the novel. They actually seem to like the girls and identify with them, although they are just as helpless as the older women were in the novel to prevent Paulie's self-destructive and violent descent. In the early days of the filmmaking, Judith and I on occasion read our versions of the same scene from the novel and screenplay at literary festivals. Inevitably, I was struck by how little she needed to say to evoke a character. For instance, once after I read the novel's opening pages (in which Mouse explains to the reader who she is and then sets up Paulie's crime as "a bizarre, Napoleonic act of self-assertion"), Judith brought down the house—theatrically speaking— with her terser version in Paulie's voice, "I killed him for his dick."

The film of *The Wives of Bath* changed both directors and production companies twice before the option to make the film was given to the award-winning independent director Lea Pool and Montreal producers

Cite-Amerique, who premiered the film to great acclaim at the Sundance Film Festival and Berlin International Film Festival in 2001. Half a decade after I agreed to a present-day setting, I was lucky enough to see Lea Pool's film *Emporte-moi*. When Cite-Amerique came in with an offer that included matching the talent of Lea Pool with Judith Thompson's original screenplay, I accepted readily.

If Judith understood how to make the passion of teenage girls live in scenes and dialogue, Pool, in her turn, appreciated the Sapphic quality of their teenage love. However, as Pool told an audience member at Sundance, she never saw the novel or her film as a lesbian coming-out story. For her, it is a story of adolescent love at a time in girls' lives when they are unaware of sophisticated political and sexual preferences. This was very much how I saw the story too.

The representation of adult sexuality in *Lost and Delirious*, as the film was eventually called, is openly celebratory, unlike the alienated sex scenes in the novel which reflect the repressions of the early 1960s when boarders were so embarrassed by their bodies that they undressed in washroom cubicles or took their uniforms off under their nightgowns. Consider the scene in the novel when Mouse spies on a fellow boarder, Ismay Thom, struggling into her merry widow. "She appeared to be stuck in the tight, elasticized material, which squeezed her blubbery thighs together like breasts. A gross kind of leg cleavage, you could say." The sexuality in the novel has little in common with the stunning sex-positive scenes that had film critic Roger Ebert remarking in a *Chicago Sun-Times* review (January 2001) that, "You're absorbed from beginning to end because the characters are enormously interesting and likable. And because they are gorgeous. And because you could hear a pin drop in the 1,400-seat Eccles Center during the sex scenes which are not explicit, but are erotic." Despite the beautiful sex scenes in Pool's film, the actors nevertheless express the girls' frustration with their female roles, and their need to make what is perceived as unheroic, heroic. In the film, the girls discuss Lady Macbeth in class (a scene that's not in the novel) in a way that underscores, comically and movingly, how young women can see femininity as something weak and passive.

I was inspired to base the conclusion of *The Wives of Bath* on a heinous crime that took place in Toronto in 1978. A seventeen-year-old girl, who regularly passed herself off as a male gas jockey, murdered an elderly Toronto taxi driver. Dressed as a girl, she lured him to her room on the pretext that she needed his help with some luggage. Then she killed him with a baseball bat, cut off his genitals and pasted them on her body with Krazy Glue. In this woeful garb, she presented herself to her girlfriend's father who had accused her of not being a real man.

Although you won't see this crime portrayed in Pool's brilliant film, you will see something equally surprising and stirring in its place. When I found out late in the production of the film that Pool had left out the novel's ending, I suspected the producers of watering down the story for commercial reasons. As the credits came up, and my film agent, Tina Horwitz, and I staggered happily from our seats, I realized I was relieved that Pool had chosen another ending. The crime in the novel was a device to reflect on the characters' thoughts and feelings about themselves as girls, but Lea Pool's camera didn't need the crime to convey these same things. To stick with my ending might have tipped her powerful drama over into the genre of film horror because cinematic effects are so much more visceral and immediate than words on a page. To portray something so horrific in the film might have interfered with the audience's ability to stay with the story.

It's rare for novelists to be shamelessly satisfied with their book's journey into film. However, I feel as if my story about boarding school girls has passed through the imaginations of three women sitting around a campfire, each one adding their unique knowledge to my tale of female rebellion and adolescent love. Writers and readers should never hold it against a film if the film isn't exactly like the book it was based on. The question is—is it a good movie? That, in the end, is film's truest service to a work of literature.

Susan Swan
New York, 2001

Tell me also, to what conclusion
were the generative organs made,
And fashioned by so generous a maker?

—from the prologue to
The Wife of Bath's Tale,
by Geoffrey Chaucer
(author's translation)

Part One

Part One

The ghostly woman on the giant tricycle stared down at me like an old friend. Only "stared" is the wrong word. The lids of her eyes were collapsed inwards—puckered the way a pair of lips look when all the teeth are removed.

"You," I said, but the figure didn't seem to hear me. I began to tremble and sigh. Now this odd creature made an excited clicking sound, the kind of coaxing noise you make to a horse. She lifted the handlebars of her bike so the front wheel reared up on one end.

"Where did you bury him, Mouse? Is he in the geranium garden? Or did you hide him in the old hockey shed?"

"I can't remember," I said in my meekest voice. Scowling, she settled her shoulders into a racing hunch, as if a hundred unseen bicycle riders were about to overtake her, and pedalled vigorously through the doorway. In the dark below I could hear the clank and rumble of the heating pipes. There was no other way out now. Rising around me on all sides, instead of the grey sandstones of the school—I saw rows of shiny eyeballs with slowly nictitating lids. I swallowed fast and went through the door to find her.

1

My name is Mouse—Mouse Bradford. Mary Beatrice Bradford, if I want to be long-winded about it. I'm sixteen now, the same age Paulie was when she performed her weird, Napoleonic act of self-assertion. It was my father's scalpel she used, not the X-Acto knife mentioned in the news—a B-P Rib Back surgical blade, one and three-quarter inches long and brand-new. My stepmother, Sal, must have ordered it for Morley from the Hartz medical catalogue. I kept it in his doctor's bag in my room at school. The bag was hardly bigger than a lady's purse. A real dandy in black natural-grain cowhide with a wrap-over lock and double handles of solid leather. I needed to have it around to remind me of Morley. Otherwise I had nothing to prove I was his daughter except for my deep-set eyes with their odd, luminous stare, and my queer five-inch fingers. "A pianist's hands"—that's how the guidance counsellor described them. She didn't say I had surgeon's hands like my father. She didn't expect girls like me or Paulie to have a serious profession. Even our headmistress, Miss Vaughan, believed a backup skill was all we needed. I can't say their views bothered me. I didn't want to own hands that could wield a scalpel with semi-murderous precision. I mean—yes, I'd better be clear about what I mean or Alice will have my head—if you could slice precise little rips in the right places so nobody would know you'd carved your patient up like the Thanksgiving turkey, well, then, you'd be capable of carving up anybody, anytime.

Luckily, for me a medical life was never in the cards. I faint easily, for one thing. The sight of blood does me in. Even the word "needle" makes me feel lightheaded. I can't imagine my own hands on Morley's scalpel cutting out a new identity for myself.

I'm five foot four and a half in my stocking feet—not really what you'd call big, although I have met many girls shorter than I am. The main mouselike things about me are my slender, fan-shaped ears and my long, pointed nose, which makes me look older and wiser than I am. I am clever, though, and I don't take up much room. My left shoulder is also slightly rounded—some would say I'm humpbacked like a rodent, and I can't argue with that. I call my hump "Alice," after my real mother; it's from the German name *Adelaide*, meaning "of noble birth." Alice, poor soul, is not as smart as I am, but she keeps me on my toes. She won't stand for anything but the truth.

For instance, I know Alice would feel better if I told you about my part in Paulie's crime, because there is no one else who will listen. I can't talk to Sal, whose shaming voice is more than I can handle. You see, Sal took me out of school when Paulie did what she did and sent me off to stay with my uncle in Point Edward (or Punk Edward, as Morley used to call it). Sal says it doesn't matter that I did nothing legally wrong. Where there's smoke, there's fire, so it's better if I stay out of sight.

I wasn't born with gross spinal curvature, or kyphosis, as doctors like Morley call it. Polio caused the muscles in my back to atrophy and made my spine torque to the left, as if somebody had twisted it too tightly with a screwdriver. Morley thought I might outgrow the torque in my spine, but the specialist the school sent me to said I needed chiropractic treatment. Morley meant to take me to a specialist sooner or later. Morley meant to do a lot of things.

As Sal likes to point out, shoemakers' children don't have shoes. She used to tell me this as she pushed me out the door of our kitchen in Madoc's Landing, right after she'd muffled me in a headscarf wrapped around my mouth, like the veil of Islam. On the way to school my breath would coat the scarf with moisture, and the moisture would freeze into tiny ice balls, and the icy material would rub my nostrils, already raw and pink from too much nose blowing. I'd want to cry, but that would only make my nose wetter and rawer, so I'd lurch down our front walk, past the snowdrifts that rose as high as our windowsills, devising ways to raise my temperature. A fever was the only symptom Morley respected.

A half a line higher than 98.6 degrees Fahrenheit and I could stay home. When I turned twelve, I experimented with hot cloths and small mustard plasters on the forehead. Masturbating made my forehead hot, too. Only I wasn't organized enough to pull it off. And I was afraid Sal would walk in and catch me with the evidence on my forehead or my hand where it wasn't supposed to be.

The cold is a funny emblem for unrequited love, but that's how it is with me. I get three doozies of a head cold a winter because of the unresolved feelings I have about my father. I guess some people have dead saints to worship, and I have Morley. At least the common cold isn't as embarrassing as amoebic dysentery, whose description in Morley's old medical text as a severe disturbance of the gastrointestinal tract sounds like a weather condition. I used to pretend I'd come down with the symptoms so Sal would take me to see Morley. It was hard to believe the huge, distracted man balancing on an office stool, his white coat smelling of starch and chemicals, was related to me.

At first, Morley went along with the charade. He'd wink at Sal and scribble out a prescription for me. I'll say that for my father: he could relate to anything in a medical textbook. Then Sal told him he was training me to be a liar, and he stopped.

Whenever I start coming down with a head cold that would lay even the great doctor Morley Bradford flat, I hear Sal's voice talking about shoemakers' children. If I'm feeling hard on myself

I'll let her go on for a while. But if I'm in a nicer mood, I'll say to myself, Oh, poor Mouse, have a good cry, you dear soul, bawl your heart out. And then, of course, I can't cry a drop.

There are other things to know about me, but I wanted to bring up the main points first: my hopelessly unrequited love for Morley and my unsightly back. The other notable feature is my shyness.

Usually I don't talk much, but when I do, Sal claims I go off on tangents, like a tomato plant that grows too many tendrils. "Back to the root now, Mouse," she says whenever I get to the good part of my story. Sal likes me to stick to the main subject and avoid tendrils like the plague. I like tendrilling, but it's a suspicious pastime to a farm woman like Sal, who grew up on the Elmvale flats and happened to be hanging around Madoc's Landing after my mother, the first Alice, went and died on my father. But Sal has more imagination than you'd expect. For instance, she's good at making up sayings you'd never think of yourself. Most of her sayings are about dogs. As in "You can't teach an old dog new tricks." Or "It's a dog's life." Or "You can lead a dog to water, but you can't make it drink."

When the scandal blows over, Sal says I can come back and help her run the rooming house she's made of Morley's home and mine in Madoc's Landing. Until then I have to stay here in Point Edward with my uncle and my companion Alice, who is like a mother to me. Except no mother I know tells off-colour jokes.

— That reminds me, Mouse. Why don't girls have penises?
— Because they don't want them?
— Don't be a dope. Because girls think with their heads.

So you see, Sal is right: I'm going off on a tendril now when I should be getting back to Paulie Sykes and how she played her little game of pin-the-tail-on-the-donkey at Bath Ladies College.

2

Morley's scalpel was Exhibit 3 at the trial. Paulie's trial, of course. The trial between Her Majesty the Queen and Pauline Lee Sykes. Exhibit 1 was the photographs, seven of them, showing the deceased lying behind the old cycling trunk in the heating tunnel. I don't know why the photographs came first, before the murder weapons. I'd have started with the hockey stick myself. As it turned out, the stick, whose long handle had been wrapped many times with black construction tape, was Exhibit 2.

HIS LORDSHIP: Those are photos of the room in which the crime was committed and the weapons used?

INSPECTOR GOSSAGE: That is correct, my lord.

HIS LORDSHIP: Seven photographs.

INSPECTOR GOSSAGE: Yes, my lord.

HIS LORDSHIP: And the body of the deceased was concealed behind the trunk at the extreme east end of the tunnel?

INSPECTOR GOSSAGE: Yes, at first.

HIS LORDSHIP: It was hidden from view, then, was it?

INSPECTOR GOSSAGE: It was hidden from view because of the trunk being there, and also because of the way in which the body had been prepared for concealment. It was wrapped up in various garments—a lady's skirt, and so on.

HIS LORDSHIP: And before that, it was placed in the trunk?

INSPECTOR GOSSAGE: Yes, my lord, but it wouldn't fit. So it was placed as we see here, behind the trunk.

HIS LORDSHIP: And the lacrosse stick? And the knife?

INSPECTOR GOSSAGE: Two corrections, my lord. You are looking at a field-hockey stick and a scalpel.

HIS LORDSHIP: And placed in the trunk, were they, afterwards?

INSPECTOR GOSSAGE: That is correct.

HIS LORDSHIP: How would you describe the field-hockey stick?

INSPECTOR GOSSAGE: Weighing about three pounds, my lord. A good blunt instrument that could be put to a variety of uses.

HIS LORDSHIP: And the knife? Is this the knife in the photograph?

INSPECTOR GOSSAGE: Scalpel, my lord.

HIS LORDSHIP: And how would you describe, the, uh—scalpel?

INSPECTOR GOSSAGE: It looks like an X-Acto knife, only it's more sturdy. A series of tiny curved blades that fit into a Bakelite handle, my lord.

HIS LORDSHIP: It's plastic-handled—

INSPECTOR GOSSAGE: Bakelite, my lord.

HIS LORDSHIP: And the knife—blade, is about, what, five inches?

INSPECTOR GOSSAGE: I believe, my lord, it is only one and three-quarters. B-P Rib Back blade number twenty—very sharp, my lord.

HIS LORDSHIP: It was the property of another student, I believe?

INSPECTOR GOSSAGE: Yes, my lord. A student named Mary Beatrice Bradford, my lord.

HIS LORDSHIP: What sort of school was this? A training ground for doctors or psychopaths?

INSPECTOR GOSSAGE: I don't know, my lord. [Laughter]

That wasn't the only mention of my name at the trial. I sat at the back of the courtroom, glad Morley wasn't there. It felt like I was at one of the endless morning services at Bath Ladies College. The voices of counsel addressing the judge intoning—yes, my lord—sounded as if they were addressing God himself.

3

I didn't meet Paulie right away. Not as Paulie, anyhow. If I'd had any idea what was going to happen, I'd have asked Morley to turn back the day he and Sal drove me down to Bath Ladies College. It began to rain as soon as we left the Landing. See, Mouse—pathetic fallacy, I told myself.

Nobody said a word as we rolled farther and farther south, passing farmhouses that weren't really farmhouses but mansions, with high green hedges and white fences for horses to jump over, and little shops with wagon wheels positioned by the door to let you know they sold antiques. It was the sort of namby-pamby countryside you could imagine Virginia Woolf walking through in her long skirts. I often thought of Virginia when I felt low, because she was so depressed she drowned herself in a stream with her pockets full of stones. In my opinion, it always helps to remember there is somebody sadder than you.

All three of us were staring grumpily at the rain-soaked windshield of Blinky, Morley's new turquoise Olds 98. I called it Blinky as a joke, because its convertible top went down slowly, like a hydraulic lift, instead of in the blink of an eye. Even Morley called it Blinky in his relaxed moments, but that day he was cross, because the rain was forcing him to drive without his beloved fedora. With its top up, Blinky didn't have enough headroom to accommodate Morley in a hat.

His fedora sat crumpled and lonely on the top of my steamer trunk, which was jammed into the back seat beside me. The car trunk was too full of junk Sal had collected from the church rummage sale.

I was out of sorts myself. That afternoon Sal had made me dress in the school uniform, although there was nothing in the school brochure asking girls to wear it on the first day. But she bullied me into putting on the green tunic and white blouse. (I'd negotiated myself out of the dumb-looking tie.) Just look at yourself, Mouse, I thought. You're as conspicuous as a convict. Set apart from normal people by a little dress that nobody in their right mind would wear.

Of course, Sal wasn't happy, either. She always got carsick, although she didn't think it was ladylike to say it out loud. Sal believed that suffering in silence was a woman's lot. To look happy was a show of bad faith, a way of letting your sex down. Sal said we were born martyrs. Maybe we were even martyrs in the womb.

In front of me, Morley pressed his push-button window, and now the rainy breeze was tugging at Sal's knotted black bun. It nestled like a furry slug under the silly pillbox hat she kept in place with a pearl-studded hatpin. She sighed and fidgeted with the black strands of hair that fanned out across the white skin of her neck like sea anemones in a current. Her little dark head was hardly higher than Morley's shoulder. I liked to wonder how a woman her size could have sex with a man as tall as Morley. I often sneaked looks at him when he walked down the hall without his pyjama bottoms, on those mornings he thought I was still asleep, and the size of him shut down my imagination. I guess Morley's penis set a standard— something for other men to aim at.

Morley accelerated over a small rise, and suddenly we were in a long, winding ravine. I saw a sign that said "Wilbury Hollow" and a parking lot where people carrying umbrellas were hurrying out of the rain onto red-and-grey buses. On the hill to the west, a medieval-looking stone house squatted in a grove of spindly trees. I recognized Bath Ladies College from the school brochure. It said the building had been commissioned by a Sir Jonathon Gilbert Bath, who'd hired a British architect to design it like a Norman castle, because he wanted a home in which to entertain Queen Victoria. Sal figured Sir Jonathon was a ne'er-do-well, because he'd only got as far as tea with the queen's third son, Prince Arthur, before his debts forced him to sell the place. It was bought by a board of Anglican trustees who wanted to start a girls' boarding school on the outskirts of Toronto. They kept the name of its original owner because the place was already known in the city as Bath Castle.

"My God! It looks like a prison," Morley said quietly to Sal, who was sitting in my place, the seat next to Morley.

"All schools do," Sal said, and she quickly turned up the radio so we could hear a news broadcast about the American president, John Kennedy, celebrating his wedding anniversary with his family. His anniversary was a little sad this year, the announcer said, because the Kennedys had lost their new baby son, Patrick, in August.

"The poor tyke," Morley sighed, and Sal turned the radio off. Slowly we climbed the ravine hill, until we came to a green sign on tall metal poles that said "Bath Ladies College" in purple and gold letters. On a grassy field behind a tall wire fence, beefy women with curved sticks were whacking a ball in the rain. Then we turned into a narrow drive lined with weeping willows. Their wet boughs dragged close to our windshield, like the soggy ears of English sheepdogs.

Morley pulled up in front of the turreted building that we had seen from the road, and Sal and I stared at the front tower, which poked skyward like a disapproving finger. A flock of grey pigeons suddenly flew up from its roof and settled on the ivy-covered archway. The ivy had been partially cleared off over the door, and there, under a carving of the spiky tassel of a clover flower, I read the words, *"Built in 1890 as a residence by Sir Jonathon Gilbert Bath and shortly thereafter converted to Bath Ladies College for the instruction of Christian gentlewomen. Our daughters shall be useful and ornamental, like the clover that smells sweet in the meadow. Anno Domini 1896."*

I noticed skinny black strips of metal strung across the school windows. Bars—the school had bars. I didn't ask myself why. I've always been too suggestible for my own good.

The Trouble with Morley

I want to make this clear. I was sent to school for two reasons:

1. Its headmistress, Vera (the Virgin) Vaughan, was a distant cousin of Morley's.
2. Morley's unfortunate inferiority complex about bringing up females.

Naturally, this put me in a bit of a jam. Anybody related to Vera Vaughan was a traitor and a scum at school. And there was another problem: I didn't want to be locked up with people I didn't respect—i.e., girls, my least favorite gender. I didn't know how to explain this to Morley.

You see, Morley had never had a sister, and my mother died of a brain tumor four years after I was born, and he'd been counting on her to bring me up. Not that Morley looked down on women, like I did. Maybe he thought in secret that my mother had let him down, but he never said an unkind word against the female sex; he was just guilty of a failure to understand them, which turned out to be no favour to me.

I wish I could say I felt neutral about them, like Morley. I wanted to be as reasonable as possible. But girls were only mock boys as far as I was concerned. My embarrassment started with the American cowboy movies I saw in Madoc's Landing. I didn't like it when the whiny girl star would trick Audie Murphy into kissing her; I wanted him to get on with leading the cavalry charge. I'd ask Sal why Audie allowed girls to be in his movie. And she'd say: "To upset complainers like you."

Basically, you understand, Morley sent me to Bath Ladies College because Sal suggested it. He'd never have thought of it himself. She knew about his relative who ran a girls' school in the city, and she wanted to get rid of me.

"Do you see what I mean, Sal? There are bars on the windows here," Morley said. I felt smug. The school didn't impress me. It wasn't decrepit enough. And it didn't sit in a nasty-smelling marsh like Lowood, the school in *Jane Eyre* where girls dropped dead like flies of typhoid fever. I knew Morley didn't have time to read, so he wouldn't know about Lowood, and Sal said the books I read were for people who went to university. Except for the Eaton's catalogue, which she consulted each fall so she could order me a new winter coat, Sal is almost an illiterate.

Of course, my feelings for Sal are a little complicated. I needed her because she was the only person I knew who would take me shopping for a new posture corrector without feeling sorry for me. A little hump here or there was nothing to Sal. She'd been to Africa, where she'd nursed women with tapeworms, Dumdum fever, and lymphoedema of the breast. Once she'd treated a man with elephantiasis of the scrotum. She'd shown me a picture of what he looked like in *Manson's Tropical Diseases*. The poor guy's privates swelled up like a garden hose tied in a knot.

And Sal needed me because she had a secret. She drank. Only in her "C" mood, of course. She also had "A" and "B" moods. In her "A" mood, when Morley was around, she trilled her voice like an Irish colleen (Sal's word for anybody pretty). In her "B" mood, when Morley wasn't around, she talked gruffly, like the farmers who came to town to buy hip-length waders for smelt fishing. It was her "C" mood, the nightmare mode, that caused trouble for me. In her C mood, she fell asleep by supper, and I had to tell Morley she was tired from waxing the floors. Morley saw so many sick people every day in his office, I didn't want him to come home and face taking care of a drunk wife, too.

The worst thing about Sal, though, wasn't her drinking but her shaming voice. She always found something wrong with me and Morley no matter what we did. Morley would shrug it off, as if he expected it, but I took it to heart. You see, nobody's perfect. So no matter what Sal said, I felt she was right in general, even if she'd singled out the wrong thing specifically.

Meanwhile, in the front seat, Sal was turning her shaming voice on Morley. She tucked a large hunk of black hair back under her pillbox, her pearl hatpin between her teeth, and sighed. "Isn't it a little late to be having a change of heart, Morley?" I sat up. Was Morley going to utter the one sentence he should have spoken when Sal had come up with the idea in the first place? *My daughter will go to that school over my dead body.*

Naturally, I didn't want to go away and leave Morley. Maybe my father wasn't everybody's idea of Captain Courageous, but he came closer than anybody else to my all-time favourite hero, John F. Kennedy.

From what I'd read about Kennedy, I knew he'd never send his daughter, Caroline, to a girls' boarding school. If Sal had tried that on him, why, he would have slammed the door of his bubble-top limousine and hurried up the steps in that way of his which kept people from noticing his sore, stooped back. Then he would have thrown himself across the entrance, barring the door with his body.

"Look he-ah, Sal," he'd say. "It's not natural to stick anybody in a girls' school, cut off from her family. It's not how the real world is, Sal, back where I come from." And Sal would crumple up like a used Kleenex and throw her arms around my knees and beg my forgiveness.

The Trouble with Alice

Alice has always caused me problems. Children don't like her because she's a hump. I hold Victor Hugo responsible. And the actor Lon Chaney. Quasimodo had a hump in the back *and* the front. Plus protruding teeth and the zits that Victor Hugo politely referred to as "wens."

I don't look like Quasimodo, but when children notice me coming, that's who they see—Lon Chaney in the film version of *The Hunchback of Notre Dame*. A double-humped, one-eyed creature with legs that touch at the knees, like sickles. Never mind how nice Quasimodo was in his heart. Children don't think of that. They see a monster when they look at me, and then they behave in ways I'd still rather not talk about. When I was twelve they threw rotten oranges at me on my way home from school. That was when Sal first mentioned Bath Ladies College.

"Won't the girls treat her worse there?" Morley asked.

"Don't be silly," Sal said. "They like misfits at those sorts of places."

And Morley, the fool, replied: "Well, Sal, you're a woman. I guess you know best."

In the front seat, Morley answered Sal's question. "Yes, Sal, it's too late to change our minds now."

"Good," Sal said, and fiddled with her hat for the tenth time. "Because Mouse doesn't want to go back to the Landing. What would Norman Vincent Peale think about a girl who gave up on a place before she even tried it?" Sal paused. "He'd think she was a quitter, wouldn't he, Mouse?"

I had to hand it to Sal. Norman Vincent Peale and his persistence principle was an old favourite of mine. I used to read his column in *Life* magazine with the same intensity that Sal read her favourite feature in *The Ladies' Home Journal*, "Can This Marriage Be Saved?" Once I made the mistake of consulting Reverend Peale about Morley.

Dear Mr. Peale,

Sal and I have tried every way we know to perswade my father to take a full day off for Christmas. He hardly ever vacations. He is an elderly man and is not as young as he used to be. I am afraid he may dye from an attack of overwork. PLEASE give me some advise.

Hopefully yours,
Mary Beatrice

I didn't get an answer for two whole years, and I knew I'd got the address right: 488 Madison Avenue, New York, New York. Then I found my letter in Sal's corsage cupboard, and my big ears burned over the laugh she and Morley must have had about it. I didn't say a word to her about the letter. I slipped it into my pocket, and later I corrected the spelling mistakes and sent it off. Soon enough, Reverend Peale wrote back.

Dear Miss Bradford,

Keep working on your father. Remember! Plugging away will win the day.

Yours,
Norman

His answer should have made me feel better but I never wrote to him again.

Morley was doing a very Morley-like thing, revving the engine of the Olds. It wasn't a good omen for me. Morley usually revved a car when he was uncomfortable.

Finally, between a long *vroom-vroom-vroom*, he said: "You're a good old girl, aren't you, Mouse?"

Morley only called me a good old girl when he wanted something from me. And for a tenth of a second, his big, sad eyes found mine in the mirror. I nodded without thinking. Relieved, he lumbered out of the Olds and walked around to open the door for Sal. It was embarrassing the way Morley forgot about my presence. He stood in front of the school, grinning down at Sal as she tottered out of the car on her spike heels. She caught her balance, and in perfect "A"-mood form, the little flirt smiled up at her great god Morley.

I prayed in the back seat that Morley would look over at me and say he'd reconsider. Oh, Morley, I muttered, if you take me back home, I'll worship you like Sal. I'll even rush over to you with the Madoc's Landing *Bulletin,* the way the nurses do when you walk through the door of Lennox Street General. Yes, cross my heart and hope to die, I'm ready, like Sal and all the others, to serve the legendary Morley Bradford, the tallest doctor in Guilford Township—six feet seven inches in his stocking feet. A giant who stays up all night playing poker with the boys at the Grand and then operates next morning fresh as a daisy. Morley, please. If you do me this favour, I'll be as devoted to you as I am to President Kennedy.

But standing on the steps of Bath Ladies College, Morley looked like he always did: a big Morley balloon who'd float away if he weren't anchored to the ground by a pair of huge oxblood wing tips. The rest of my father, starting with the wide cuffs of his baggy grey flannels, billowed upwards out of my reach. Morley was a human dirigible growing in volume through the vested midriff and ending far above me in a big distracted balloon head. His smoky blue eyes were fixed on a spot on the horizon I couldn't see.

Then Sal pointed at me and Morley did a double take. He

mumbled, "Oh, there you are, Mouse," as if I had deliberately disappeared from view when I fumbled with my door handle. I glanced down, as if I didn't mind him overlooking me, and handed out my crutches. Then slowly, very slowly, I swung my feeble legs out of the car.

4

"To dig a hole, you must use a spade properly. Push with the ball of your instep—the ridge just behind your toes. See, Sergeant, how I hold the spade with one hand and kick it once into the ground?"

In a grove of elms, a large, white-haired woman was showing an odd little man how to dig a garden. She was twice his size and dressed in strange clothes for gardening—a tailored charcoal suit and high heels, although her snub-nosed pumps were the kind of shoes Sal calls "serviceable." Not the fancy kind, with toes so pointed you could kick out the eye of a snake. The little man's feet were hidden inside a child's pair of rubber boots. His overalls were kid-size too and he wore a Glengarry tam, or what the curlers in Madoc's Landing call a bonspiel hat. Every so often he bent down and patted a little corgi dog who sat at his feet. He was a dwarf.

Two figures stood nearby, a tall man, close to Morley's height, whom I guessed was European because he had a long, wilted moustache, and the men who wore moustaches in Madoc's Landing always came from Poland or someplace like that. He stood crouching over a wheelbarrow, handing chrysanthemums to a slender teenage boy in an old peaked hunting cap and khaki pants, who plopped the flowers into the freshly dug holes the older woman was digging. The boy looked gloriously wet and dirty.

The tall woman spied us and stopped digging. Smiling, she held up one of her palms to the heavens and I realized it had stopped drizzling, although the sun was nowhere in sight and the sky was still oyster-coloured behind the school's moisture-soaked lawns and stone buildings. Morley and Sal waited awkwardly, as if they, too, were new girls, while the woman lurched over to us, taking a short cut through one of the flower beds, so that the heels of her sensible pumps sunk halfway into the earth.

"Hello, cousin Morley." She held out a large hand to Morley, who shook it shyly, shifting back and forth on the pavement from one wing tip to the other. "And this must be your new wife, Mrs. Bradford." Her whispery voice sounded like the sulky voice of a girl. And yet the size of her made me think of a man. I looked at her curiously. Was she one of those creatures Sal calls a half-and-half? I'd never seen any man or woman quite like her. She was as big and round as a giant Toby jug, and I thought she looked the way Chaucer's Wife of Bath might have looked if she had stepped into the twentieth century: broad in the behind and out for herself, and the rest of the world could go hang. I knew there was a special breed of women like this who lived outside the rules of men, and I guessed she was one of them, whether she loved women in private or not. She wore her white hair parted in the middle and held flat against her large head with a pair of child's barrettes. In the back, it was twisted into a sausage roll that was kept in place by a black hairnet. Her suit was rumpled, the way my clothes look if I stay outdoors too long. Its jacket was cut too loosely around her large shoulders, and she hadn't bothered to wipe off the chalk smudges I noticed on its cuffs. I could tell Sal didn't know what to make of her, either, and I saw her move just a little closer to Morley.

"Hello, Miss Vaughan," Sal said nervously.

"Call me Vera, Mrs. Bradford." She saw Sal looking at her muddy heels and smiled. "If Sergeant would only use a spade properly, I wouldn't have to ruin my Sunday shoes. But I can't have him getting one of his backaches." She chuckled, and Morley and Sal and I all made chuckling sounds, too.

"Aye-aye! Only blisters." The dwarf sauntered over to us, the corgi at his heels. The little dog capered twice round the tiny man, who made a funny, two-fingered salute at the headmistress behind her back, but she turned and scowled at him with her aggrieved, circle-ringed eyes. He stopped dead in his tracks and hung his head, and his little dog squatted down too, like Lady, our golden retriever, when Morley tells her to sit.

"And you must be Mary," the headmistress said, turning her back on the dwarf. "It's always a pleasure to meet a member of the family." I felt my chest tighten. I didn't know how to answer her.

"Mary Beatrice is very shy," Sal said. "She won't talk until she feels at home."

"I understand. I'm shy, too." The headmistress waved at the teenage boy planting mums with the tall gardener. "Mary Beatrice," she said, "I want you to meet Lewis. I've put you in a room with his sister, Paulie."

The boy strolled over, clenching and unclenching his fists. His hands were large for his size and muscular and he walked like the boys in Madoc's Landing, who always shuffle their feet, as if the impulse to move starts with their big toes. Girls, where I come from, walk with a swaying pelvis and put their toes down last. "How do you do?" he said, and bowed. I couldn't take my eyes off the back of his neck, where his hair below the cap was shaved as short and sparse as the hair in front of a kitten's ears. I wished I could shave my hair like that.

"Having a good look, are yuh?" he hissed under his breath. He sounded spiteful, as if he wanted to hurt me. One of his front teeth was missing.

He's uneducated, I thought. And he thinks I'm looking down on him. I turned my head away shyly and pretended I didn't hear what he said.

Then he pointed to the Olds, where my steamer trunk sat in the back seat. "Can I carry in the new girl's suitcase?" he asked. In my heart of hearts, I admit I felt pleased.

"Thank you, Lewis. This is a job for Sergeant," Miss Vaughan said.

"That half-pint!" Lewis made a grab for the dwarf's hat, and the corgi rushed at the boy and tried to bite his pantleg, but the headmistress grabbed the dog's collar and pulled it back.

"Lewis—that's enough! Now get a move on—both of you!" the headmistress snapped, and then she smiled hugely again, as if she'd come to her senses and remembered we were still listening. "When Sergeant has shown Mary Beatrice to her room, he'll bring her to the tea party so she can join the other girls."

Now the headmistress pointed toward another stretch of apple-green, and for the first time I dared to look at the group of girls and their parents I'd heard chatting to one another in high, excited voices under a dripping canopy. Not one girl had on a green tunic; they all wore long navy tea dresses. I looked down anxiously at my shiny black oxfords. What an overeager idiot they'd think I was, coming to school already in uniform.

Morley looked at his watch. "I'm afraid we must get on our way," he sighed. "I've got surgery back in Madoc's Landing." He leaned over and patted me hard on the cheek with the back of his hand—Morley's way of kissing good-bye.

"Good-bye, Daddy," I whispered with my best fake smile.

I didn't really need crutches. I used to pretend I did to make Morley take pity on me. Then Sal got it in her head that I should never go anywhere without them, and I was too proud to admit I'd been faking. Of course, sometimes my lower back did get tired. And my left side gave out a bit. I liked to go to bed when that happened, but Sal wouldn't let me. "Pretend you're a victim of a skiing accident, or a hero who's been wounded in the Second World War," she told me.

That first morning at Bath Ladies College, the dwarf named Sergeant and I stood together in a huge stone reception foyer. The dwarf pointed out the niches in the wall where suits of armour had once stood. Another large reception area, to my left, had been cordoned off, as if to protect its shelves of library books, a slew of high-backed garden benches, and a dilapidated billiard table the size of a swimming pool—leftovers from Sir Jonathon. Meanwhile, all around us girls in navy dresses rushed at one another, shrieking and embracing. I clenched my teeth and pretended I didn't hear when the dwarf told me to look at the parquet floor. Its herring-bone pattern changed from shades of light to dark, depending on where you stood. As if I cared about its stupid design. It was bad enough to be wearing the wrong thing and carrying crutches, but to be paired up with a pint-sized man made me feel mortified.

I followed him silently down a long corridor whose polished blond floors felt slippery underfoot and smelled to high heaven of fresh paste wax. I tried not to look at our reflections in the shiny wood: his short torso rolling from side to side like the sailors on the government wharf in the Landing, and mine rolling with a slight forward teeter. On either side of us, the walls were festooned with pictures of old graduating classes and plaques listing scholar-ship winners in gold script. On one plaque I saw the words "The Ten Commandments of Friendship." I just had time to read number five ("Be cordial—speak and act as if everything you do is a genuine pleasure") and number six ("Be genuinely interested in people—you *can* like everybody if you try").

Then we turned a corner, and before us, rising up over our heads, floor upon floor, was an old staircase whose railings seemed to spin skyward in endless circles that finished finally in a huge round skylight. It was like looking up into a scrawly drawing of a giant eye. I dreaded the climb on my thin legs, but we went up slowly, the dwarf puffing and staggering under the weight of my old steamer trunk. It bumped loudly over each step, and I began to feel sorry for him.

At the first landing, he stopped to catch his breath. "Blasted bloody things," he said. "They're worse than hauling a coffin." Then he took off his curling cap and gestured with it toward an oil painting. "The English headmistress," he said. "Our first and last." A robust woman dressed in Edwardian cycling clothes stared back at us. She appeared to be sitting on a large tricycle.

"Isn't she a holy terror?" The dwarf genuflected in front of the picture. I didn't know if he was mocking her. The fierce pop eyes under her dome-shaped forehead made her look as if she could see right through you. Startled, I read the words inscribed in stone beside the portrait.

My dear girls,

The work our maker has assigned for you on earth must be carried out to the best of your abilities until that great day when material symbols are replaced by the reality of life everlasting.

Yours in faith,
Viola Higgs
(1874–1957)

I wondered why she was riding such an odd-looking tricycle but I didn't want to gratify my guide by asking questions. We began to climb again, going higher and higher into the strange tower. The dwarf had started to flip my trunk ass-over-teakettle, although I couldn't see how that made the climb easier.

At the top of the fourth landing, I heard giggles. Young girls' heads suddenly peeped out of doors that opened along a narrow corridor with a low ceiling.

"It's only the grade sevens," the dwarf said. He let my trunk crash down in another flip. Immediately, a frightened-looking woman in a housecoat flew out one of the doors and ran toward us waving her arms. Her dyed red hair was in curlers, and both her cheeks looked abnormally swollen, as if she had stuffed them with cotton batting.

"You have no business disturbing the blue wing," she said in a high, nervous voice. "The girls are having their nap. Please leave at once!"

The dwarf began to giggle and wave his arms back at her, and the laughter of the girls grew louder. He shook his big head at them and pursed his tiny mouth. *"Ssssh-ssssh-ssssh!"* he said. He was half the matron's height, and hardly taller than her small charges, now standing boldly beside me in the corridor. Then, before she could say another word, the dwarf yanked my trunk toward the next flight of stairs and in an unexpected show of strength dragged it out of sight without stopping for a breath.

I dragged myself up the last flight of stairs into the tower. My lower back ached a little now, and I took one of the aspirins from the bottle I carried with me for these occasions. We stood facing a narrow circular corridor lined with tall doors. The dwarf said these rooms used to be the servants' quarters, but the school had made them into music cubicles. Some of the doors bore little brass plaques with religious inscriptions by Anglicans like Frances Ridley Havergal, whose hymns we sometimes sang at the church in Madoc's Landing. These inscriptions used military phrases, such as "standard bearers" and "chosen to be a soldier," and their cheerful tone made me sad for no good reason.

The dwarf pushed open the last door and tugged me by the sleeve into a high, narrow room.

"Haven't you got all the luck!" he said, and giggled. "You're in the bedroom of the English headmistress—the best room in the house." He lowered his voice and pointed at the ceiling, where I saw a dusty globe fastened to a metal hook. "That's what she hanged herself on." Anxiously, I looked around. I wondered if he was teasing me. It might be the best room in the school, but I didn't see much to be glad about except the view. The east window looked down on a parking lot and a two-car garage (where the dwarf told me he and the other janitor, a Czech named Willy, had a tiny room). Beyond lay the dark, leafy mass of the ravine, which crawled up the hill like a rash toward the manicured grounds of the school. The south window overlooked a very grand stone patio surrounded by the funny spindly trees whose name I found out later was camperdown elms. Off to the southwest I could see the silver towers of the city, which sat like the Land of Oz on a merry blue stripe of lake water.

Directly below, on a knoll beside the patio, I saw the canopy where the parents were still having their tea party. The sun was now almost fully out, and I could hear the adults' happy voices chattering like birds after a rainstorm. I walked around my room aimlessly. It was plainly furnished: three continental beds evenly spaced between three dressers. Lined white cards were stuck inside the mirror on each dresser. On one I read the name Victoria Quinn, and on the other, Pauline Sykes. A bulletin board hung over each bed. A grainy old poster for the movie *King Kong* was pinned to the first board. The second displayed a picture of the Calypso singer Harry Belafonte next to a scroll in embossed yellow script, which read: *"Woman is descended from Adam's side to be his equal, near his arm to be protected and close to his heart to be loved."* I guessed the poster belonged to Victoria Quinn. On her dresser sat a framed photograph of a blond boy in a brush cut. The photo was signed, "As always, Rick." Next to it I saw a matted hairbrush, a bulging makeup case, a crockery pot spilling over with alpine flowers, and a package of Cameos. I smiled. I had something in common with one roommate.

"Aye, that's the spirit," the dwarf said in a friendlier tone. He handed me a black licorice in the shape of a pipe. "Would you have one of my sweets?"

I shook my head no, even though licorice candy was my fav, and he laid it down anyway on top of my trunk.

"Now, don't mind if you're homesick for a bit. It passes. And then one day—bingo! You wake up and, just like that, you're an old girl." He stood on tiptoe, looking up at the Cameos. "The matron will have Victoria's head for that. She's a careless girl." Suddenly we both heard a noisy commotion outside the window, and the dwarf stood on one of the trunks to look. "What have we here!" He clapped his little hand to his forehead. "Trespassers! Don't they know old Sergeant is king of the castle?"

Behind the tent, a row of male bodies was slithering over a tall wire fence, which I realized must encircle the full length of the grounds. I watched as, one by one, they dropped to the ground, some falling on their sides or backs. Their bodies looked toy-sized from my high window. Quickly they unfurled a banner and began to chant in unison at the startled tea-party guests.

> Ripping folly!
> Beastly jolly!
> Bath Ladies College
> is ours—rah!

On the lawn, some of the girls in navy tea dresses screamed as their parents stood looking at each other in confusion. Then the boys began to chant their verse again, even more loudly. A few of their members shook cowbells. In front of me, the dwarf banged the window with his fist. "Now where is that bloody Lewis when we need him? Wait! There he is! No, by God—it's the Virgin!"

I looked down. The headmistress stood in the midst of the crowd. In her hands she held a garden hose. She stood with her legs squarely apart and pointed the hose at the intruders, who stared for a moment in shock at the iridescent spray of water falling on their heads. A moment later, they turned and scrambled back up the wire fence. The water soaked their banner, changing the words "Bath Ladies College is ours" into a watery smear.

Then I noticed a turquoise convertible winding its way through the weeping willows. I made a little choking sound and looked around, in case Sergeant was listening. But he'd disappeared. I heard him cursing as he ran down the long hall, on his way to chase off the last of the intruders.

5

Mouse, you are grotesque, I told myself in the drafty bedroom. I stood staring into the mirror, hating the sly, wise face that stared solemnly back at me. The lips of its thin, lopsided mouth didn't move. See, it agrees with you, I thought.

I lay down on my bed. I didn't want to unpack or do anything else that felt like admitting I *was* there. I decided not to change my clothes. The moment I took off my blouse, some girl would walk in and see my twisted shoulder, Alice Hump.

Most of the time I hardly knew she was there. Of course, Alice aches a little when I've done something like climb five flights of stairs, and there are days when she wears me out entirely; she's like a suitcase that gets heavier the longer you carry it. But she's not really a nuisance. It's only when I undress and notice my vertebrae sticking out like tractor treads on my left shoulder that I know for sure that Alice will always be with me.

Finally, I sat up and stuck my best photo of Morley in my dresser mirror. I also put up one of my real mother and a few of President Kennedy. Then I opened my trunk. On top of the neatly folded tunics, Sal had left the school's list of outfits, each checked off with her messy blue ballpoint:

Navy winter coat
Green woollen tunics

Navy woollen knickers
Navy beret (for use with tunics)
Cotton bodices or brassieres (for older girls only)
Navy afternoon dress for teas and church
Purple Viyella long-sleeved blouses with collar (to wear with tunic)

Beside the list lay Sal's going-away present to me—a new copy of *The Power of Positive Thinking*. I slammed the lid of the trunk back down and went off to find the washroom.

He was standing in front of the bathroom mirror, a cigarette dangling from his lips. Lewis. He looked slighter in the shadowy cubicle, washing his face. He had the kind of insolent mouth fathers and ticket takers hate. A full mouth that spread like a hostile ripple across his bony face.

He wasn't making a sound, although he was obviously enjoying his masculine ritual. He was lost in it, daydreaming, the way I'd seen Sal do as she sat for a perm, or he'd have noticed me by the door. First he pulled out a brush from a brown shaving pot and began to smear white foam over his cheeks and neck. Then he took out an old-fashioned long-handled razor and began to shave slowly. He used one hand to pull the skin up by his left eye as the other scraped the razor down his left cheek. He did the same thing with his throat, only here he used his hand to pull the skin down while the razor slowly shaved up his neck. Then he pulled his upper lip down over his front teeth so he could shave under his nostrils, careful not to cut his lip. He moved now to his right cheek, pursing his lips the way I'd seen Morley do when he didn't know I was watching.

Now he stopped and wiped his hand on a towel, sucking on his cigarette so deeply that it pointed to the floor. After this virtuoso act, he took what was left of his fag and placed it on a window ledge, where it began to burn a black mark into the wood. I must have made a startled sound, because he looked up and saw me.

Before I could stop myself, I let out a little screech. Lewis quickly threw his butt out the window and sprayed the room with hair spray from a nearby shelf. Pushing past me, he hissed: "Say a word about this to anyone and you'll be sorry."

I listened for his footsteps, but the tower seemed to have swallowed Lewis up. The scent of hair spray lingered around me.

My screech attracted two matrons. I didn't mention Lewis by name, but I said I'd seen a boy in the washroom. They set off in a panic, flinging open bedroom doors up and down the hall. Their peevish voices questioned the other new girls, who must have been unpacking. And then they came back and questioned me all over again. I began to feel uneasy about protecting Lewis, and the second matron misunderstood my evasive tone. With a snakelike flick of her tongue, she loosened her front teeth from her gums and then snapped them, clacking, back into place. I realized she was too angry to speak. Then she said: "We don't appreciate practical jokes at Bath Ladies College. Any more complaints like this and I'll give you a gating."

6

That evening I was sitting on my bed with my hands over my ears when my roommates walked in. A bell as loud as a fire alarm was reverberating through the tower. Now it died away, and the school seemed weirdly quiet except for the sound of running tap water coming from the bathroom. Up and down the corridor, girls were getting ready for bed.

I didn't know what to say to these two grade-eleven girls. I'd skipped two grades, so they looked years older and bigger than me. One was very tall, with dark, heavy-lidded eyes and a skinny, sneering mouth. She moved with the confidence of an acrobat and wore her oily black hair combed across her forehead, while a long braid hung like a tassel between her shoulder blades. She reminded me of somebody.

The beauty of the other old girl made me stop breathing. Her milk-blond hair and high, plump cheeks made me want to hum Morley's favourite song about the girl that he marries having to be as soft and as pink as a nursery. I guessed she belonged to the gold-script poster and the alpine flowers—Victoria Quinn in the flesh. And her friend had to be Pauline Sykes, whose brother, Lewis, I'd caught shaving in the washroom.

"Are you goin' to get your bath ticket?" Pauline Sykes asked, breaking our silence. I noticed she dropped her *g*'s the way people did in Dollartown, a village outside Madoc's Landing. When I don't eat my vegetables, Sal always asks if I'd like to move to

Dollartown, where all people have to eat are Dollartown steaks—
i.e., slabs of fried baloney.

I didn't answer. I felt a little frightened of Pauline Sykes without
knowing why.

"Do I have to tell you again? Get your bath ticket."

"I don't want a bath," I whispered finally.

"C'mon, Paulie. Drop it," Victoria Quinn said.

"Spoilsport." Pauline Sykes withdrew to her side of the room
and sat down on a chair facing the wall. Then, slowly and loudly,
she began to bang her head against the wall. Each thump made the
wall quiver with a little ringing noise, and the mirrors above our
dressers shook. Almost immediately our door opened, and the
frightened-looking matron seemed to fall into the room. She'd
taken out her rollers, and two springy kiss curls sprang out of her
forehead like the coiled horns of a ram.

"Who is making that racket!" She looked angrily around the
room. "Is it the Sykes girl?"

"I hate this hole," Pauline said. Her back was still turned to us,
but she'd stopped her awful head banging.

"Are you listening to me, Pauline?" she said. "You realize that
this term Miss Vaughan expects you to play your part in the
boarding school. And that means thinking of others besides yourself. I expect you haven't given a thought to looking after the new
girl, have you?"

Pauline made a rude sound that the boys in the Landing call a
raspberry. I wasn't sure if I should take it personally, and I sat on
my bed, my head in my hands. The matron sighed and walked
quickly past me to my dresser. I smelled a funny odour, like lamp
oil. "Who's this?" she sniffed, and snatched up my magazine
photograph of John Kennedy with his daughter, Caroline, aboard
his yawl, the *Manitou*. His nice wavy hair was lying flat and thick
against his scalp, even though a strong wind was blowing the
boat's flag straight out like a banner.

"The American president," I said in a small voice.

"He's a Catholic, isn't he?" the matron said. "He's very young to be president." She pulled down the photo of my real mother and my favourite picture of Morley, a colour snap taken last August. It showed Morley and Sal and me picnicking at the Indian reserve near Lennox Point. Morley was sprawled in a deck chair on *Thebus*. (Next to Blinky, Morley's cruiser was his second-favourite top-down toy.) The colour photograph had turned Morley's two shiny gull wings of grey hair the same shade as the golden fur on Lady. Lady had her nose over the gunnel, wagging her tail. I was sitting far away from Morley, stuffed into an orange life preserver. Sal, in dark green sunglasses, was sitting in a deck chair beside Morley.

"Oh, Miss Phillips. Why don't you let us leave our snaps up?" Victoria said as the matron took down my photographs. "What harm does it do?"

"There are to be no personal effects on your mirrors," Miss Phillips said. "There's a bulletin board over your bed for that purpose."

"But then our photographs get holes in them from the thumb-tacks," Victoria continued. "It's better if we can slide them inside the mirror frame."

The matron used two fingers to pick up Victoria's matted hairbrush and dropped it inside my roommate's top drawer. "Victoria, you know how your father and Miss Vaughan feel about you smoking on school property."

"Oh, don't tell my father about the cigarettes," Victoria said. "Please, Miss Phillips. I just had one puff of the first cigarette. I was buying them for someone."

"I'm afraid you've left me no choice." The matron snatched up the pack and put it in her pocket. "You can take up the matter with Miss Vaughan."

"Miss Vaughan doesn't give a shit, and you know it," Pauline said, jumping to her feet. "And anyways, those are my fags. Not that it's any of your business."

"Is that true, Victoria?" The matron ignored Pauline.

"What are you asking her for?" Pauline said. "I told you the fags are mine."

"Very well. Pauline's foul mouth has brought her an orderly mark." Miss Phillips sidled out of the room, her back to the door so she could watch my tall roommate. "And there will be lights out early for this room." The overhead light flicked off as she slammed our door.

I couldn't see in the sudden darkness, but my two roommates appeared to be lying on their beds staring at each other and whispering. I thought I heard Pauline tell Victoria she'd always be there for her and not to let the matron get her goat. Then the two of them stood up and began to rummage in their dressers for their pyjamas, as if I weren't there. Victoria noticed me still sitting in my tunic and smiled. "You'd better hurry," she said, "or old Phooey Phillips will catch you." She giggled. "Doesn't she smell fusty? It's because she uses naphtha to take the stains out of her clothes."

Another bell rang, and the door opened. A sudden circle of bright light blinded me. "I hope everyone is settling down nicely in there," a singsongy English voice said. The flashlight beam waved wildly across the room until it lit up Pauline's bed, where she lay with the covers over her head. "I don't want to hear that you are up to your old tricks, Paulie. I should think someone in your position would want to be more careful." A grinning, disembodied head hovered above us, lit from below by the beam of the flashlight. Its plump, powdered cheeks made me think of the giant puffball mushrooms that grew in the farm meadows outside the Landing. "And why is the new girl not undressed?"

"She's having trouble with the lights off," Victoria said, and I felt a sweet blush spread up my spine to the top of my torqued shoulder. Oh, Alice, I thought, she likes us.

"I see. Well, perhaps she'll do better when I close the door," the new matron said.

"May I please be excused?" Pauline said. "I have to answer a call of nature."

"So do I," I said miserably.

"Both of you should have thought of that before. We at Bath Ladies College need to think ahead. No toilet privileges now." She shut the door.

My eyes began to water. Mouse, don't be a baby, I told myself in Sal's meanest shaming voice. Button up, now. If Morley knew what they were putting you through, you wouldn't be here for a second. I turned away so that Victoria couldn't see me and lay with my eyes tightly shut.

"Don't worry," Victoria whispered from her bed after what seemed like ages. "That's only Mrs. Peddie, the English teacher. She's harmless. She lives up in the tower and Phooey lives down in the Blue Wing. Mrs. Peddie is supposed to look after us but she's so busy she asks Phooey to do it."

"Victoria, I think I have to go to the washroom now," I replied.

"Call me Tory," the other girl said. "And listen. You can pee in a glass, then. Paulie and I have done it before." She pointed to the glasses on our dressers and giggled. "I'd recommend two for floating bladders."

Silently I took a glass from my dresser. I pulled down my knickers and squatted over the glass. I missed by a mile and warm pee spilled over my hand and gushed down onto the side of my bed. Pauline made a groaning noise in her sleep.

"It needs a bit of practice." Giggling, Tory helped me strip my bed and spread out the sheets on the red-tiled window ledge.

"You'll get used to this place," she said, and opened the two narrow windows. They swung outward on hinges, away from the metal bars that kept you from sticking your head outside. "That's the ravine," she said. "There used to be a hole in the fence, but they patched it up. We aren't supposed to go there because sometimes a man stands in the woods at lunch hour and opens his coat

at the day girls." She lowered her voice. "Paulie's brother told
me."

"Lewis?" I whispered.

"Yes. The Virgin lets him do odd jobs on weekends because
he's too old to be in high school. And he's not much on books.
But wherever Paulie goes, Lewis goes. Paulie and Lewis don't have
parents."

"Oh," I said, impressed.

"Paulie was at an Anglican home for problem girls when the
Virgin found her. She persuaded the board to let Paulie come here
on a scholarship. Before Ridgeley House, Paulie had been living on
the street. Can you imagine? And her brother, too."

"Is he nice?" I asked, thinking of how he looked when he was
shaving.

"Lewis and I are in love," Tory whispered huskily. "You know
what that's like."

I nodded as if I did, and we stood for a moment, shyly letting
our shoulders touch. In the ravine below, I noticed the dark
feathery tops of two old jack pines. I listened for the wind in their
boughs, but all I could hear was the noise of car horns and motors
rising up from the highway in muffled waves. Oh, Morley, I
thought, how could you let Sal lock me in a place where you can't
even hear the wind! It had started to rain again, and a moment later
Tory closed our window, to keep my sheets from getting soaked.
She gave me her extra blanket, and I crawled under it, shivering.
"You still haven't got undressed, Mary," she said softly. I heard
her clear her throat. "I understand. You're shy. Well, good night,
then," she said, and turned to the wall.

"By the way, my name is Mouse," I whispered, but the small
room was quiet now and smelled horribly of pee. I was afraid to
fall asleep. The tower's cavelike silence made me uneasy, and I felt
a heavy sadness rise out of my chest and float off down the long,
wavy corridor like a woebegone spirit searching for a way out.

7

I awoke to a whirring noise—a delicate mechanical sound like the *flap-flap* of tiny metal wings. And then I heard the voice of my dead mother, the other Alice, singing hymn number 576 in *The Book of Common Prayer*. It was by Frances Ridley Havergal.

Take my life, and let it be
Consecrated, Lord, to thee:
Take my moments and my days,
Let them flow in ceaseless praise.

Trembling, I crept out of bed and looked down at Tory, longing to wake her. But I didn't dare. I stole out into the pitch-black corridor. About ten yards from me, a small yellow light no bigger than a firefly bounced along the walls of the tower. Not far behind the tiny bobbing light I saw a ghostly form pedalling a giant tricycle. The odd-looking bike consisted of two small wheels at the back and a large one in front, like a child's tricycle, only the front wheel was three times as large as the back wheels. I recognized the tricycle and the rider from the woman in the portrait Sergeant had shown me on the stairs. The woman wore the same long black dress with a lace collar that made her look like a maid. Only I knew she wasn't. Somebody like her wasn't anybody's servant. She had the same gleeful carelessness about her appearance as the headmistress, Miss Vaughan. Her cheeks had been messily powdered, and a mannish leather suitcase was strapped to her back. As I watched, she made her bike zigzag slowly back and forth, to avoid the stripes of moonlight on the floor of the tower. The old coach light on the handlebars was swinging crazily from side to side.

Then she saw me and slammed on the brake. Her snowy head jerked forward, and I thought she was going to fly over the handlebars, but she quickly composed herself and turned her powdered face in my direction.

"Do you know where I left this world?" She pointed a crooked white finger to the door at the end of the corridor. "In that room—your room."

"Where's my mother?" I whispered. I could no longer hear her singing, and I thought that if I was polite, this odd personage would tell me what I wanted to know. The figure didn't answer. She sat down again and began to pedal away. The whirring noise grew louder and louder, until the figure was racing full tilt, her shoulders hunched, her arms akimbo. Just before she reached the last music cubicle, she rang her silver-plated bicycle bell, and the door swung open. There stood my dead mother, her hand on the knob.

She looked young and startled, the way she did in the photograph the matron had taken from my dresser mirror. Her soft blond hair—the hair I had liked to hide under when I was a baby—lay in gold puffs across her slender shoulders. I recognized the ruffled silk blouse and long, tailored skirt, whose hem reached halfway to her calves. The ghostly figure dismounted from her bike and turned her broad back to my mother, who proceeded to unbuckle the leather suitcase and take out a great number of objects. I identified an oilcan, a tool that looked like a wrench, and a pair of gardening shears. When this was done, my mother sat down on the piano bench and folded her hands in her lap. And carefully—very, very carefully—the older woman lifted up the oilcan and tilted it just by my mother's neck, until a thick, slow stream of oil bled down the front of my mother's frilled blouse. My mother opened her mouth and started to sing:

> Take my hands and let them move
> At the impulse of Thy love.

Then the older woman put down the oilcan and picked up the gardening shears, and I knew she was going to do something horrible to my mother. Before I could shout a warning, the figure cut a hole in my mother's blouse, just above her heart. A single tear dribbled down my mother's cheek. Then I did shout, but I couldn't make the words come out of my mouth; I tried to move, but my bare feet were stuck to the cold wooden floor. Now the older woman began to hack out large clumps of my mother's hair, as if she were clipping fur balls from a cat whose coat was hopelessly matted.

Then, at last, I could move, and I ran on my spindly legs toward my mother. But just as I reached the cubicle, the headmistress slammed the door in my face. I rattled the knob, but it was locked. I heard the snip of the shears and little cries. Then, nothing. I listened for a long while. Still nothing. And then, so faintly that at first I wasn't sure it was her, I heard my mother's gentle voice. It didn't seem to be coming from inside the cubicle now, but from the walls of the tower itself.

> Take my feet, and let them be
> Swift and beautiful for Thee.

8

The next morning, after the 7:30 bell, Miss Phillips made us kneel on the floor so she could measure our tunics to see if they fell to mid-knee—perfect school-regulation length. Then she gave me a new set of sheets without mentioning the reason why and sent us out for a morning walk around the hedge. Tory said Miss Phillips was always nice to you after she'd lost her temper; sometimes she even gave you a stash of gum, which was against the rules. Meanwhile, Pauline—or Paulie, as I dared not call her—looked at me suspiciously from under her puffy bangs, and I guessed that she was scornful of my act of desperation.

After breakfast, the three of us walked together down the winding flights of stairs to the infirmary for our medical checkups. Inside, a line of girls stood with their heads down. All of them had stripped to their bra and underpants, except for some of the fat girls, who tried to get away with wearing their school blouses until the last minute. A few girls turned around to stare at us with fearful faces, and I realized they were looking at Paulie. She sucked her teeth and pointed her index and baby fingers in their direction—the sign that means you're full of it. One or two laughed, and I heard the phrase "that Sykes girl" whispered among them, as if Paulie's name were a swear word. Paulie abruptly turned her back and pulled down her purple bloomers, mooning the crowd. Then she yanked at the handle on the wall behind us and a panel door slid up, exposing what looked like the insides of a cupboard. "See you later, suckers," Paulie called, and ducked quickly into the dumbwaiter, pulling its door down with a bang. All around us, girls giggled or talked in low, astonished voices.

"Won't she get caught?" I asked.

"Paulie will stop it before it hits the kitchen," Tory whispered. "The dumbwaiter goes through a tiny classroom nobody uses." The line had moved up, so we rounded a corner in the hall, where two nurses stood in white uniforms. The first nurse weighed and measured each girl and called out the results to the nurse holding a clipboard. Then, in a loud voice, as if she wanted us all to hear, the first nurse asked each girl if she had started menstruating.

The embarrassed girls answered in whispery voices. I could tell when one of them said yes, because the second nurse waved her clipboard to indicate that she should step into her office and fill out the date of her last period. Every one of the fat girls had removed her blouse by now. Ahead of me, Tory stood on the scales. Her round shoulders were dimpled in the same places as Bess, the Betsy Wetsy wet'um doll Morley had given me when I was six. I winced at how vulnerable she looked when the nurse called out her weight—a hundred and forty pounds.

Soon it would be my turn. I didn't want to take off my tunic and let everyone stare at Alice—or at my new posture corrector. I'd bought it with Sal at Starkman's. We'd gone in together, Sal in one of her pillbox hats and me on my crutches. I'd walked in fast, my eyes on the ground, not wanting to see if there were any cripples hanging around. But, sure enough, right beside us, a sad-looking, pock-faced man was staring off into space inside a little cubicle stashed with boxes. His legs looked shrunken, as if they'd been in too many of Sal's washes. Then a saleswoman came over to us. She glared at Sal with cold, watery-blue eyes when she caught Sal looking at her bleached hair, and then stepped into the sad cripple's cubicle without excusing herself.

"Oh, it's in use," she said. She took down a box and pulled out a crisscrossed harness and showed me how to tighten the belt slowly at the base so it didn't draw me up too fast. "Your breathing will get better," she said.

She wanted me to put it on, and I refused. "There's no reason to be embarrassed," she said. "Not in here." She said this in a scornful, authoritative way, turning her head all the way around to show that she meant Starkman's. I looked all around, too, and saw tables of boxes that reached to the ceiling and folded-up wheelchairs. Sal made me use the cubicle as soon as the pock-faced cripple had left, and I felt better with the harness on—stronger, like an angel getting its wings. I could float above the head of the saleslady, who couldn't see my sly beauty.

"You haven't taken off your blouse," the first nurse said. "It's better for measuring." I didn't say anything. Out the window I could see the wire fence the boys had crawled over the day before and the four-sided clock tower of their school, Kings College. Tory had told me at breakfast that the clock was called the four-faced liar, because pigeons sat on its huge, black hands so that it didn't tell the time properly.

"Oh, modest, are we?" the first nurse said, grimacing. She took a measuring tape from her pocket. "Please take it off. Or do you want me to do it?" I stared down at my new oxfords and did what she asked. Then Alice was naked for all the world to see. And my poor, flat, sunken chest.

"Twenty-six," the first nurse said, and the other nurse wrote it down on her clipboard. The first nurse looked me in the eye. "Have you started menstruating?"

I looked her back straight in the eye. "No."

"How old are you?"

"Thirteen."

"But you are in grade eleven. Most girls in grade eleven are fifteen or sixteen."

"I skipped two grades."

The first nurse looked at me coldly. "It may surprise you to know this, but I'm aware you have a liking for practical jokes, Mary Bradford," she said.

I stared at her blankly, and the first nurse whispered something in the second nurse's ear. I heard the phrase "deformed chest." I cringed, wondering how much the girls behind me could overhear.

"Is there a medical reason for your condition?" the second nurse asked in a gentle tone.

"Kyphosis," I whispered.

"Speak up, please."

"It's called kyphosis. Doctors say it affected my development. I may never have a period."

Down the corridor, I heard the silly girls whispering like idiots. I hung my head. Their voices sounded unfriendly. Go ahead, I wanted to scream. Gasp as much as you like. I like being under-developed. You can grow up and become women. Not me.

"All girls menstruate," the first nurse said quickly. "When you start, I want you to come to the infirmary and enter the date on the book we have set aside for that purpose."

The second nurse led me off down another corridor. Behind us I could hear the girls still whispering about me. We stood in a narrow rectangular room. I was surprised to see girls in cots reading or sleeping. I didn't know how they'd had the chance to get sick so quickly.

"Your brace looks relatively new, but you need an instep in your shoe," the nurse said. "And I will speak to Miss Vaughan about sending you to my chiropractor. There's no reason for your condition to be so extreme."

"I don't want a funny-looking shoe," I said and began to weep. She put her arm around me and asked if I wanted a hot milk. I whispered yes into her soft breasts and let her help me off with my clothes. I knew that whatever reputation I'd been developing as a rebel was shot to pieces.

9

A Conversation with Alice

All my life I have heard Alice's voice in my ear. I may not want to listen to her and I may not want to believe what she says, but I hear Alice the way you hear what your mother will say about something before you do it. So I figure I may as well talk to her since I'm going to hear what she says anyhow. I don't know what I would have done without Alice at Bath Ladies College. Or President Kennedy, for that matter.

— Alice, you know I never wanted to become a woman.

— I know, but you didn't want to be a man, either.

— Well, not exactly. I wanted everything a man has except his penis. It was the other way around for Paulie. She already had everything a man has but that.

— You mean she didn't want a penis?

— Other people thought she needed one—not Paulie. Not to begin with. Oh, Alice, have you ever met a girl who didn't giggle when you asked her if she wanted one?

— That reminds me. Why don't girls tell jokes about boys' private parts?

— That's not very helpful. Seeing how I don't have a real mother. You know I can't count on Sal. And I've already heard that old joke of yours, anyway. Because they don't like gags on penises.

— I was only trying to cheer you up, Mouse. And remember, I'm the same age as you.

— I beg your pardon. I grant your grace. I hope the cat will scratch your face.

— You don't have to bite my head off. By the way, what's the difference between a penis and a prick?

— Alice, please.

— Don't be such a fussbudget, Mouse. A penis is what a man uses to make babies, and a prick is the rest of him.

— This time you've gone too far. No wonder I liked to talk to President Kennedy. I bet he didn't tell stupid jokes.

— Sure he did, Mouse. And you know it.

September 16, 1963

Dear Mr. Kennedy,

You don't know me, but I know you. So let me get to the point. I'm in a bit of a pickle. I'm locked away in a prison for women disguised as a Canadian boarding school. My own father should be the one to get me out, but he's too overworked and too kind to his patients, so he doesn't have anything left over for his family (i.e., me). For instance, I have never had even a five-minute conversation with him by himself. There isn't time. He allows only half an hour for each meal at home and then sleeps another half-hour. Then he goes back to the office. He works from 7:00 a.m. to 11:00 p.m. On Sundays and holidays, too. Frankly, Morley (my father's name is Morley) is beginning to look a little the worse for wear.

He should lose fifty pounds and dye his hair black. It would do wonders for his olive complexion and stop his cheeks from sagging like old rubber tires.

You never look pooped in your photographs. Well, maybe a little uncomfortable now and again—I know you have a bad back. But you never look as if you are on your last legs, which is the way Morley looks every day.

You always look brand-new, Mr. Kennedy. Whether you are

clapping at Caroline doing a handstand in your office or smiling down at her in her nice white party dress at Hyannis Port.

The only time I've seen her look the littlest bit lonely is in the photograph on the South Lawn of your White House. You're nowhere in sight, but she's sitting with her brother taking afternoon tea with her English nurse.

Of course, I could be wrong. Mostly she looks happy. Particularly in the snap that shows you both in a car. She's snuggled up against your shoulder, and the two of you are watching the road ahead. You look like you couldn't care less about the world around you.

Your friend,
Mouse Bradford

September 18, 1963

Dear Mr. Kennedy,

After I wrote you my first letter I realized I could tell you anything and you would have no way of knowing if I was telling the truth. For instance, I could tell you my mother is Marilyn Monroe and I live in Canada, a country that was discovered by the singer Paul Anka. He runs it from an igloo on Baffin Island when he isn't making records, and our main industry is shipping ice cubes to keep your White House cool!!

Anyway, I promise to always tell you the truth, Mr. Kennedy. (You'd only find out if you came up here, anyhow.)

The following—all true, cross my heart—is just to give you an idea of what a day in this hole is like.

A bell wakes us at 7:00 a.m. and we have to be in our tunics for inspection at 7:30 a.m. Then a matron inspects our rooms from 7:30 a.m. to 7:40 a.m., when we are walking around the hedge next to the hockey pitch. Our lights must go out at 8:00 p.m. The army's got nothing on this place.

Once in a while, on what they call an "out" Saturday, the matron takes us shopping at Eaton's. That's a big department store downtown, and all the boarders load up on gum and cigarettes when she isn't watching. The rest of the time we can't go into the city. We get to stare at it through the bars of our windows. It is situated three miles to the south of us. At night, I can see its lights strung out like a necklace of Christmas bulbs on the shore of Lake Ontario.

To be honest, Mr. President, I feel a little blue. I'd like to ask my father to send for me, but I know he won't listen. I bet I'm the last thing on his mind as he drives about Madoc's Landing doing his calls. If I close my eyes, I see him driving our Olds convertible to the concession store on County Road 14. It's run by French-Canadians. My stepmother Sal says they think our dog Lady is his new girlfriend. That's because Lady sits as close to Morley as she can. So when Morley drives by, all you see is a ridge of blond leaning against his shoulder. I pity Sal. If I were her, I'd take the distracted way Morley treats her personally. A man that tired is capable of letting anything happen to him. Well, I see the eagle eye of my form mistress upon me.

As ever,
Mouse Bradford

September 25, 1963

Dear Mr. President,

I'm writing this in morning prayers. Yesterday Miss Vaughan gave us a little talk about the hymn maker Frances Ridley Havergal. She read us a boring chapter from a book called *Morning Bells* and talked about how we should give ourselves up to God—i.e., not just our minds but, Mr. President—our hands, feet, lips, eyes, ears, and so on. What for? So we can become instruments of righteous-ness. "The little hands will no longer serve Satan by striking or pinching; the little feet will not kick or stamp, nor drag and dawdle, when they ought to run briskly on some errand; the little lips will not pout; the little tongue will not move to say a naughty thing." Personally, Mr. President, I'm going to keep my hands, so that I can write you. This morning the talk is just as bad—i.e., the history of Bath Ladies College. Apparently, this dumb school is modelled after Cheltenham Ladies College in England, like a lot of girls' schools in Canada. Some of our teachers—i.e., Miss Vaughan and Mrs. Peddie—taught at the British school. Now Miss Vaughan is reading us a funny poem about two British headmistresses from the olden days.

> Miss Buss and Miss Beale
> Cupid's darts cannot feel
> How different from us
> Miss Beale and Miss Buss

All the girls laugh, and Miss Vaughan is laughing, too, as if she didn't realize the girls thought the same thing about her.

In a row against the north wall sit the grade thirteens and the prefects in their yellow knotted belts. The teachers sit in a row against the south wall. Every old biddy has her ankles crossed, her hands cupped in her lap. We're supposed to sit like that, too. If our deportment isn't good, we let down the reputation of the school. Queen Elizabeth's portrait is hung on the wall behind the lectern. She has nicer hair than Miss Vaughan, better makeup, and she has a *husband*.

At least I know the names of all the teachers now. And, more important, the names the girls call them behind their backs. The Virgin is the nickname for our headmistress, Miss Vaughan. She's called the Virgin because she is untouched by the male hand. The girls here say they wear their virginity pins in her name. These are circular silver pins that everybody wears on their clothes when they aren't in uniform. Miss Charlotte Ibister, our gym mistress, is called Hammerhead, because she looks like a shark and has very big thighs. Hammerhead makes the fat girls cry when they can't do the splits over the horse. Mrs. Peddie is called Lola the Les, because she's in love with the Virgin, who arranged for her to have quarters near her in the boarding school. Mrs. Peddie teaches English plus sex and scripture. Because she is a divorcée, some of the teachers think she's a loose woman. (Not me. A man would have to be crazy to ask out somebody who looked like her.) She smiles so hard you can see her gums, and she wears tight wool sweaters when her breasts are way too big. They look like torpedoes about to burst out of her brassiere. Everybody giggles when she and the Virgin walk together down the corridor. They both have big, fat bodies that jiggle when they move, and it doesn't seem to bother them one bit. The big difference between them is in their height. Mrs. Peddie is short and always smiles, and the Virgin is tall and scowls. They're like the figures in a Swiss cuckoo clock: one predicts sunshine, and the other, showers.

I know I shouldn't be so familiar with you, when you are a high official of the land, Mr. President, but do you think I'll turn into an old hag if I stay here? A few years in this dump and you don't notice you're wearing the same stupid shirtwaist you wore to prayers twenty years before. There are no men to say you look nice, so you forget you have a body and face which the world sees. (Nobody, of course, except another les.)

The matrons in the boarding school are dogs, too. Miss Phillips, or Phooey Phillips, doesn't use underarm deodorant. She uses lamp oil to clean the spots off her dresses because she's too cheap to send them to the cleaners. I hate her because she gets the rules mixed up and doesn't let us go to the bathroom after lights out. So you see, Mr. Kennedy, I'm getting to be an old hand. I don't know the names of the girls yet. They all look the same to me in the school uniform.

Warmest regards,
Mouse Bradford

September 26, 1963

Dear Mr. Kennedy,

Morley's a writer, too, by the way. He hasn't had two books published like you. (I know, for instance, you published *Why England Slept* when you were only twenty-three—ten years older than me!) Morley publishes every week in the Madoc's Landing *Bulletin*. His column is called "Bedside Manner." Example:

Despite claims of chiropractors and osteopaths to the contrary, there's no reason to ascertain, from the evidence at hand, that few doctors take these quacks I have mentioned seriously.

Morley's sentence structure gets a little tangled. You, Mr. President, write more rhythmically. Example:

> And so, my fellow Americans, ask not what your country can
> do for you; ask what you can do for your country.

I notice you like using the principle of parallel sentence structure. You use balance to create a sense of reason and fairness. It's the trick of a good rhetorician. I can't say the same for Morley, but he's not in your line of work. He has to get people's heart rates lower. So a lot of jumbled words make them slow down, if you see what I mean. They have to stop and think about what he's saying, don't they? So for a doctor, Morley writes just fine. On the other hand, he could try a parallel sentence or two, and maybe you could vary your sentence length, if you don't mind my saying so.

The worst thing about Morley being a writer is that he never writes me. Well, c'est la vie.

Luff,
M.B.

P.S. Other parallels between you and Morley. In the hero department. Morley won the Intercollegiate Football Championship for Varsity against McGill. With only two minutes to go in the game, he kicked the winning three-point field goal from 43 yards out. Morley saved the day. Just like you did when you towed one of your men away from the sinking P.T. boat, a rope between your teeth.

At least these letters stopped me from waiting for Morley to tell me I could go home. I knew this wasn't a real possibility. Not after Sal's postcard the second week at school.

Dear Mouse,

By now you must be getting used to your school. Your headmistress told us the girls often find leave-taking hard, but soon settle in. Morley says to tell you he is taking the three of us to Nassau for Christmas, and we will have a fine time then. (That's what the last of the big spenders says now, but we shall see what we shall see, won't we?) Don't get your heart set on a lot of visits from us, Mouse. I don't like Toronto, and neither does Morley. Too many clip joints that prey on folks from out-of-town. Morley couldn't wait to get home and see Lady.

Yours,
Sal

An unreadable sentence had been scratched in at the top of the card. I knew it was a greeting from Morley. His handwriting was illegible because he wrote so many prescriptions.

10

I know, I know, I'm tendrilling again when I should be getting on
with what Paulie did. But adjusting to boarding school wasn't easy.
First of all, new girls had to learn the vocabulary. That meant
learning words you'd never heard of before, words that stood for
feelings and things you would never dream you could say out loud.

Spastics, Finks, and Leses

a les—what everybody thinks the girls are here
spastic or spaz—fun, crazy
nooie-noo—a boy too cute for words
fink—a boy or girl who's not
bananorama—the chunks of too-ripe bananas that Paulie wings at
 other girls' heads
bore-eng (on an up note)—life inside old Before Christ, i.e., Bath
 (Ladies) College
weird—the only word I knew before I came (besides fav)

Secondly, you had to learn a whole new set of manners, which
exaggerated every polite gesture you'd ever learned in the first
place. And then, when the matron's back was turned, you had to
be brave enough to throw all these new rules out the window.
Eating bananas was a case in point. We had Jell-O desserts every

Thursday and bowls of fruit every Friday, which is how Paulie got her hands on the bananas she aimed at Ismay Thom's head every Friday afternoon in math class.

"Would you like a banana, Mary Beatrice?"

"No thank you, Miss Vaughan."

The Virgin looked dolefully at the bowl of fruit the kitchen maid had put on the head table. Across from me, the English girl Ismay Thom watched, smirking.

Ismay Thom was a star music pupil and Paulie's pet peeve. She lived in the next room down the hall. She smelled overwhelmingly of talcum powder and practised the "Jamaican Rumba" every day on the piano in the music cubicle next door until our walls shook and I was sick to death of a piece that used to move me to the bottom of my Mouse heart. It was Ismay Thom who snickered at Paulie and me as we put on our navy hats and coats for the Sunday church service, because her parents were atheists and she was allowed to stay home. And it was Ismay the know-it-all who scolded Paulie for dropping her *g*'s in *-ing* endings.

"Would you like a banana, Miss Vaughan?" Ismay simpered.

"Thank you, Ismay. I don't mind if I do." Miss Vaughan set the banana down on her plate as if the fruit was singeing her fingers. And then she speared it with her fork, crooking her baby finger just the way Sal tells Morley not to do. I'd never seen anyone eat a banana with a knife and fork before, and I wondered what Sal would think of Miss Vaughan's etiquette. Maybe Sal would be impressed and make Morley and me eat our bananas that way, too. Now, in a quick, aggravated motion, my headmistress hacked off both tips with her knife.

"And how are you liking our school, Mary Beatrice?" she said.

"Oh, it's very different from what I'm used to," I replied, watching her hands peel the banana so that its skin collapsed on her plate in long, sloppy strips.

"The strangeness will wear off, won't it, Ismay?" the Virgin said.

"Oh, yes," said Ismay the Simp. The Virgin's banana lay on her plate like a swollen tongue. And now, very slowly and methodically, the Virgin began to chop the banana—*whomp, whomp, whomp*. In a moment it lay diced in eight precisely matching chunks, as if by a machine-shop tool.

Up and down the table the porcelain rang with the sound of girls chopping and eating bananas without touching them. Somewhere in the dining room Paulie was doing this, too, only I never thought to look.

The next thing I knew, the Virgin carefully laid her knife and fork side by side at the left of her plate and stood up. All talking stopped and the girls scrambled to their feet in a thunderous explosion of scraping chairs. I stood up, too, and Miss Vaughan scanned the tables with her unblinking eyes. She smiled. It was as if the sun had come out after a rain squall. Everybody relaxed, and Miss Vaughan said grace in her whispery girl's voice and walked out, all our eyes on her broad-shouldered back. A smiley Mrs. Peddie jiggled after her carrying two cups of hot cocoa for them to drink in the staff room. There goes Lola the Les, I thought, trying out my new vocabulary. From across the table, Ismay Thom called my name.

"Mary Beatrice, you didn't get her cue. When she asks you if you'd like a banana, you're supposed to say, 'No thank you. Would you like a banana, Miss Vaughan?' That way, she gets to have it first. Understand?" Ismay giggled nastily. "I thought she would have told you this before you came. She's your aunt, isn't she?"

"She's only a third cousin," I said, and kept my head down so I didn't have to see the other girls staring at me as they filed out of the dining room. I always stayed behind until the last girl left, because I didn't want anybody to notice I walked favouring my left side. To make matters worse, the nurse had ordered new orthopedic oxfords for me. Ordinary oxfords were bad enough, but these oxymorons were as heavy as a man's dress shoe, and the built-up right heel made my foot look deformed. And then, wouldn't you know, just as I was feeling really sorry for myself, somebody whacked me on the bum.

"Don't be a snob, Mouse! Wait for me."

I jumped, all nerves. It was Tory. You could have knocked me over with a feather. I thought I was alone in the dining room, but there she was, lurching along and giggling because she hadn't finished stuffing her feet into her oxfords. The backs of her shoes were broken down, so that she could step into them like slippers without bothering to do up the laces. It was these broken-down oxfords plus the ripped-out hems on her tunics and her knee socks that bunched like a pair of droopy drawers around her ankles (not to mention her school tie with the purple threads all picked out) that made Miss Vaughan sigh "Oh, Victoria" when she saw Tory in the hall. Somehow, her slobby uniform didn't make Tory look ugly, though. She always looked feminine—with milk-white hair you could die for and plump, high cheeks that coloured up the second anybody teased her.

Now she took my arm and leaned into me the way Lady sometimes leans against Morley and whispered how glad she was I was a full-time boarder. Pauline went home on the weekends to visit her grandfather, so Tory had nobody to talk to except me and Lewis. Of course, they had to be careful, or else the Virgin wouldn't let him do odd jobs around the school. And then she confessed that she was scared because Miss Ibister had asked her to replace a forward on the field-hockey team who had the flu.

"There are the Amazons we have to play—out there!" she said, squeezing my arm. And, sure enough, through the dining-room window I could see a crowd of tall women with wide, thick torsos massing on the hockey pitch. They were the same big women wielding the curved sticks I'd noticed the first day I arrived. Tory said these big women were phys-ed teachers from the university imported by Miss Ibister to give our first field-hockey team practice for the finals. She didn't know how she could be expected to hold her own against the likes of them, and neither did I. Not that I knew much about the sport. I'd never played it before and would be watching from the sidelines as Miss Ibister's number-one helper. I couldn't play sports on account of Alice, so Miss Ibister had cooked up the helper idea as a way of including me.

I told Tory it was a real shame that enthusiasts like Miss Ibister didn't know when it was best to leave well enough alone.

11

Now see here, Mouse, I told myself in Sal's sternest voice, you have to stop thinking about how you look in your weird shoes. There's no point cringing around like an old dog who wants to crawl away into the ravine woods and die. It's true you have a poor excuse for a body, but someday Morley will realize how much you have suffered and make it up to you. So hang in there the best you can. Never mind that it's October in Madoc's Landing, your favourite time in the whole world. Cut up the oranges for the players and pretend you're interested in this dumb sport.

In front of Miss Ibister and me, the beefy phys-ed women galloped up and down the pitch, their sticks slashing the air left and right but never raised quite high enough to get a foul. Just as Tory said, our girls looked reedy and small in comparison, even though most of our players were chunky, with big muscular thighs like Miss Ibister.

Behind us, on the embankment, the sporty girls jumped up and down, shouting "Go B.C.! Go!" A bunch of day girls sat in an exclusive group on the grassy hill sneaking looks at Lewis. He didn't give the silly whispering things so much as a glance as he lounged against the hockey shed, his peaked hunting cap twisted on backwards.

Now, suddenly, our team was in the other team's end zone, and even the day girls jumped to their feet, shrieking their heads off.

I guessed they were putting on a display for Lewis, because it didn't sound like their hearts were in it. They knew this was only a girls' school, not a boys' school, where sports were practice for the grownup-man's game of war.

I Am Honestly Not Sure

Now I need to tendril a little and point out Tory's place in the hierarchy we lived by at Bath Ladies College. The hierarchy depended on two things: your appearance and where you lived. For instance, the chunky girls ran our clubs and our school teams and the school houses. They were usually boarders, and I am honestly not sure whether they got chunky from the starchy boarders' diet or whether they were that way in the first place. The pretty girls were mostly day girls, and they were the followers, who did less-important jobs. They had boyfriends, and they didn't do things to uphold the school reputation like being the first in the crowd to offer a seat on the bus. Only our school leaders and the prefects did that. They knew how to hold up the side, as they said at school.

Nobody said it out loud—it was just understood—that Tory was a pretty girl who would never make a prefect. Not only was her tunic a mess, but she wore silver keepers in her pierced ears, and when Miss Phillips told her jewelry was against school rules, Tory argued that she had to wear them or else the holes would grow back in. And she wasn't responsible: she left old apple cores in her underwear drawer and was always losing her brown homework book, in which we kept a daily list of our assignments. But she treated everybody the same way she treated me—as if you mattered. And she always made little jokes about how hopeless she was when anybody gave her a compliment. And if somebody criticized her, she'd only smile in her nice, kind way and agree with what they said. No wonder Paulie loved her and tried to protect her by tidying up the mess she left behind. Paulie remade Tory's bed every morning so she wouldn't get a gating for untidiness and listened for hours to Tory complain about her father, who was the principal of Kings College and expected Tory to excel in her schoolwork.

Paulie had no place in the hierarchy. Nobody knew what to do with her. As for me, I was a new girl with a funny little limp and a hunched shoulder. Perfect fodder for Miss Ibister, who stood beside me, a clipboard in her hand and a whistle in her mouth, ready to blow your eardrums out when the players did something wrong.

Meanwhile, back at the game, our players were charging toward the rival goalie, who lumbered toward them, her knee pads bunching and unbunching like the body of a centipede. Viciously she kicked the ball out of her territory. And then a tall phys-ed woman with the physique of an ape broke from the pack and loped toward our goal post, and everyone on the embankment screamed.

The Virgin suddenly appeared on the stone steps behind the pitch and began to pace the edge of the embankment, angrily calling out to our defense to get their sticks on the ground. She was dressed in her unflattering charcoal suit.

I looked at the field. One of our guards had stopped the forward, and Tory was running with the ball. Now the hefty forward was chasing Tory, waving her stick as if she wanted to smack the bum of my roommate, who seemed to be running away from us all—running to victory in a whir of white dandelion hair and green bloomers and purple knee socks pulled up over her shin pads, so even her nice ankles looked fat.

Then suddenly, something went wrong. The stick of the ape-woman hooked Tory across her right ankle, and she fell flat on her face on the grassy pitch. Miss Ibister sounded her whistle, and the players came to a standstill like pieces in a shattered clock. "Tory's down!" somebody shouted. Everyone rushed toward the middle of the pitch, and Tory disappeared behind a phalanx of female bodies.

On the embankment a few girls called: "Two, four, six, eight! Who do we appreciate? Tory! Tory!"

Miss Ibister pipped her whistle in my ear. "Don't just stand there like a ninny! Cover her with this while I get the nurse!" She handed me a coarse wool blanket and pushed me, stumbling, over to where Tory was lying in an awkward crumple on the grass. Her lips were blue, as if she were cold. I bent down beside her, pretending I was Morley on a house call.

"She's had the wind knocked out of her," I said to nobody in particular, and I tilted back her head and lifted her jaw. Immediately her cheeks went pink again and she began to breathe. Her tongue had been stuck in the back of her throat. I am good with my hands, Sal always said so, but I don't know how I knew to do this. I must have read it in one of Morley's textbooks and stored it away to use in a fantasy that featured me as the rescuer. I was borrowing his manner, too. The I-will-make-you-well set to his shoulders he put on in front of a patient; the reassuring taking of the pulse.

Tory weakly raised her head and somebody cheered, and then two prefects carrying the tray of oranges pushed me out of their way and back into the crowd. On every side of me, women's bodies shut out the sky. My head was barely higher than the rows of breasts bulging out of their blouses—some pairs large and jolly as pumpkins; others, in the stiff, pointed cups of their bras, narrow and sharp, like dangerous instruments that could slice open your skull.

Across the field, a skinny fair-haired woman with a face like a minnow's was hurrying toward Tory. One of the school nurses and a doctor accompanied her. All the girls and the thickset phys-ed women turned to stare. She was what Sal called "a looker." Even Morley would have been impressed by her tight navy suit, high heels, and lean legs sheathed in the russet gossamer of Haines stockings. I guessed she was Tory's mother. She stood watching silently as Willy the janitor and Lewis lifted Tory onto a stretcher and carried her off.

A crowd of girls began to follow them, but the Virgin called everyone back. She stood quietly for a second, the skirt of her old chalk-stained suit fluttering in the breeze. Finally she said, "The game's over, girls. There'll be doughnuts and soft drinks in the cafeteria for everybody." The school's crullers were my favs, but nobody asked me to join them so I walked off slowly, my head down, hoping one of the girls in the stricken crowd would call me back.

12

I sat down in the long grass near the ravine fence. It was just the spot Virginia Woolf would have picked if she'd gone to Bath Ladies College. Granted, it wasn't real countryside, like the windy beaches and pine-fringed islands where Morley and I come from; but at least milkweed and wild asters grew there, and the fence around this part of the grounds was made of fieldstone, not wire. The rumour was that Sir Jonathon had paid a dollar a stone to the farmers who brought them to him from their fields. At one time there'd been 250,000 stones in the fence, and a dollar was almost what those farmers made in a week.

I liked Sir Jonathon's extravagances—not just because it would shock Sal, but because I was starved for news of somebody who could get away with doing what they wanted. I checked to make sure nobody could see me, and then I lay back in the grass and pulled out a pack of Sweet Caps. Oh, Mouse, aren't you wicked, I told myself as I lit up. I was barely into my first exhale when I jerked up with a little cry. Lewis, the grounds boy, stood grinning down at me. I couldn't help noticing his missing front tooth. Paulie's teeth were in better shape, but the family resemblance was more obvious now that I knew the two of them were brother and sister. He squatted down beside me, his bum touching the backs of his ankles.

"You could get expelled for that." He looked impressed.

I nodded. "I wouldn't mind that," I said.

Lewis began to roll a fag from a package of Drum tobacco. He seemed to know I was watching him and didn't mind. I'll have to be careful, though, I thought, not to make him think I'm interested in him sexually. I wasn't, was I, Alice?

"I saw what you did." He deftly lit his fag from a match inside a rolled-up match cover. "Nice work."

"Will she be all right?" I asked.

He shrugged. "I don't know." He stared sullenly at the school rising from the lawns to the west like a prison. "Maybe she'll get to go home and get out of this joint. By the way," he said, "I have a favour to ask of you."

"Oh?" If he wants my body, I thought, he's got another thing coming. I waited nervously, in case I had to deny him.

"Give her this, will you?" He handed me an envelope covered with weird little stick drawings of a girl and a monkey with a long tail. On the front, in big block letters, I read the words, "To my girlfriend, Victoria." I saw more drawings and some initials on the back. At first I thought they spelled out something like SWAK (sealed with a kiss). But when I looked closely, I made out the phrase "KONG LIVES. LONG LIVE KONG." He laughed at my face. "Don't worry, kid. She understands my jokes. We're two of a kind."

"And what kind is that?" I asked, carefully putting his letter in the breast pocket of my school blouse.

"Free spirits. Like James Dean. You know who that is, don't you?" I nodded, and he spat and then squashed his cigarette with the heel of his shoe. I looked down at the butt; it was totally demolished. Then I did the same thing—squashed out my cigarette with the heel of my big, heavy oxford. My butt kept smoking.

"Filters take longer to burn out," he said, and stomped on it. He stared at me as if he wanted to kiss me, so I put out my hand for him to shake, and instead he kissed it with a mocking laugh.

I watched him walk away down a path through the trees. At the bottom of the ravine, he turned and waved. He looked like the stick figures he'd made in his doodles: two legs, two arms, and a head. A boy. There goes the person Tory loves, I thought. She has Lewis, and I have nobody. And I felt terrible again.

13

"Bradford, make it fast," Pauline hissed as I crawled behind her into the dumbwaiter. Paulie pulled down the door with a scary bang and we sat crouched together, knees up to our chins, in a space no bigger than the inside of an old icebox. Now Paulie began to pull on the heavy hemp ropes, watching me suspiciously, as if she expected me to cry out and give us away. So I stared up into the darkness at the top of the shaft, trying not to notice the way the platform swayed slowly from side to side like a subway car. I heard little rattling sounds and squeaks, and then the platform stopped and something clicked into place. Paulie pried open the outside latch with a screwdriver, and we stepped out into a dark hallway whose windows looked down on the ratty little space behind the school where we weren't allowed to go. Nobody except the tradesmen used it.

Paulie put her finger to her lips, her hooded eyes measuring me as she pointed toward a closed door. I recognized it as the door to one of the infirmary bedrooms. She opened it cautiously, and I followed her into a large dormitory. A girl with frizzy blond hair lay sleeping in the second bed. It was Asa Abrams, the only Jewish girl in the school. Poor Asa spent most of her time in the infirmary. We crept past her slowly breathing body. Ahead of us, the night sky in the narrow window beyond the beds glowed pink from the lights of the city. Luckily for us, Tory was awake. She was sitting up in a pair of polka-dot pyjamas and a pink Viyella housecoat. When we got to her cot, Paulie put her hand on Tory's arm, and the two of them stared and stared at each other. At last, Tory motioned to me to come closer.

"I asked Paulie to bring you, Mouse," she whispered. "Thank you for helping me Saturday." Tory never called me by my last name, the way the other girls did. I hoped it wasn't because she felt sorry for me. Now she nodded at Paulie, who hadn't taken her eyes from Tory's face. "Mouse will help you with your essay, won't you, Mouse?" I whispered "Yes" without knowing exactly what Tory meant, but I realized she was making me a substitute for herself. I felt pleased. I was finally being included. "My left leg is broken in two places." Tory threw back the covers so that we could see her legs stretched out stiffly in plaster casts that looked like giant white pupas. "I've torn the ligament in my right ankle, which is almost as bad. I'm being sent home for the rest of the term." I felt my pleasure shrink. The idea of boarding school without Tory made me feel lost. Paulie must have felt the same way, because her dark head sagged a little, too. Then I remembered Lewis's note.

I handed it to Tory, and Paulie and I watched her read it. "Lewis wants me to give him a picture," Tory whispered. She handed the note to Paulie, who put it in her pocket without reading it. "And he wants to know why I've got a photo of a boy on my dresser," Tory said. "How does he know I have my brother's photograph there?"

"Lewis has the run of the school," I whispered, to their surprise. Then I told them about seeing Lewis in the bathroom on the first day. They both listened carefully. Particularly Paulie.

"Oh, that's so nervy!" Tory said. "Going into our washroom like that, right under Phillips's nose!" She grabbed my hand. "Do you think he lay on my bed, Mouse?" She started giggling uncontrollably. "Maybe he looked in my laundry bag!" Suddenly, at the end of the room, Asa coughed twice, very pointedly. "Get on the floor!" Tory hissed. Paulie and I flattened ourselves under Tory's cot and listened. The coughing stopped, and now a door squeaked open.

"Is everything all right in here?" the nurse asked. "I thought I heard voices."

"You did," Tory said. "I'm afraid I was talking in my sleep."

"Well, settle down now, Victoria."

The door closed, and I happened to look over at Paulie. She was watching me again—no longer with hostility but with an expression I didn't understand.

14

In my heart of hearts, I knew that Bath Ladies College wasn't a school but a time machine that trapped you for good. The outside world kept changing, but inside the boarding school nothing ever altered. That's why the matrons and teachers looked the same as they did in the yearbooks twenty years before. And why girls like me didn't have a hope in Hades of going home in one piece.

I was sure old Sir Jonathon never intended things to turn out like this—i.e., for his nice home to be used as a prison for six hundred girls. His original plans, before he ran out of money, called for a large Scottish tower (besides the mock-Norman tower I lived in), a bowling alley, a stable for one hundred horses, and a deer park exactly like the Queen had at Windsor Castle.

The Virgin tried to make a little extra out of the old place by opening the reception hall and foyer to the public over Christmas and the summer holidays. The board didn't think she worked hard enough at this, but their charge was unfair. She did the best she could, under the circumstances. As it was, we all had to set up chairs in Sir Jonathon's mammoth library for old girls' weddings.

The older girls who acted as tour guides on public occasions passed on to us information about what a fanatic Sir Jonathon was for cleanliness. He'd installed gas-fed fireplaces because he considered wood-burning fires too dirty. And he put the coal furnace outside the castle for the same reason and built an underground heating tunnel to connect it to the house. He'd even installed a central vacuuming system, which depended on a water-suction machine in the basement. The system cost too much to run now, but you could still see the brass fittings over the suction holes on the walls of our classrooms.

Sir Jonathon was a bachelor. Maybe, like me, he didn't think much of girls. What would he say if he knew how we sweated and cursed old Hammerhead under our breath when she made us hang from ropes and jump over the horse in his conservatory? It used to be the showroom of his castle: he'd installed a vast stained-glass dome in the ceiling and run special steam pipes through the dirt in the planters to keep his exotic flowers warm. Now only a few rubbery houseplants grew there. And how would he feel about the wastebasket in his grand bathroom stuffed to the top with little brown bags containing used sanitary napkins—the bathroom with a shelf cut into his white Carrara marble for the first telephone in Toronto? He couldn't have had much fun with the women who went to his tea parties. In the photographs of gatherings on the castle lawn, they wore dresses that looked like heavy coats, and hardly any of them smiled except for one or two and only then in such a vague kind of way that it was hard to tell if they were really smiling at all.

I couldn't help thinking how different they looked from President Kennedy's wife, Jackie, in her snug Dior coats and pillbox hats. I may have been wrong, but I didn't think Jackie would enjoy herself at a party like that. Of course, I didn't know Jackie personally. My relationship was with her husband, the president, and that's the way I wanted to keep it.

October 4, 1963

Dear Mr. Kennedy,

I know you have been working too hard refuting Senator Goldwater (keep up the good work on your nuclear test–ban treaty!), so

I'm sewing a pillow for your poor sore back. It's green calico to match your smiling Irish eyes! Plus—guess what!! My roommate Paulie likes you. Yesterday in church, she told me she saw you on TV debating Nixon and thought you were pretty nifty for a Catholic. That's high praise, Mr. President. Ordinarily, Paulie never has nice things to say. I was so surprised, I nearly fell out of the pew. (Wouldn't that have been a riot?) I hate going to St. Paul's, by the way. I can't concentrate on the sermon, because I don't know when to kneel or stand. The congregation jumps up and down when you least expect it, so that's a bit nerve-wracking. Plus we have to line up on the front steps in pairs and then file in wearing stupid navy dresses and coats while everybody watches. The only good things about church are: (1) getting to wear a hat with a dark veil (that makes me feel mysterious, like Greta Garbo); (2) staring at the hats of the pretty women who sit in the front of the church; (3) imagining how good our chicken à la king lunch will taste; (4) riding in Sergeant's bus. Its seats are shot, so we bounce up and down like crazy, and he teases us when we drive by the boys' school. He says, Would you like me to turn in here, girls? And everybody squeals yes, yes! And Miss Phillips just looks nervously out the window and pretends not to hear.

All in all, Sunday is a pretty slow day for us at Bath Ladies College, Mr. President. Paulie says it will be better next year, when we can teach Sunday school in Marly Hall. Of course, the little kids scream and do stuff that gets on your nerves, but at least we get to munch on arrowroot cookies and drink apple juice, while the rest of the school has to listen to another sermon about the low points of being human.

But enough about church. I know *you* like it, and I will try harder to like it, too.

Paulie hates church like I do. I help Paulie with her homework assignments, so she's nicer to me now. But I'm a little afraid of her. She's an unusual girl, a bit strange—maybe even too strange. It's hard to know for sure, because I don't have anybody here to talk to except you. My other roommate, Tory, tore a ligament in her right leg and broke her left one, so she has gone home for the term.

And, what's worse, a drip named Ismay has asked to take Tory's place.

To tell the truth, I guess I don't have many friends here. So it's hard to know what's real. There are days when I feel as if the tower could swallow me whole, like the Blob. (Have you seen that film?) You see, there are days when I'm not sure who I am, Mr. President. I feel like my Mouse head and body could belong to anybody. Do you know what I mean? Maybe it's because I feel other people's feelings so much, I can't tell my emotions from theirs. I'm just floating around inside a great big pile of old stones, and a whole lot of girls are floating around in here with me.

Your devoted friend,
Mouse Bradford

Men Were Hard to Come By

Men were hard to come by at school. Only two kinds were allowed inside: funny-looking janitors who had B.O. and ministers, who were more interested in God than sex. Still, both kinds wore trousers, and that was good enough for us. If President Kennedy had ever visited, the whole school would have died.

On the second Friday in October, Mrs. Peddie brought Tory's father, Canon Quinn, to our Family Life class. I wanted to like him because of Tory, but he had eyebrows like a pair of unfurled bat's wings. And bad fingers. It was hard not to stare at his fingers. They were rounded at the end like the blind heads of worms. Maybe that's why he kept them clasped on his lap. He even held them there when he walked.

He was holding his fingers like that when Mrs. Peddie introduced him.

"We're here to discuss your future role as wives and mothers. An educated woman is of great benefit to her children, isn't that true, Canon Quinn?" She turned a huge, gummy smile at the minister. The trouble with Mrs. Peddie was that she always wanted everybody to agree with her. Her optimism was depressing because if you didn't agree, you knew you were going to hurt her feelings, and if you did agree, then you were lying to her and letting her down anyhow. I wondered if Canon Quinn found it as much of a problem as I did.

"I second that, Mrs. Peddie. Heartily."

"Although I daresay a few of you will go on to make your mark on the world," Mrs. Peddie said. She didn't look at us. Instead she smiled girlishly at Canon Quinn and heaved herself onto the edge of her desk. She was wearing one of her infamous sweaters pulled tight over the shelf of her enormous bosom. "Perhaps right before our eyes sits a famous composer?" (Oh, it's not me, I thought, but Ismay Thom.) "Or a doctor of divinity." Mrs. Peddie was suddenly looking in my direction. She often caught my eye in class, hoping I'd answer a question. I never did because she said we didn't know what we thought about something until we could put it into words and I was dead sure she was wrong about that although I couldn't exactly say why. That morning I smiled back at her even though I wasn't interested in something so finky. Not for a second.

"I will read a little about the history of our school, and then our visitor for today has a few words to say to you. You should know that our former principal, Miss Higgs, was engaged once herself." (There were a lot of gasps from us girls, and Mrs. Peddie giggled too.) "So she was very partial to husbands. Of course, she could never remember the names of her girls' husbands. But let me quote to you the words of the school historian: 'Miss Higgs felt it was wrong that girls should look forward to marriage as their only possibility in life.'" And here Tory's father shifted uncomfortably, moving his clasped hands off the desk and onto his chest. "'She desired to see every woman equipped, if the need arose, to maintain herself in dignity . . .'" Mrs. Peddie began to swing her ankle up and down—as if she thought she was our age—right under Canon Quinn's nose. He regarded Mrs. Peddie thoughtfully. " 'Each of you has some particular gift of your own'—Miss Higgs wrote—'which can be pressed into service for human betterment while at the same time permitting a small allowance for the unfortunate woman in question.' "

"Which, I trust, in good faith, did not happen often," Canon Quinn added.

Mrs. Peddie wheeled about, her thick leg still swinging, her lower lip wobbling. "I fear it happened more often than we'd like to think, Bruno."

"Oh." The Canon stared down at his clasped hands. By now his two index fingers were waving like batons, and he looked as if he were seeing Mrs. Peddie at a great distance. His passivity surprised me. I expected him to sneer at her for flirting with him, maybe push her off the desk. I wanted him to fulfill the promise of his nerve-wracking eyebrows. But he did nothing of the sort. He just sat there the way he did in prayers, looking out the window, his index fingers oscillating. So I began to read the English essay Paulie had given me to check over. Mrs. Peddie had asked us to write a speech by a famous person in history. This is what Paulie wrote:

Guess Who

I am the star of a movie you all saw. You know it's me because I don't wear clothes and I beat my chest every time I see a pretty little blond. I love blonds. There is a real nice blond who goes to a girls school I know. Tory Quinn is her name, my name is (wouldn't you like to know). I love T.Q.

I can roar louder than Tarzan. Do you know who I am yet? Yesterday I went to Tory's school while she was playing field hockey. I caused a sensation. A bad woman had knocked Tory down—a real bad woman. So I beat my chest and ran out to where my favourite blond lay dead as a doornail.

I kneed the creep who did the dirty work right where it hurts and then ran to my Tory.

Her cute little pink face was white as a ghost! So I picked her up and carried her up to the top of the school. My hairy feet climbed the outside of the tower with no problems. When I got to the top, I saw they had got the fire engine after me. It was like the battle with the fighter planes at the top of the Empire State building all over again.

The little red men put their ladders up against the tower and started to yell dirty words at me. So I pushed over the first one and the second and the third but they only brought in more trucks with more ladders. So I kissed my poor little Victoria good-bye and then I beat my chest to show I wasn't scared. Me, King Kong, scared of measily humans? Now you know who I am. Then I jumped—hairy feet first. Good-bye cruel world. Good-bye you bunch of suckers.

I could hardly believe my eyes. I read it twice, and then I wrote a reply.

Dear Paulie,

I think you have a great imagination! If only I could think up ideas like that! It will make Ismay Thom green with envy. Seriously, though, I did notice a few errors with spelling. "Blonds" should be *es* because it's females you're talking about, and "measily" is spelt "measly." Also, "measly" is slang, which Mrs. Peddie won't like.

In fact, I think Mrs. Peddie may have a few objections. Maybe you should read the essay Ismay wrote for her on why civilization depends on good manners (or mine about the joys of gluttony. You know how we stay behind on Thursdays to eat the leftover jellos! The only dessert that won't make us fat.). Ismay's essay is a little long (11 pages), but it has a lot of adjectives and adverbs, which Mrs. Peddie likes. For instance, how about—I am a tall magnificent creature who stands on the edge of the parapet, a fierce glassy stare in my proud eyes . . . my noble furred arms hanging slackly at my side . . . ? (It would be nice to feel sorry for King

Kong, you see.) Also, I think you should leave Tory out. Mrs. Peddie doesn't like personal references in an essay. Thank you for doing me the honour of showing me your writing. I personally consider John F. Kennedy to be my ideal man, but there are things to be said in favour of King Kong.

Your roommate and friend,
Mouse

I saw a shadow on the page. I looked up, and who was standing there but Mrs. Peddie herself. She didn't say anything; she just picked up Paulie's essay and walked away, leaving me to wait for the axe to fall.

15

I sat in a hushed classroom at a slanted desk with black cast-iron sides, painting my nails with Tropical Dawn. All around me girls read their books or looked out the window toward the ravine, where the orange-red maples and yellow beeches shimmered in the watery afternoon sunlight. Then, from far down the corridor, I heard a rhythmic pounding so faint I paid no attention. Behind me, one of my studymates started slapping the top of her desk. A moment later, all the girls were slapping their desks with their palms, like oarmasters in the movie *Spartacus* beating time for the slaves who rowed old Roman galleys. And now, just as quickly as it had started, the noise of the girls' hands died away. I looked up and found myself staring right into the Virgin's eyes. The desk slapping, which imitated the sound of the Virgin's footfalls, had been a warning that everybody except me understood. The Virgin pointed to the nail polish on my desk and beckoned to me. I couldn't move. My legs had turned to water, the way you find yourself in dreams, when you try to run and can't.

Angrily, the Virgin flung open our study door.

"Mary Beatrice, may I see you in my office, please?" I stood up and went out without looking at anybody.

The Virgin sat down behind her desk and I stood, trying hard to settle my face into a remorseful expression. She cleared her throat awkwardly, as if she was trying to cover up a moment of nervousness, and brought out a piece of paper. I recognized the handwriting on the paper as that of Mrs. Peddie's. Suddenly, the Virgin whipped off her half-moon reading glasses and sighed.

"Now, Mary Beatrice. I see here you have a few gatings from the boarding school. Putting nail polish on during study. Going to the bathroom against Miss Phillips's wishes. Being late for morning inspection. Do you really think I should be cross over things as silly as this?"

The Virgin rested her chin in her hand and gazed at me as if we were sharing a confidence. I began to stutter. I didn't like to think I was unreasonable.

"I guess those are silly things to do," I said.

"Yes, yes!" the Virgin said. "I know you have more common sense."

Now the Virgin brought out Paulie's essay and my reply. "Don't you think passing notes in Mrs. Peddie's class is a silly thing to do?" The Virgin read softly: "Dear Paulie. . . ." I began to perspire.

"You don't have to read it. I know what it says," I said.

"It's very interesting what you said about Paulie having a good imagination, Mary Beatrice. I think you're quite right." She chuckled and looked at me as if I should chuckle, too, and I managed a twittery nervous sound. "You know, of course, that Pauline is a very troubled girl? The staff—well, I'm sure you've noticed the troubles they have with her."

"I guess it's hard when you don't have a real mother," I said, and then wished I hadn't given myself away like that.

"Paulie has a real mother," the Virgin said. "She just isn't able to cope with Paulie. She's in a mental institution." The Virgin sat back and looked out the window. She suddenly seemed very sad. "Let's talk about something else for a moment, shall we? Mrs. Peddie says you are very well read but you don't speak in her class. Why is that?"

"She thinks we don't know what we think until we can say it."

"Yes, that's a challenge, isn't it?" The Virgin paused. "Of course, Mrs. Peddie and I differ about the nature of knowledge. Speech is an intellectual tool, and we know some things intuitively without being able to put them into words. Spiritual knowledge, for instance. But you write well, Mary Beatrice, so you will soon learn to speak well too. I understand you have written a very good essay on *Pride and Prejudice*. Personally, I prefer Charlotte Brontë to Jane Austen. Do you know what Charlotte said when a critic told her she should write like Jane?"

I shook my head no. " 'Miss Austen is shrewd and observant, but she cannot be great because she is without poetry.' " Miss Vaughan smiled cozily, as if she and I were just girls together. " 'One sees there only a highly cultivated garden but no open country.' No open country. Isn't that wonderful, Mary?" I couldn't answer.

The Virgin stood up. She put her hand on my shoulder and smiled graciously. "Any friendship you can show Paulie will help. However, all this aside, I am afraid, Mary Beatrice, I am still forced to give you an orderly mark."

I felt lightheaded. Mouse Bradford has a black mark! Mouse Bradford is in disgrace! And I thought I was a coward, a scaredy-cat who lived in dread of rule breaking and punishments? Well, now Paulie would respect me. I lowered my head and waited to receive the wrath of the Virgin. Instead, she nodded cheerfully.

"There's no point saying any more to a bright girl like you, Mary Beatrice. I'll expect sensible behaviour in the future." She paused and dropped her sulky voice to an even more whispery whisper. "The staff want me to send Paulie back to Ridgeley House, but she's better off here with us. Will you be my scout and keep an eye on her for me?"

Without knowing how I got there, I found myself in the hall, where Paulie stood at the front of a line of girls that wound all the way down the stairs outside the Virgin's office into the junior school. These girls looked me over, as if checking for physical signs that the Virgin had manhandled me, and then went back to their anxious whispering. Paulie wouldn't look my way. I guessed she suspected me of spinning incriminating tales about her. Behind me, I heard the Virgin step out of her office and whisper in the bullying tone she reserved for the janitors or any girl who resisted her logic, "In here, Paulie. At once."

When the door to her office closed, I began to clump off down the long winding corridor as fast as my heavy old oxymorons would take me.

16

The Virgin gave an orderly mark to Paulie and then issued a strange order: Paulie was to walk off her frustrations with the school every evening after study. And I was to go with her. The Virgin said the exercise would help my legs get stronger.

I felt shy about walking with Paulie. I was sure she wished some other girl had been chosen. The first night, we set off in silence toward the ravine. We walked past the grove of camperdown elms, whose twisted branchlets hung down like witches' fists. I knew from English class that Sir Jonathon had also planted Chinese junipers in the grove, golden yews, English oaks, and eight types of willow, including the cricket-bat willows, whose wood is the best for making cricket bats. Mrs. Peddie made us memorize the names of trees and plants so we would be able to refer to flora and fauna as expertly as the British novelists we studied. She sounded so earnest, I thought it was impossible to be a writer unless you could reel off the names of all the flowering deciduous trees, know which tree was the only deciduous pine in the world (the larch), and know how to treat the sting of a blackthorn bush (rub it with the leaf of a burdock). At the edge of the grounds, Paulie finally stopped.

"I don't know what you told the Virgin, and I don't care. But you're not going to get anything out of me," Paulie said.

"All right," I said.

Paulie pressed her face into the wire mesh of the ravine fence, like a convict gazing at the outside world. "Did she make you promise anything?"

"She said my detentions were for silly things and that I should be more careful next time. She said—" I stopped, flustered. "She said I should let her know if you did anything strange." My big ears felt hot. "But I won't, Paulie. Honest."

"I bet," Paulie said. "Well, I'm not going to fucking tell you if I do do something strange."

"All right," I said.

"All right? All right! Is that all you know how to say, Bradford?"

I hung my head in shame. I was in awe of her fierceness, and frightened of it, too. She seemed so much older and bigger than me. She must have realized by then that I was no threat, because I heard her sigh, and we walked on along the top of the ravine without talking. The ground was beginning to feel slippery from fallen leaves. Above our heads a light burned in the tower where Miss Phillips stood behind her curtain watching us.

For the first week, we hardly talked. I took Paulie at her word and walked with her silently, watching her kick out at the shiny chestnuts that littered the school lawns. I wore my school sweater—the green one with the crest on the breast pocket—and the scarf that Sal had knit for me. Paulie wore nothing but the kilt and blouse we were allowed to wear after the school day was over. Often we stood at the edge of the grounds and stared through the fence at the ravine. Sergeant kept the holes patched, so there was no easy way off the grounds except by climbing the fence. I wondered if I could escape from the school by digging a hole under it, the way World War Two prisoners had escaped from Stalag 17. Once I was over on the other side and into the woods, the Virgin and her army of matrons could search and search, but they'd never find me.

One night, as we stood near the ravine, a fog rolled in from the lake. It swallowed up the ravine and the clock tower of Kings College to the south. I stared back in the direction of the school, searching for the bright pane of Miss Phillips's window. I saw only foggy bits of lawn and a shape rising in the gloom like a dark ship. When I turned around again, Paulie was gone. I began to walk quickly in the direction we'd just come from, calling her name.

The mist kept filling up the school grounds, like the moist breath of a giant. Here where I stood, the ivy ran over the floor of the grove like a ground cover and then up the south trunks of the ravine's elm trees, where the plant was sheltered from the coldest winds. A few minutes passed. I called Paulie's name again. No sign of her. I turned to go, and there was Lewis sauntering toward me, clenching and unclenching his fists. He wore his old hunting hat, the chin strap dangling loose from one of the far side-flaps. And in the fog, his teeth sparkled and glistened like a werewolf's. Get a grip, Mouse, I thought. This is the grounds boy. What do you think he's going to do? Rape you? Down in the ravine, where nobody can see you—not even the Virgin. Who seemed as far away now as Morley in Madoc's Landing.

Lewis smiled and beckoned for me to go with him. I shook my head no.

"Got the willies, have yuh?" He pointed to the darkest part of the ravine, toward the heating plant. "Paulie's waiting for you over there. She asked me to get you."

"Paulie? You know where she is?" I asked.

"Here—she asked me to give you this." He handed me the large safety pin she used to do up her kilt.

I took the pin and stared at it wonderingly. Perhaps Lewis had killed Paulie and now was going to do the same to me. He must have read my thoughts, because he patted my shoulder.

"Come on," he said. "Paulie told me you don't have much time left on your walk."

It was true—only another eight minutes. Wordlessly I followed him down the path. He stopped at the old coal shed that stood behind the heating plant near the school fence. On the other side lay the ravine, which stirred with funny rustling noises I couldn't identify. I listened for a moment. It was the wind in the ravine trees mixed with the soft whooshing sound of traffic on the highway bridge to the north. The whooshing sound rolled toward us like the roar of surf. Lewis called "Paulie—Paulie." Nobody answered. Then he kicked open the door of the shed and went in to find her while I stood at the entrance shivering.

I thought of going after Lewis and decided against it. I peered into a darkened room. A huge boiler sat in one corner, its door open so I could see a stack of firebricks inside. A creepy feeling came over me that Lewis was hiding in there. That he was not who he said he was. That he'd lied. I wanted to run back to the tower. Then I felt a hand on my shoulder. When I turned around, Lewis was smiling at me, a cigarette drooping from his bottom lip. In the background, I heard the sound of whatever dilapidated machinery the Virgin used to heat her school. For a second, I felt irritated. Nobody used coal furnaces anymore: even the school in Madoc's Landing had switched to oil. Now sharpen up, Mouse, I told myself. It doesn't make sense to be thinking about a rundown furnace just now, when you're about to get yourself killed. And then Lewis leaned so close I could smell the Brylcreem on his hair. He put his hand on the back of my head. I didn't move; I was too frightened. He tilted my head back and stuck his tongue in my ear. His mouth stank of nicotine. I tottered back, waving my arms, and he grabbed me and held me close. He put his bony face right next to mine and hissed: "Bradford, don't you know who I am?"

Lewis took off his cap, and a thick black braid fell down his back. Then he popped in one of his front teeth and smiled. I didn't know what to say, and Lewis began to laugh. He said he hadn't meant to scare me—he'd just got a little carried away because he liked practical jokes. And then he took my hand and yanked me into the dark shed and closed the door.

17

It wasn't the boiler I heard. It was the automatic coal feed, Lewis said. He made me listen to its rhythmic clink—a sound like a bicycle chain going round and round, of metal hitting metal in the darkness. I stood trembling beside him, my ear still wet from his kiss.

Then Lewis—I mean, Paulie—struck a match, holding it between her muscular thumb and forefinger. I stared at her, breathless, not sure what was going to happen next, and not caring. The flame crept slowly down and burnt out soundlessly between her fingers. I smelled something funny under the sulphur, and then I realized she'd put the match out with her own skin. Paulie lit another match and handed it to me. "Your turn," she said.

The match burnt down halfway. I felt the heat before the flame touched my fingers. "Ow!" I said and dropped the match.

"It's not that it doesn't hurt; it's that you don't mind if it hurts," Paulie said. "Lawrence of Arabia—remember? That's what he said in the film."

"Yes," I said meekly.

Paulie lit a candle this time and held it so close to my face I couldn't see a thing except the halo of its flame. Fingers suddenly poked my left bicep.

"You're flabby, Bradford—like a girl," Paulie said. She handed me the candle and flexed her arm so her muscles squirmed like small moles inside the casing of her skin. I'd never seen Paulie's biceps before; they'd been hidden in the sleeves of her school middy. But I'd seen Lewis's arms. Oh, yes—a few times. It was impossible not to notice Lewis's arms, dangling like twin cobras from his rolled-up sleeves. No girls I knew had arms that grew like snakes from their torso. And now here were Lewis's arms on Paulie.

Or *was* this person Paulie? Maybe it was a creature who could move with the authority of a man one minute and giggle like a girl the next. The sight was confusing and interesting—like watching a wizard melt into male and female shapes before your eyes. And every change in Paulie provoked a change in me. When she acted like Lewis, I wanted to exhale responsibility for myself like a sigh; when she acted like Paulie, I was myself again. Well, almost myself—as much as a Mouse can be. And then I heard Sal's voice in my ear—see, Mary Beatrice, you're a girl after all—deferring to a man the way a woman should. And I felt sick. Was I no different from the dummies at Morley's hospital, who followed him into the operating room carrying his surgical tray?

Bewildered, I let Paulie lead me past the hills of coal into the boiler room. It smelled of male sweat, and I saw the white coats of the janitors hanging on the wall. They had made a kind of sitting room for themselves next to the boiler. Two broken-down chintz armchairs spilled stuffing like seeds from a burst milkweed pod. On an overturned Kotex carton somebody had arranged copies of *Playboy* in a row, the way Sal arranged Morley's medical magazines on our coffee table.

Behind this makeshift sitting room stood a door draped with the same striped olive-green curtains the Virgin hung in her office.

Paulie went right over to the curtain and lifted it, and inside I saw another tiny room, with wooden sides like a horse's stall. The clink of the coal feed grew fainter as we stepped inside, me still holding the candle. We were standing in an old coal chute. In the middle of the chute was a piano stool with a stack of bananas sitting on top of it.

Beside me, Paulie lit an incense stick, then dipped her knee and crossed herself, genuflecting as expertly as the High Anglicans we saw at St. Paul's. Then she made me hold the candle close to the wall, and I saw a creature with mad, raging monkey eyes. His hairy arms held lightning bolts, as if he were about to hurl them into our hearts. I nearly dropped the candle.

"Give them to Kong," Paulie said, and tapped my pocket where my Sweet Caps nestled. I just stared at her, and she snatched them up for herself and put them next to the bananas on her altar, the pack open so my fags spilled out onto the floor and shone in the gloomy room like white fingers. I was looking at a movie poster of King Kong—an old one, from the thirties. In the dark, I could see New York at Kong's feet—a silhouette of bumps no higher than his massive calves.

Oh, Kong was terrible to look at if he was mad, and lovable as a teddy bear when he was doing things he liked, such as holding Fay Wray in his fist and gently peeling off her clothes. I could see why Paulie liked him. I was fond of him myself.

Near my cigarettes I spotted one of Ismay Thom's scarves, some dead geraniums from the Virgin's favourite plot, a *Book of Common Prayer*, a sheaf of new school notepaper with the school motto and the tassel of the clover, and—I had to look again—the book by Norman Vincent Peale that Sal had given me.

Before I could say anything, Paulie pounded her chest and swung her arms back and forth the way Kong does when he's protecting Fay Wray from danger—like the time he ripped apart the jaw of the *Tyrannosaurus rex*. "Kong the beautiful, Kong the bold, Kong the brave," Paulie bellowed. I shrank back into the furnace room, embarrassed for Paulie and her strange behaviour.

"I fooled you, didn't I?" Paulie followed me out, smoking one of my Sweet Caps. "And I fooled the Virgin, too. She swallowed every lie I told her about Paulie having a brother. The Virgin thinks she's so smart, but she swallowed it all, hook, line, and sinker."

Despite my uneasiness, I was impressed. Oh, Mouse, I thought, here you are with a master rule breaker, you, who bows down to authority like a willow tree in the wind! What a job of mimicking! In her own way, Paulie was a genius. "And Tory?" I whispered.

"Yeah." She squinted, as if she were seeing me for the first time. "Kong likes you, Mouse," she said. "He says you can be a boy, like me."

"You mean dress up?" I said nervously.

"Yeah." The cigarette flipped upside down and then disappeared completely inside Paulie's closed mouth. "But you have to pass his tests first, okay?" she mumbled. Wisps of smoke escaped from the lit cigarette inside her mouth and snaked upwards into her nostrils. How could Paulie stand holding the hot cigarette in her mouth? I waited for her to start coughing. Instead, she clamped her lips tightly together so no smoke could leak out. Maybe the moisture from her tongue kept the cigarette from burning the roof of her mouth. And, then again, maybe not. I waited for the smoke to start coming out of her ears.

"I don't know."

"Sure you do." Paulie flipped the cigarette out of her mouth with a fold of her tongue. "You'll look better as a guy." She nodded toward my hump. "It'll be easier to cover up—that." She put her hands on my shoulder, and for a second I swear she was Lewis again and she was going to stick her tongue in my ear or do something worse, like French-kiss me on the mouth. But she only laughed and sat me down on the shabby old chairs and outlined what I had to do.

18

Here are the preliminary tests of Kong, just as Paulie devised them.

1. Lift a full five-foot-square carton of Kotex boxes over one's head and balance it there like a bunch of bananas. (Estimated weight: forty pounds.)
2. Hold a match between thumb and forefinger and let it burn down to the skin without crying. (I got a second chance on that.)
3. Stand (only sissy girls sit) on a swing in the junior playground and take it over the top.
4. Walk along the tower wall twice without looking down or stopping.
5. Adopt an I'm-all-right-Jack attitude no matter what.
6. Eat six bowls of fish eyes and glue (tapioca pudding) without puking.
7. Practise shaving with Paulie's shaving kit. (If shaving the hair off your legs only makes the hair grow in heavier, then shaving your face would make you grow a beard, Paulie said.)
8. Pee standing up.

I completed the first two preliminary tests and missed the third. (Lucky for me, Sergeant had taken down the swings for the winter.) I did the other tests the next evening. I won't say how well

I performed—not in detail, anyway. Let me put it this way. Kong liked Mouse and closed his eyes to the pee dribbling down my thigh and wetting my shoes. So I could sneak past his exacting standards the first time around.

Why did I do the tests? I was scared to say no to Paulie, and maybe I wanted her to be Lewis. Lewis was a bully-tease, and I found that exciting, because, although I didn't know it, I was beginning to develop a taste for fear. Fear makes you feel alive. Without a drop of fear now and again, life wouldn't be worth living.

There was one other reason. It was true what Paulie said about Alice: I *did* look nicer in jackets with padded shoulders. As for what she said about Kong—I thought of it as Paulie being Paulie. We at Bath Ladies College (as Mrs. Peddie would say) felt grateful to each other just for being there to share the misery of school life.

Although the preliminary tests were finished, I still had three more categories to go.

Mastery over Nature.
Mastery over Other Men.
Mastery over Women.

19

Nobody suspected that Paulie was Lewis, because nobody expects a girl to be a guy. Ismay Thom didn't suspect that Paulie was Lewis, and she was our new roommate. Ismay was the first to point out that I wore the heels of my oxfords into half-moons because I didn't walk like a girl; I walked jaw and stomach out, the weight on my heels, like a man. Well, of course I did. Paulie and I both did. We practised until it was second nature. Basically, you understand, Ismay couldn't have given me a nicer compliment. But what I didn't want to happen happened anyhow.

Alice and I Discuss the Hard Facts

— I think it's too late, Alice. I've even got—groan—hair down there.

— You mean that patch springing out between your legs, as if it's electrified?

— Yes. And look what happens if I press my breasts together with my palms!

— Yikes! Cleavage!

— Well, it's not movie star cleavage. It's more like what you get when you squeeze two very old tennis balls together. I mean, you can see hollows on the outsides of my breasts, but there's still a genuine little valley in the middle. And only women and fat men have that.

— Maybe your breasts will deflate like old inner tubes.

— That won't happen until I get old and you know it. Oh, Alice, why do we need separate sexes anyway? We all start off as girls in the womb.

— Not me. I grew out of your shoulder.

— You're not listening. I'm talking about the tiny lump Morley's textbook calls the genital tubercle. It looks like a girl's privates when it first shows up on an unborn baby. It's not until much later that this swelling develops into a penis.

— I thought you didn't like girls.

— That's beside the point. Don't you see, Alice? If somebody could only arrange it so that lump didn't develop, we wouldn't need two sexes. It would save us all so much trouble.

One night, Ismay walked into the washroom and caught Alice and me doing the nightly once-over. "You're starkers, Mary Beatrice! Oh, you make me sick. Showing yourself off like that." I shrank away, my arms shielding my hateful new breasts, which I longed to bind flat, like Paulie. "And you should wear a bra," she sniffed, "if you don't want them to sag like a Ubangi's." Her ringlets quivering, Ismay marched to her dresser and began the nightly ritual I knew by heart.

1. Pull the long flannel nightie covered with apples over her head and do it up to her chin. Then slide out her underclothes, one by one, like a magician discovering doves and oranges inside your ears.

2. Sprinkle talcum powder down the open neck of the nightie and move the material in and out so the powder sifts out the armholes and under the hem and makes you choke and the room smell like freshly changed babies.

3. Brush her black-as-earth hair a hundred strokes, front, side, and back. Scotch-tape two kiss curls—one to each cheek—and curl the rest of her mop with tiny, spiky wire rollers.

4. Polish her oxfords with her own spit, like a soldier in boot camp, and then iron her tunic on her dresser top. (Ismay liked her tunic to hang in hideously neat folds, without wrinkles, just the way the new girls who didn't know any better wore them. With Ismay, it was a point of pride.)

5. Open the barred windows as wide as possible. (The more night air you have, the better your complexion. Ismay thought she had cheeks like an English tea rose. Personally, her papery white skin made me think of English warthogs. But at least the open windows made the smell of her baby powder fainter.)

6. Pull the covers up to her chin and read out loud to nobody in particular Douglas Bader's autobiography *Reach for the Sky* until Paulie tells her to shut up.

Halfway through number three that night, Ismay put down her iron and held up her tunic. "Somebody here hates me, Mary Beatrice," Ismay cried. "They have to—to do a disgusting thing like this." The back of her tunic was thickly coated with something like chocolate. There was a great big circle of it right on the part that fell over her bum, as if Ismay had bled through the material during her period. I looked closely.

"It's only dried ketchup," I said finally. "The school laundry will take it out."

"Do you really think so?"

"Absolutely. They use so much detergent and starch, there's no way this won't come back clean as a whistle."

"You're a bloody optimist, Mary Bea." In no time at all Ismay was at number six—my most unfav part—while I retreated to my bed to lick out the vanilla fillings from the Oreos I kept stashed in my underwear drawer. Ismay had her regime to get by on; I had my cookies, which I stole from the matron's night tray in handfuls—with Paulie's approval.

Number six: "It was a glorious spring morning when Bader

drove to Roehampton to take delivery and his spirits were soaring at the prospect. He thought it must be the way a woman felt on her way to pick up a new fur coat."

"What's he going to get?" I wasn't quite brave enough to tell her I didn't want to hear about her idol Douglas Bader. Bader sounded pompous, not kind and smart like President Kennedy.

"New legs, of course," Ismay said. "Wooden ones. Two of them. Bloody exciting, I'd say."

"I wouldn't feel excited about getting a new fur coat," I said. "I don't like them." In my heart of hearts, I felt worried. Maybe Sal felt exactly like that when Morley had given her a fur stole last Christmas. But I didn't say so to Ismay. Even though women were the most embarrassing gender, it still bugged me when I thought of Sal and the way she seemed to fit those descriptions of fluffheads who liked nothing but clothes and jewels. Not even Sal—from what I could see—was that simple. Not deep down, not truly. Not when you got to know her. And that was when the most surprising thing happened: Paulie walked out of the closet. She always undressed there, and nobody dared to say anything about it. Ismay and I both yelped because neither of us knew she'd been hiding there, listening. And then I felt ashamed for acting like a girl.

"You babies," Paulie sneered, and began to tie her hair off her forehead with an elastic from her bloomers. Her remark made me feel even worse.

"You're bloody inconsiderate, Pauline Sykes. A decent person wouldn't surprise us like that," Ismay said. She picked up her tunic and waved it at Paulie. "And don't think I'm going to let you get away with this. I expect you to pay the blasted cleaning bill."

"I didn't touch your stupid tunic," Paulie said. She was applying white zit cream to her pimples. "You did that yourself. You just don't want to admit it. Isn't that right, Bradford?"

I wish I could say I told the truth. Just between you and me and the gatepost, I liked Ismay. In a lukewarm sort of way, of course.

Because she didn't care what the other girls thought. Because she liked me and secretly gave me her stash of Oreos when Paulie wasn't looking. If I'd been Ismay I would have died at the way the other girls avoided sitting next to her at our meal tables and snickered behind their fingers when she sang too loudly in prayers. I will never forget her English voice trumpeting over our soft Canadian sopranos: "Like the dancing waves in sunlight make me glad and free . . . like the straightness of the pine tree, let me upright be." I had Paulie to stop me from getting picked on, but Ismay didn't have anyone.

Anyhow, I mumbled something like "Maybe so" and kept on polishing off the Oreos. I'd gone through all the white fillings, and now I was eating the crunchy black wafers, one by one. Ismay looked at me as if her heart were breaking and went back to reading out loud. "Dessoutter had a set of three shallow wooden steps with bannisters, and when he put the legs on and tried . . ."

"Would you stop reading that stupid fucking book!" Paulie lurched at Ismay, and I swear she was going to sock her one, so I shouted, "Ismay, watch out!" (It was the least I could do.) And Paulie glared at me and grabbed the book about Douglas Bader and threw it out the window. Ismay began to squeal and sob, and our bedroom door opened. In came Miss Phillips.

"That'll be enough, Ismay. Pauline, you will report to Miss Vaughan in the morning."

In the middle of the night, I woke up and saw Paulie standing by our open window, smoking. She looked so much like Lewis right then that I pulled the covers over my head and did what I often did in my bedroom at Madoc's Landing—i.e., masturbate.

I'd like to set this straight, just for the record. As far as I was concerned, playing with myself had nothing to do with Paulie or boys. Or even sex. Because nothing I saw in the movies suggested a connection to what the curvaceous women did when they lay in men's arms. Masturbating was a game, like pick-up sticks. You could play it by yourself over and over, as many times as you liked. In boarding school, all of us needed our solitary pleasures. And next to Oreos, this was mine. Sad to say, just as I was getting warmed up, somebody pulled off my covers.

"Okay, Bradford. Get up."

"Why?" I whispered.

"Because Kong says so."

20

At the fifth-floor landing, Paulie made me stop so we could catch our breath. Below us, we could hear Phooey Phillips complaining to someone about the "troublemakers" who had just coated her toilet seat with Vaseline. Then, to my dismay, the talking below stopped, and echoing up the old tower stairs I made out a drumming that could mean only one thing: any second now, and the Virgin's white head would rise like the moon out of the dark stairwell.

"Quick," Paulie hissed. "Up there." Paulie dashed headlong up the stairs no student was permitted to use, and I limped after her, looking left and right to make sure nobody saw us. I hated myself for caring if I was expelled for breaking into matrons' rooms; I wanted to be like Paulie, who put tacks on the Virgin's pew at St. Paul's when the Virgin stood up to sing. I didn't want to be like the other simps who thought they had guts because they hiked up the skirts of their tunics and dared the Virgin's army of matrons to give them a uniform mark. Trembling, I stood on guard while Paulie pulled something out of her pocket. "Ye olde master key," she whispered. A moment later she pushed me in.

It was cold in Mrs. Peddie's small parlour. Her rooms were plainly furnished like ours, except for the large Heintzman piano, which she liked to play for us on Sunday evenings after the Virgin had given us a talk.

Paulie bolted the front door from the inside and began to rummage through Mrs. Peddie's desk. I didn't know what she was looking for. I could hear the Virgin's cough in the hall below. "Hurry, Sykes," I said. I'd never dared to use her last name before, and Paulie grinned and held up another key. Then she rummaged around some more and produced a package of caramels and a diary stuffed with letters. Snickering, she emptied the rest of the drawer onto the floor and tossed the diary to me. "The old bag's love letters," she said. Then, with Mrs. Peddie's key, she opened a tall door beside the piano and pushed me through.

I followed her on my tiptoes down a creaking set of stairs wide enough for Sir Jonathon's regiment. We went three flights, maybe four—and then we were standing in a little room with two doors. The first door said "Voltage," and the other didn't have a name. There was no sound except for the dull rumble of the heating plant.

"Get ready," Paulie whispered. "You're about to see the land of the little toilets."

The unmarked door slid open to reveal a dim tunnel that looked as long as a city block. It wasn't really dark but the ceiling was low, and the heating pipes undulated in the gloom like fat, dark worms. And then I saw a curious thing: row after row of miniature toilets lined up against one wall of the tunnel. The toilets were coated in dust and looked to be too small even for Sergeant.

"They were left over from the time the junior school was renovated," Paulie whispered. "The Virgin will never find us down here."

We began to creep slowly along in the darkness, careful not to touch the hot pipes. Their surface was covered with a coarse cheesecloth that had been glued onto corrugated cardboard. At the second bend in the tunnel, the pipes split into pairs—a return pipe and a flow pipe—heading off in different directions, to various wings of the school. The ceiling was higher here, and there was dust over everything—thick dust that I could feel in my nose.

A banging noise started up, and Paulie and I jumped. The noise got louder and louder and passed over our heads in a rush of wind and metallic clatter, as if some creature were hitting the insides of the pipes, clamouring to get out and attack us.

"I'm turning back," I whispered.

"It's just the furnace," Paulie said in a normal voice and grabbed my hand. I let her pull me slowly around the bend.

A giant tricycle, like the one in the portrait of the English headmistress, stood against the wall beside a large trunk. It was hard to believe anybody could ride such an awkward-looking contraption (although I know people will say exactly the same things about our bicycles fifty years from now). The headmistress's bike looked to be a very good model of its kind. It was outfitted with a handsome bell and a leather-covered headlight that hung off its bars like an old coach lamp.

Paulie opened the trunk beside it, which turned out to be full of cycling gear. She pulled out a pair of old goggles and put them on me. She pointed to something that looked like a rectangular tombstone and told me to get on it. She said Sergeant had told her it was the old mounting block Sir Jonathon had used for his horses. I didn't want to sit on the teetery old bike, whose kidney-shaped seat rose far above our heads. But, as Alice knows, obedience is my worst failing. Sal raised me to do what she said when she said it, although I can't put all the blame on her. I am a slow thinker, and doing what somebody else says first often saves me the worry of figuring out what I really think until I have the time to puzzle it through properly.

So I was starting to climb up onto the mounting block when Paulie motioned for me to stop. A little way down the tunnel a thick, deep voice was singing in a language I didn't recognize. I backed into the bike, and one of its wheels began to spin round and round, clinkety-clink. About twenty yards down the tunnel a man's body appeared. It was Willy, the other janitor. I don't think he could see who we were in the murky light coming from the boiler room, but he saw something because he began to march toward us waving his arms and shouting incomprehensible words at us in a thick accent. I stood shaking beside Paulie, who threw something at him—I think it was a wrench she must have grabbed from the trunk.

"Stay away from us, you dirty foreigner!"

Willy stopped and stared at the place where the wrench had grazed his leg. Paulie pulled out a string of small firecrackers from her pocket—the bad kind that Sal says will put out babies' eyes. The next thing I knew she had lit and thrown them at Willy's head. They exploded in the air, and when he ducked, screeching, she lit and threw another batch into an old garbage can beside the boiler-room door. The second explosion sounded like a machine gun going off half-cocked. Willy put his hands over his ears, and Paulie took my arm and pulled me through a small passageway I hadn't noticed before. I recognized the coal shed when I saw the old chairs with their split sides and the ugly curtains Paulie had put up to hide her altar to Kong. Paulie pushed open a hinged door, and we walked out into the night.

It was raining heavily—too heavily to see much except the shape of the old box hedge and the tops of the trees in the ravine. But the sky to the south had partially cleared and shone softly orange from the lights of Toronto. The spire of Kings College was also visible. In the falling rain, it looked like a privileged kingdom far beyond our simple lives as boarders at Bath Ladies College. Then Paulie poked me, and we hurried away from the mass of the ravine and up a stone path to the front entrance, where a long figure in a bulky overcoat was sitting on the stone railing. I saw a frieze of white hair and a bobbing prick of orange light below a pair of glinting spectacles.

"We're in luck," Paulie whispered. "We've caught old Cock-shutt smoking. She won't dare to report us now."

We walked up the front steps and, sure enough, the switchboard operator only frowned as we slipped past her into the vaulted stone foyer and crept up Sir Jonathon's grand staircase, still carrying the goggles and the diary Paulie had stolen. I expected to find the Virgin waiting for us. But the pillows arranged under the covers to look like our bodies were still in place. And our bedroom was empty except for Ismay, who was snoring next to the wide-open window. I knew, without Paulie saying so, that I'd passed another test. I, Mouse Bradford, of all people, was a troublemaker, a bad girl, a rule breaker—and I owed it all to Paulie, who had helped me outfox the Virgin in the game of us against the old biddies.

21

The next day, Paulie and I read the letters she had stolen from Mrs. Peddie's apartment. They had been written by Miss Vaughan and Mrs. Peddie.

November 16, 1953

Greetings, dear one,

Finally my arm is strong enough for me to write to you. Late yesterday afternoon the surgeon dropped in and told me I must stay two more weeks for bed rest and observation. Two more weeks, Lola! And I am to do water therapy for my sprained shoulder. The concussion is not serious, even though it kept me unconscious for a day. Dr. Tully says the body has its ways of healing, and as long as I do not overexert myself, my poor head will mend on its own. I am still having headaches, but the doubling of my vision seems to have gone. Dr. Tully says he hopes the person who did this to me will be locked up for years to come. For some reason, I cannot bring myself to tell him it was a police officer. I shall not tell father either. I am afraid what happened would break his heart. We are so close, and yet he cannot—would not, Lola— understand. Do you know, he doesn't even believe that I can balance my own budget? As if I don't know anything about figures! I, who excelled in mathematics at school! Lola, he used to ask my youngest brother to go over my bank account with me. It is puzzling, isn't it?

However, it is true I do not value money. In fact, I am guilty of excessive frugality. Perhaps that was what my father was getting at with Jason and my budget. I travelled through Europe for less than £40, staying at youth hostels. And now we are teaching at Bath Ladies College for the glorious sum of $2,000 a year. That is two-and-a-half thousand less than what an English teacher gets at a Toronto high school, Lola. I thought it was going to be $2,000 a term. I think I shall have to tell Miss Higgs at Christmas that I am finding it awfully hard to manage on this.

Your Vera

P.S. I'm afraid I am not ready to talk about what happened, Lola. If you were here, no doubt you would chide me with that graceful smile of yours, and press me to unburden myself. It also pleases me to think of all the things you would find to say about how one can pass one's time productively in a hospital. I would pretend not to take any of your optimistic talk seriously and then off I'd go to my water therapy, secretly cheered up. Rest assured, I am doing my best to make myself strong so I can hold you in my arms again and kiss the corners of your dear mouth.

November 21, 1953

Dear Vera,

Miss Higgs came into the staff room yesterday bringing your news. As I suspected, she said you are rushing things—ordering everyone about and refusing to listen to the nurses when they tell you to lie quietly. Now, Vera! You are very strong-minded, and you know you always overestimate your strength. Oh, I can cope, you like to tell me. Nonsense. You are as in need of tender care as anyone else. You simply must take things slowly. There, now I've scolded you properly. I am coming down with some bed socks and other assorted woollies. Just the thing for the Toronto General's cheer-less beds.

With all due,
Lola

P.S. Of course, I wish I had stayed in the hotel lounge. He couldn't have beaten *two* women that savagely. And I am terribly terribly angry about what happened, Vera. It is an outrage that a woman of your stature has been subjected to an attack and possibly disfigured because of prejudice. Unfortunately, the students seem to know something of this. Neither Miss Higgs nor I can put our finger on who is spreading the story, but there is gossip in the boarding school that you were the victim of a rape.

November 30, 1953

My darling Lola,

I am sorry my little outburst of affection made you uncomfortable when you came to see me. It is just that I have been in here so long, Lola. And now the prospect of staying in over Christmas for more tests! I do, of course, realize the incident at the Continental has made you more cautious. And I curse the brute for making you feel that way. I know, I know, we ought to be more prudent now, but my stubborn heart does not want to give that constable or anyone like him the satisfaction of interfering with the love you and I feel for each other. I am so grateful I have you in my life. Do you remember the day we met at Cheltenham Ladies College, Lola? You thought I looked like a bluestocking because I'd walked onto the grounds at Cheltenham in my trousers and rucksack. I was used to hiking in Europe, you see. Meanwhile, there was Miss Higgs in one of her funny old dark dresses riding her ancient three-wheel bike round and round the botany pond. She was going at quite a fast clip, and she was being followed by you and Charles with a tea tray. You did not seem to be bothered in the least by the sight of an elderly woman in strange clothes traipsing about the lawn on what looked like an oversized child's tricycle.

When I mentioned this to you later, you pointed out to me that Miss Higgs was doing the sensible thing. She wore Edwardian dresses because they were roomier than our modern clothes, and she rode an old three-wheeler because she could keep her balance on it better. She is getting on, you said, but she needs her exercise like everybody else. And didn't I realize three-wheelers used to be a serious sport round the turn of the century. In short, I was the iconoclast in my trousers. Ah, well! Who would have ever thought that day that you and I would come to mean so much to each other. And that we would follow Miss Higgs back to teach in Canada, the land of my birth.

Your Vera

P.S. I do appreciate your outrage, Lola. I myself do not feel angry. I refuse to take prejudice personally, you see. And I have always known of the dangers. I am referring to Zooey Armstrong's dreadful experience at Cherry Beach. Punched and raped by our own police officers in front of Nan Tyler (who could do nothing to help her dear one). It is abominable, Lola, but at least you and I were spared that.

January 9, 1954

Dear Vera,

Miss Higgs has caught the culprit who was spreading the stories about you. It started with an article in the *Hush Free Press*. Apparently, Jellie Godsoe's father works on this smut rag and showed Jellie the clipping which described your beating at the hands of the police. The *Hush* office is near city hall, next door to the Continental, and one of their reporters witnessed the assault firsthand. *Hush* has no idea you were beaten because you love a woman. The paper is on a crusade against violence on the police force, and they see you as a middle-class victim who was wrongly attacked. (All true enough, as far as it goes.) I have given the clipping to Miss Higgs, who says she will send it to you later. It is too long for me to go into here. The headline reads, "Decent Citizen Dragged, Pushed, and Knocked Unconscious by Ruthless Cop." The article says you were attacked because the police officer thought you resembled a Teresa McClusky, who was being sought on a charge of kidnapping a Mississauga baby. The officer thought he had found the missing girl and imagined arresting her would work to his credit when the merit badges and promotions were being handed out.

The paper makes no mention of the fact that the officer saw you kissing me in the booth when he walked in to have a coffee. (Oh, Vera—and I had picked that booth because I thought no one could see us there.) There was a lengthy description of the constable twisting your arm and ripping your blouse and then banging your head over and over against the doorjamb. His lack of experience was pinpointed as the cause of the misunderstanding. Take heart, my love. We shall soldier on.

Your own
Lola

We read these letters in silence, passing the pages to each other in wonder. It thrilled and frightened me to think we had stumbled on secret documents that proved the gossip about the two women was true. Paulie said it was like getting your hands on the secret of the atom bomb. She said she intended to use the letters to get the Virgin to do whatever she wanted, and she hid them in a Kotex box she put in my drawer. She said nobody would suspect me of taking them. But when I went to check on them after breakfast, the letters were gone. Miss Phillips, I guessed, had discovered them during morning inspection and taken them to Miss Vaughan. We waited for me to be called on the carpet, but the weeks passed, and although nothing happened, Paulie and I continued to puzzle over the matter in private.

22

A week after Paulie stole Mrs. Peddie's letters, I had the opportunity to see the two women's love for myself. When it happened, I was in the leaves room—our way station between the school and the outside world. Alone there, I always felt a little closer to Morley, as if he and Sal and Lady were just over the next hill and not a hundred miles or so up the long, thin asphalt highway that connected Madoc's Landing to the strange life I lived in the city. The room consisted of an oak desk, scales for weighing parcels, and a big, black telephone, which you could have all to yourself if you buttered up the switchboard operator, Miss Cockshutt. And, of course, there were the leaves books. Each boarder had to let the school know in advance what her plans were for the weekends and sign her guests in in one of the green leaves scribblers labelled "out" or "in." The guests had to be one of the hosts approved by your parents, or you couldn't go. There was no problem in my case, since my host was my uncle. He was my dead mother's brother and a man of the cloth, as he liked to say, whose annual salary was the equivalent of his brother-in-law's insurance payments. I had his letter in my pocket to prove it.

Nov. 2, 1963

Dear Mary Beatrice,

Your stepmother has written to ask Margaret and me if we would take you out for the weekend when I am in Toronto for our diocese meeting. She is unable to have you home for the long weekend, as she is having an operation for a collapsed bladder.

Your aunt and I have engaged a room at the Park Plaza so that we will be able to treat you in the style which you are accustomed to at home.

With best wishes and affection,
Uncle Winnie

For no good reason, the table stacked with our leaves-room books suddenly started to shake. I heard the sound of an aggressively cleared throat, and heavy shoes hammered Sir Jonathon's miraculous herringbone floor. The Virgin was on the warpath again. She couldn't see me behind the frosted panes of the leaves-room door. I stood squished and trembling against the wall, watching her through the bevelled edge of the glass.

"Now what is the matter?" the Virgin snarled at somebody I couldn't see. You know George Orwell's picture of the future? The heel of a soldier's boot coming down on a human face? That's how brutish the Virgin sounded that day. As if she were going to step on me or the next poor soul who got in her way.

"Oh, Vera, is it true? Are we going to merge with Kings College?" I recognized the British accent. "You know what happened at St. Mildred's when they went coed. The girls chew gum in their uniforms and show up for debates in slacks."

"Look—I've heard just about enough of this." Now I could see Lola the Les, the Virgin's girlfriend, in one of her too tight sweaters. She reached up, as if she and the Virgin were someplace else, anywhere but Bath Ladies College, and patted the Virgin's cheek. "You poor thing. It must be so hard on you." To my surprise, the Virgin bowed her big, snowy head and began to tremble all over like Lady when she crawls under the bed during a thunderstorm. I heard little gulping noises. I think the Virgin was sobbing.

"All the staff feel the way I do. It's so underhanded," Mrs. Peddie said. "Replacing you with a man."

"I can't make a fuss, Lola. Think of how the school's reputation would suffer."

"Now, Vera—I won't have this. You must stand up for yourself and tell Canon Quinn we simply won't have him for principal."

I stood transfixed behind the door. Before Christ merging with a boys' school? And the Virgin crying? Unthinkable. Plus the two women seemed so sad and broken up, I admit I felt pretty bad for them. In fact, I was a little discombobulated and when I backed up without realizing it, one of the leaves books fell off the table. The Virgin opened the door and saw me, and Mrs. Peddie whirled around and saw me, too.

But it was too late for them to scold me for eavesdropping. In the school foyer the male teachers were arriving for a curriculum meeting, filing through the front door one by one. Legs in baggy tweeds, legs in creased grey flannel—some with shiny bums on their cheap trousers and some with bums wrapped in expensive Donegal plaid.

And then I forgot about the Virgin and Mrs. Peddie because Paulie was in the foyer, watching the male teachers from the shadows. I glimpsed her loitering behind one of the spreading stone columns—a nondescript schoolgirl with runs in her black school stockings. Except for the ladders in her hose, you'd never have picked her out in a crowd.

Meanwhile, the male teachers were filing into the library. They glanced around the foyer slyly, some like schoolboys, hastily picking lint off their Kings College blazers, not sure they'd measure up in front of the girls. Most of them were British. Canon Quinn believed in the English tradition of a classical education. And they seemed to come in two varieties: short and stocky, or tall and rangy.

The short, stocky ones looked like the English bobbies whose pictures I'd pasted into my Coronation scrapbook—working-class. Small, with pudgy faces under metal helmets that made me think of wastepaper baskets turned upside down and moustaches springing from under their noses like dark, bristly toilet brushes. The tall, rangy ones were upper-class, or at least hoping to pass as well-bred. They talked in high, piping tones that rose skyward and crashed about the ceiling like trapped birds.

Then Paulie was at the door of the leaves room. She looked haughtily down at Sergeant. "Didn't you hear Mrs. Peddie calling you? We need more chairs in the gymnasium." Setting up the chairs for morning prayers was one of the duties Sergeant performed each day—Virgin's orders. He walked off, swearing. Paulie didn't even notice that she'd insulted him. She was staring at the male teachers. At their zippered flies—all ten of them. And behind each one of those flies, what set them apart from Paulie and me.

23

Alice and I Discuss Penises—Again

— Alice, I never wanted a penis. Nor did I want breasts, and the second-class status that goes with them. Being a woman is difficult. God's bodkins.

— Well, men's penises are kind of interesting.

— They're not all that impressive. I mean, the penis of the human primate is not as long proportionately as, say, the genitals of the Horseneck clam. Consider the male clam for a minute. He is ninety percent geoduck (pronounced gooeyduck)—he has no choice if he wants to connect with his lady clam.

— Are you going to tell one of my own penis jokes?

— Don't be revolting. I'm talking about science. For instance, I read that the length of this human appendage surpasses that of all other animals and is supposed to make man the lord of creation. You see, men owe their penis size to us. When women stood upright, our vaginas swung forward and down. And the male penis, following the same principle as the giraffe's neck, grew in order to get something that was out of reach.

— That's a fine theory, Mouse. It must be nice to be brainy.

— I guess so. Still, a penis is embarrassing. It also seems vaguely inconvenient, like a last-minute detail that might get tangled up in bad-fitting underwear. Besides, Paulie didn't want a penis with a capital *P*, either. I don't know why her own psychiatrist didn't understand this. It was his job to know better, after all.

HIS LORDSHIP: Dr. Torval, you had a professional relationship with the defendant before the crime?

DR. TORVAL: A very brief one, my lord. You see, she couldn't accept any interpretation other than the one she came up with herself.

HIS LORDSHIP: Under different circumstances, that would be considered a sign of maturity, Dr. Torval. Would you tell the court what assessment you made of Pauline Sykes?

DR. TORVAL: Yes, my lord. Physically, Pauline is a normal, very well developed female. Biologically, she is a girl.

HIS LORDSHIP: But she didn't want to be one. Is that correct?

DR. TORVAL: That is correct, my lord. As a very young child, her mother abandoned her and she was taken in by an elderly man and his wife in a small village in western Ontario. When they died, she went to Toronto and began to assume a male identity. I believe she hated women, my lord, because she felt she had been the victim of one. She associated the good things in life with being a boy, and the kindness shown her by the elderly man made her feel that being male was the light at the end of her tunnel, so to speak. She called him her grandfather and kept up the illusion with herself and others that he was still alive. I believe she forged letters, my lord, so that the school would let her out to visit him. When I examined her she was reluctant to let anyone see her breasts and genitalia. She does not like them. She bound her breasts up with a tensor bandage. And she has done this since she was twelve. She has been masquerading as a boy since she was twelve, my lord.

HIS LORDSHIP: Is the defendant insane under the definition of the law, Dr. Torval?

DR. TORVAL: That is an interesting point, my lord. I believe the defendant is a schizophrenic severely affected by what Freud calls primary penis envy. It is an early and crucial stage in a girl's development.

HIS LORDSHIP: Excuse me for interrupting, Dr. Torval, but does this stage apply to Pauline Sykes? I'm looking here at the report of another psychiatrist, Dr. Julian. He says the defendant is a sane young woman who was responsible for her actions. He believes she was on her way to becoming a transsexual—a process that can lead to a collapse of judgement.

DR. TORVAL: Well, it's interesting that you should bring this up, my lord, but transsexualism is not usually combined with a psychotic break. It might benefit the court if I elaborated on gender disorder. First of all, transsexualism is not considered a major illness that would affect one's appreciation of reality. It is a type of sexual deviation. When we are born, most of us have a biologically assigned sex. If you are a little boy you have a penis and testicles, and if you are a little girl you have a vagina and ovaries. And at about the age of two or three, we have already come to feel psychologically the way that is appropriate to our sex. I mean, my lord, if you are a little boy, you do little-boy things; if you are a little girl, you do little-girl things.

MISS WHITLAW: Objection, my lord. There has been some debate as to what these little-boy and little-girl things are.

HIS LORDSHIP: Thank you, Miss Whitlaw. May I remind both you and Dr. Torval that this court is not interested in investigating psychiatric theories, no matter how fascinating. We are here to ascertain the sanity of the accused.

DR. TORVAL: Yes, my lord. But in the interests of this case, I think we have to make certain philosophical assumptions about the genders.

MISS WHITLAW: My lord, could we move away from these philosophical assumptions? As you have noted, this is a court of law, not a place for the debate of theories. Besides, many traits that were once considered masculine, such as courage and mental aggressiveness, are now seen as characteristics that can be encouraged in one gender and discouraged in the other. And if I may point out, my lord, there are psychiatrists who believe penis envy is a secondary stage of female development.

HIS LORDSHIP: Miss Whitlaw, are you introducing new medical opinions?

MISS WHITLAW: My lord, a colleague of Dr. Freud, Dr. Karen Horney, said that Freud himself exaggerated the importance of penis envy among little girls. She believed that both sexes envy each other, and that just as little girls wish for penises, little boys wish for breasts.

HIS LORDSHIP: Let us get back to the defendant, Miss Whitlaw. And I would like to remind Dr. Torval once again to restrict his statements to the facts of the case.

So much for Karen Horney and breast envy. Or womb envy. As for me, I wanted something more grand than a penis. I wanted what my hero, President Kennedy, had: courage, individual style, a life of action, and an intellect. Was I asking too much for a Mouse?

24

The day I was to achieve mastery over the female sex, I awoke late and caught Ismay in the act of putting on her merry widow. I'd only seen corsets like that in the Frederick's of Hollywood ads in American movie magazines. Sal wore a Maidenform girdle, because a lady had to hide her bum crack. (Her rule didn't apply to me—a white cotton garter belt was all she figured I needed around my skinny pelvis.)

So the merry widow, with its flecking of puckered daisies, was a revelation. I hid under my covers and watched in awe as Ismay hoisted it up over her knees and leaned against the wall, panting and grunting. She appeared to be stuck in the tight, elasticized material, which squeezed her blubbery thighs together like breasts. A gross kind of leg cleavage, you could say.

I sunk deeper under the sheets so she wouldn't notice me watching. I found Ismay's body morbidly compelling. No matter how many Oreos I ate, I stayed scrawny; my ribs showed and my hip bones stuck out. But Ismay, like the Virgin Mary, seemed designed for one use—to get knocked up, as they say in the Landing. Some girls just had no luck.

When I peeped out again, she was yanking it up with the look of a real, honest-to-God martyr going to her execution. And then the corset settled into place around her heart-shaped hips, and she leaned over and very niftily swung her breasts like bell clappers until they snuggled into the sculptured cups. Now Ismay could stand without the support of the wall. She saw me watching and made a prissy, exasperated sound, then turned her back so I couldn't see her struggle into her nylons.

I didn't want to think mean thoughts about anyone on my day of trial and tribulation, so I rolled out of bed and dressed like I always did, in one of the bathroom cubicles so the other girls wouldn't see Alice. A few of them were dressing in cubicles, too. The noise of flushing toilets was the only way I could tell the other girls were there. None of us walked around naked anyhow. It was considered showing off, like admitting you thought your old bod (as Tory called it) was hot stuff.

When I came back into the bedroom Ismay smiled at me, as if she'd forgotten I'd witnessed the war of the corset. Slowly, she pivoted for me on high-heeled black patent pumps. She wore a white polo-neck blouse and a short plaid skirt that accentuated her hips. All the girls wore them, the tall girls wore short ones, and the short girls wore long ones for no good reason that I could see.

If Sal was with us, I knew she'd take Ismay aside and pull out something black or navy, all full of whispers about how plump girls need dark colours to slim them down.

But Sal would likely be stopped in her tracks by Ismay's painted face. Ismay looked pumped up with authority. Oh, she was just asking to be deflated, if you were in the mood to take on the Ismays of the world. And then Paulie leaned in the doorway and whistled at Ismay and said, "Hubba-hubba," and I forgot about Sal's views on who should wear plaid and hurried after Paulie, who ran off down the corridor like one of the wild boys who live in girls' dreams, racing ahead and drawing me on until the tattoo of Ismay's black patent pumps grew faint behind us.

25

I stood in the gloom of the coal shed tasting new thoughts—like eating Italian olives for the first time. My kilt and Hardy Amies blouse lay crumpled in a corner. Not only did I have a mocking boy's mouth, but Paulie had pinned up my dark hair and stuck one of her baseball caps on my head backwards, and, presto: I was—well, sort of—a guy.

I christened myself Nick, as in Nick the Greek, who ran a takeout restaurant in Madoc's Landing. A Sweet Cap hung from the corner of my lopsided lips. And behind the sunglasses (which I'd borrowed from Paulie) Nick's eyes rolled evasively—sneaky and bad in pockets of shadows; dark-circle-ringed eyes up to tricks of all kinds. And the obscene gesture he instinctively made with his tongue in his open mouth seemed to say la-la-la, this is what I want to do—lick all those nifty brown nipples nestling behind Oxford cloth blouses, just waiting for me to have my way with them.

"It's easier for a girl to become a boy than the other way round," Paulie said as she tucked her long braid inside her cap and started to bind her breasts with a tensor bandage. She hadn't bothered to bind mine, because they were so small. "If you act with authority, people will accept that you're a boy. But if you want to be a girl you have to act like a dope, and acting stupid is harder. Who wants to leave behind your self-respect for a vacant kind of openness—a manner that suggests waiting for men to like you is the answer to life?" Paulie added and put on her funny old hunting cap. Now the change was complete. Lewis stood in her place. She, I mean, he, helped me slip into an old coat belonging to Willy the janitor. It was several sizes too big with padded shoulders and tucks in the back. Girls' clothes, Lewis said, were like wearing nothing, but men's clothes were tailored and made you feel propped up. And he was right. Just putting on a suit and tie changes you. You feel in control and at ease with the world. And men's shoes help, too. They're heavier, so you feel solid—rooted to the ground.

Lewis said I didn't need the real McCoy, though; my orthopedic shoes were heavy enough. Their sound pleased me. *Boom-boom*—I sounded like the Virgin in her gunboats. I was worried my hump would show through the jacket, but Lewis built up my other shoulder with extra padding. In Willy's jacket I looked bulky, not deformed. He was strict with me about how I moved: I had to stand upright, with my shoulders back and my head up. And I had to lock my knees so that I seemed to swagger. I also had to pull in my chin and, above all, never lower my eyes. I could keep my teeth clenched if I liked, but I had to make sure my jaw was tight. And pull down my lips when somebody asked me a question I didn't know how to answer. I couldn't smile much, although it was okay to open my eyes as wide as I could and bare my teeth, so that the other person couldn't tell if I liked or hated them. This confusion was threatening in itself, Lewis said.

That was the man part.

The Greek part was my doing. It was simple decoration—an accessory, like a shoulder bag. I hadn't realized I'd watched Nick so much, but I guess I always watch men, the way you watch the weather. From out of nowhere, I found I had Nick's gestures. The waggly tongue; the constantly moving hands, either swinging a little doodad or hovering protectively over the belt (as if he were about to do something primitive, like rub his balls). Sal had given me a rabbit's foot, and I'd practised swinging it constantly and staring the way Nick did, as if his eyes could suck up girls' bodies like a vacuum cleaner. Lewis thought it best if I didn't say much. I only knew one or two Greek phrases, anyway—thanks to Nick. *F. Harry Stowe* for thank you, and *endaxy* for everything else. It meant "okay."

The less I said, the less chance there was of my getting mixed up, Paulie said. The most important thing was never to look as if I'd made a mistake. I told Lewis that Nick the Greek always thought he was right, because his mother spoiled him. That's why mothers are such a problem: they can make or break you. If we had had Nick the Greek's mother, we'd be set for life, too.

Just before noon, we set off for the ravine path, which ran between the school and the nearby suburb of Wilbury Hollow. I was too nervous to speak, so I kept my hands busy with the rabbit's foot, swinging it back and forth at the level of my crotch. Far away, near the grove of camperdown elms, we could see the Virgin planting bulbs with Sergeant. She couldn't see us because we were hidden by the ravine trees. We climbed through a new hole in the fence Lewis had found, and I heard my heavy orthopedic shoes hit the paved path. *Boom-boom, boom-boom.* I was a boy. My clothes said so. My arms and legs swam through the light autumn air as we strolled whistling past the small stucco houses where normal people lived. Their little old-fashioned gardens with plots of pink cosmos and fragrant nicotiana made me homesick for Madoc's Landing. We walked by a group of kids throwing a basketball into a hoop over the garage door, and one of the boys waved at us. I waved back, and Lewis grinned.

"You see, Bradford? It's as easy as pie. Either you believe in yourself or you don't."

"Yes," I said, and laughed out loud, startling myself. "You're either a man or a mouse."

As we turned once again down the path that circled through the ravine, the warm sunshine of Indian summer on our shoulders, Lewis said he had things to say to me. About girls, mainly. About the way you had to treat them if you were a man.

You have to fool them, Lewis said. Bully them. They like it when you take charge. And you have a task to do for Kong, he reminded me. You have to feel up a girl above the waist. You don't have to touch her Down There; it's just important to get at the breasts. That's what Kong likes. Tell her that if she loved you, she'd let you do it. Guilt usually does the trick. Guilt lets you get anywhere you want to go.

We were deep into the ravine now, among fallen logs and ferns and the half-baked woods people in the city mistake for a real forest.

"But maybe girls want their breasts touched?" I said.

"They do and they don't—that's the trouble. You have to initiate everything. They don't like the responsibility."

"What girl am I going to try this on, Paulie?"

"Lewis," he said. "It's Nick and Lewis from here on in. Have you got that, Nick?"

"Yes, Lewis," I said.

"And remember Kong's words: 'A man stands alone. A man stands by his friends. A man speaks his mind and is afraid of no one.' " Lewis spat an impressive spit ball over the railing, and I busied myself again with my rabbit's foot and asked no more questions.

We came to the end of the path, and I told Lewis I had to rest my legs. Below us lay the river, the colour of agate beneath the overhanging branches. Bubbles floated like spit on its surface next to pieces of Styrofoam and dead leaves. We climbed across some old boards that somebody had placed over a swampy patch and stood by the funny small sandy shore. An overturned cement mixer lay in the grass nearby. Lewis said it belonged to Sergeant. His kiln for making firebrick for the furnace was up in the woods.

Safe from sight, we got out our fags, and I cupped my hand around Paulie's lighter flame with an ease that amazed me. Then I saw them—a whole pack. Coming toward us along the narrow beach—some pushing bicycles, some walking. A group of Kings College boys. The name of their school was not yet visible on the embossed gold crest on their navy jackets, but I knew it anyway. They were laughing and yelling as they moved toward us, pretending not to notice we were even there.

I waited anxiously for them to see through me. Sure as anything, they'd be able to tell by my face that I wasn't used to real sunlight—that I'd crawled out of a cave of old forgotten women into the real world. Lewis whispered, "It's the first punch that counts." I shrank away from him—scared to death. Lewis looked disgusted and walked over and planted himself in front of them, his legs set wide apart.

"This is private property," Lewis said. "Get the fuck out of here."

Lewis looked shorter suddenly, standing in front of the boys. The hunting cap was pulled low over his eyes, and his sleeves were rolled up so the boys would notice his muscles, as round and hard under his skin as a pair of Adam's apples.

A fair boy with a brush cut put down his bicycle. He hung over Lewis, twice his size. I recognized him from Tory's photograph. It was her brother, Rick. "Get out of our way, asshole." He spat at Lewis—not an impressive ball, like the ones I'd seen Lewis make, but a fuzzy spew of saliva that landed on his shoulder. One of the other boys laughed. Then Lewis yelled, "Nick," and now the boys turned to look at me. Oh, no, don't hurt me, I thought. You've got it wrong. I'm a girl. Can't you see? You know what we're like—we faint and preen and do all that dumb girl stuff. And I have a hunched back, too. I looked down quickly at my torqued shoulder, hoping they'd see Alice and feel sorry for me. And then Rick lunged at Lewis, and Lewis head-butted him, and Rick swore and grabbed Lewis by the neck, and the two of them toppled backwards onto the sand. Immediately, one of the other boys grabbed Lewis's arms so that Tory's brother could straddle his stomach. He laughed and spat in Lewis's face. "Bulls-eye!" Rick shouted.

All of a sudden, my stupid old Mouse heart started to thud, and I felt my neck swell, like the Celtic warrior women in the history book who puff up with rage and gnash their teeth and yell like men. The old Bradford genes must have been coming into play. And somebody I didn't know shrieked at him to leave Lewis alone, and I lurched over and jumped on Rick's back. Who did he think he was! Going to Kings College didn't mean he could treat Lewis like shit! I wanted to smash his snobby mouth—split those thin, snobby Kings College lips until I saw them bleed.

And the big idiot bucked backwards then, slamming his elbows into my face. My nose throbbed, stung. I dropped my hands and rolled off him, my arms up to protect my face. Pant legs surrounded me. I rolled to my knees just as a black high-top sneaker made a windy rush to my ear. I ducked, and then I heard a shout, and the foot went calmly to the ground. Sneakered feet and pant legs moved closer.

"Will you look at this! It's not a boy we're fighting. It's a frigging girl!" My cap had fallen off, and my hair straggled down my shoulders.

"She's got boobs under there!" he shouted, and yanked at my shirt, under Willy's jacket, ripping off my button. Lewis was still pinned under Rick. I was on my knees and afraid to look down in case I'd see the two dumb little pimples growing where I didn't want them to grow. I didn't know how Lewis had managed to keep his cap on. The chin strap, I guess.

"Leave her alone!" Lewis screamed. "Leave her alone or you'll be sorry!" The boys ignored Lewis. One of them pinned my arms behind my back. I couldn't see who it was. Then the boy with black sneakers stuck his face right into mine and started to inspect my neck and ears with his hot fingers. He acted like he was looking for cooties, inspecting me the way Miss Mullen inspected all the kids back in grade school in the Landing. I began to shake in the worst way when I felt his fingers creep under my shirt and walk plink-plink-plink in little fakey spider steps up to the nipple of my left breast. "Hey guys," he said and pressed my nipple down hard, as if he were using one of Morley's push-button windows. "Let's get us some nooky!" I could feel the tears swarming under my lids. But the other boys standing near us were no longer watching, they were whispering and pointing at the ravine hill. Hurrying down the path with his strange, rolling gait rushed Sergeant with his corgi, Spruce. He was waving his short arms.

"Lewis! Lewis! Are you in a pinch? Hey, there! Get away from my worker, you ruffians!"

The boy behind me dropped my arms, and one of them called out something about being attacked by a girl. Sergeant only waved his arms even more excitedly.

"That's no girl, you fool! That's my grounds boy, Lewis. A bunch of hooligans, that's all you are! Picking on boys smaller than yourselves!"

The Kings College boys stared at one another; then, one by one, they picked up their bicycles and began to walk off down the ravine.

"And we're glad to see the back of you, that's for certain," Sergeant called out as I jumped to my feet and started to do up my shirt. Then I remembered my cap. I grabbed it up and tucked my hair out of sight and finally went back to my buttons, my fingers all shaky. I wondered what Morley would think of me if he could see me now.

"Who's your friend, Lewis?" Sergeant asked. I stared at the river. The water smelled of old shoes and algae, not fresh like the bay at home. It wasn't even a river, really—just a gush of sewer water that came out of giant culverts.

"Nick is a Greek. He only knows a few words of English."

"A Greek, is he? Don't know much about them. It's the Frenchies I hate."

"Uh—right." Lewis nudged me. "Hey, Nick, we've got to be on our way. We're late, and we've got friends to meet at the mill."

"Don't want to keep the girls waiting, do you?" Sergeant giggled. "I reckon they'd have a few words to say about that, wouldn't they? Ah, well. Never mind, lads. That's what it is to be a man—putting up with the shit women hand you."

Sergeant tethered Spruce to a tree. Then he unzippered himself and stood with his legs apart, peeing into the river. The spray of his pee fell through the air golden and fine, like liquid coins.

"Come on, lads, no long faces now. Will you not play swordsies with old Sergeant?" He aimed higher, and I watched the spray that shot without dribbling from the overgrown pink mushroom that drooped from his fingers.

"I guess the Virgin wouldn't know what to do with that," Lewis said and whistled—a low, thrilling whistle as Sergeant shook himself so that the last drops fell to the ground. I looked off, embarrassed for him.

"Don't talk like that about your superiors, lad," Sergeant said.

"How about Miss Phillips, then?" Lewis asked. It was common knowledge that the matron hated Sergeant because he liked to play tricks on the boarding school.

"Ach, there's nothing the matter with that woman that a good pair of brains wouldn't cure." Sergeant stopped and pointed at me. "Lewis! Your friend here—the poor lad—his mouth is bloody."

I put my hand up to my face, and it came back sticky. I had a nosebleed—something I hated more than Morley's needles. Then I was doubled over, throwing up into the green spears of the burdock (thanks to Mrs. Peddie, I knew the name of the weeds I was defiling). I watched myself from a distance, as if the skinny boy puking in the bushes had nothing to do with me. When I looked up, Lewis was staring my way as if he'd never seen me before. Looking at me as if he was Kong. And sure enough, he held up eight fingers. Eight out of ten. Not bad for a Mouse. I'd passed Kong's second category of tests: Mastery over Other Men. With flying colors.

Lewis's Song to Kong

Death to the boys of Kings College! Kromp! Kromp! Kreehgar scraashh!

The mighty Lewis head-butted one in Kong's name and then and then and then—

Kunnnkk! Slam! The newcomer Nick valiantly jumped on his back—

Jagg—gkagk! And then—what! And then—shatterrk! The scum unfairly tried to disrobe Nick the Newcomer. They called him the lowest form of animal life there is—a girl!

Nick the Newcomer and the mighty Lewis were not cowed, but their enemies outnumbered them ten-to-one! And then— shwunkety-wunk! The dwarf delivered them from the jaws of trouble. Skharroomm! Arrak!

The dwarf was Victorious.

Surrounded by a sea of enemies, he conquered!

Yaeeeh! A man is somebody who is Kong in his heart. Kong. Kong. Kong.

Nick the Newcomer and the mighty Lewis saw the dwarf's sword making rainbows against the sky—holding in his hand the lost weapon of Kodo!

One foot in diameter, as wide as a redwood, as long as the sea serpents of Japan. Kong lives. Long live Kong.

26

My next test still lay ahead: Mastery over Women.

Lewis and I said good-bye to Sergeant and walked across the highway to the Old Mill. I'd never been inside a tavern before, but I'd seen the railroad hotel in Dollartown, outside the Landing. Morley sometimes stopped there to buy pipe tobacco, leaving Sal and me behind in Blinky to stare at the grubby men in dark plaid hunting shirts and peaked caps who staggered in and out of its Ladies and Escorts room. I wasn't impressed. The Dollartown tavern didn't even have swing doors like the saloons you see in old westerns.

The Old Mill didn't look like much, either—just an old brick house beside a muddy creek. It stood all alone in the north end of the ravine, which twisted off between a ridge of wooded hills toward Toronto. Once a real gristmill had stood beside the tavern, but that was over a hundred years ago. I could have been in the middle of nowhere. I wasn't in Madoc's Landing, with its string of narrow shops running down to the government wharf. Or downtown Toronto, with its streetcars and windy streets like concrete valleys, stuffed to the brim with dour-looking people. At least these sad-looking city people knew they belonged somewhere. They had an identity. Although I have to admit, I don't really understand what an identity is. For one thing, it's what makes you different from the rest of the world (which is what Alice does for me). And it's also what you have in common with others—i.e., the way I have something in common with girls.

So I squeezed my rabbit's foot hard for luck and tried not to think about what the Virgin would do to us if we were caught, or what lie I could make up if somebody nabbed us for being under the legal drinking age. And then Lewis gave me a little push and I half fell into a hall as dark as a church. Did I say dark? I mean pitch-black except for a pair of stained-glass windows on the far wall. Instead of a picture of Jesus, the windows displayed a sheaf of wheat next to a beer mug. This was the Ladies and Escorts room, where boarders were not supposed to go. I could hear people playing pool somewhere to the left of us and to the right, male laughter and the clink of glasses. To my relief, we walked into the little takeout restaurant beside the beer hall. Two St. Mary's girls in blue tunics sat smoking at one of the tables. "Behold the prey," Lewis hissed in my ear. Our dates wore pinky-white lipstick, like beatniks, and their hair was teased into thickly hair-sprayed beehives. Convent girls were wild, Lewis said, because their schools were so strict. At St. Mary's the nuns rang little bells if the girls danced too close to a boy. Sitting at the table with the two girls was one of the Kings College boys we'd fought by the river. When he saw us he stood up and whispered something to the girls, and all three of them stared at me, as if he'd told them about what had happened.

My Mouse heart quaked. The last thing we needed was another rumble.

"Get lost, creep," Lewis said, and jabbed the Kings College boy with his knee. He looked around to see if anybody was watching and then dragged himself off into the gloomy beer hall, and I realized that Lewis had succeeded in doing the unthinkable—i.e., kneeing him in the groin. Then we sat down, and the two girls put their heads together and giggled as if we didn't exist. Lewis didn't seem to notice. So that's how you act, I thought—as if what other people do is of no importance. I couldn't help wondering, just the same, if the boy had told the girls about me, and, if so, if the girls believed him. I watched Lewis for a sign that he was concerned, too, but Lewis only lit up a fag, never once taking his heavy-lidded eyes off the girls' breasts swelling under their blue tunics. They were more developed than either Tory or me, and the breasts of the girl sitting next to me looked as big as Ismay's—a 38 C, or my name wasn't Mouse Bradford.

That was because she was fat. The sleeves of her beige blouse were strained tight across her forearms, and when she raised her hand to smoke, I spotted a B.O. stain.

"Lewis, who's your friend?" the slighter girl asked. Nervously, I looked away over their bouffant hairdos, pretending I was more interested in Dave Keon's Maple Leaf hockey sweater in a glass case on the wall, framed like one of Sal's china plates.

"Lewis, why doesn't your friend talk?" she asked when I didn't say anything.

"He's from Athens, Beth."

"Well, they speak English there, don't they?"

"Not him. And he doesn't like people to draw attention to it, either."

"Oh, pardon me for breathing." The slight girl looked at the fat one, and they both started laughing again.

"His name is Nick," Lewis answered for me.

"That's a nice name," the fat girl said. "My name is Josie. It's short for Josephine." She put her hand on one of my skinny biceps. "Oh, what big muscles Nick has!" she said, and both girls snickered and hooted.

"Mine are bigger," Lewis said, and rolled up his sleeves to show them.

"Can't Nick talk, Lewis?" Josie said when they had finished ogling.

"Endaxy," I said.

"Oh, he wants to get a taxi," Josie said.

"No he doesn't," Lewis said. "He means he's agreeing with you—he can't talk much. See?"

Then Lewis ordered four coffees, and the girls smoked and whispered to each other without touching their cups. I didn't drink mine, either—my hands were shaking too much. So I just sat there like a dope, watching Lewis through my dark glasses, waiting for a sign from him that would tell me what to do.

When the signal came, I couldn't believe it. Lewis put his empty mug back on the tray and announced, rude as you please, that he and Beth were going for a walk. Beth looked a little surprised. Then they left, Lewis swaggering ahead, while the men at the counter turned to stare at the girl's nice round calves in her black winter stockings.

"Would you like to do something with me, Nick?" Josie said pointedly, and I waited for her to start up her giggling again. But she put on a show of looking serious, taking my arm and helping me to my feet as if I were a child who needed instructions.

Outside the Old Mill, the sun was turning the agate-coloured stream almost summer-blue. The air felt warm on my cheeks, and I heard bees droning in the bushes down near the storm sewers. We walked a little way in silence, and then, for no good reason, Josie stumbled against me and clutched at my hand with her fat fingers. Did she think I wanted to hold hands? How perverted! I thought. Then I remembered who I was.

"Is anything wrong?" Josie asked. For a second I almost told her. "I know I'm a little overweight," she whispered, as if she were trying to keep somebody from overhearing. "But I'm going on a Metrecal diet this weekend." I must have looked taken aback, because she giggled and said, "I can see you don't have to go on a diet." I shook my head and noisily started to chew gum, because I didn't know what else to do. Her forward manner terrified me. She smiled, as if she wanted to reassure me, all the while chattering on about how much she hated Latin at St. Mary's. I didn't say anything, and after a while she stopped talking, and we walked in an uncomfortable silence toward the wooded end of the ravine.

The river ran quite fast here through a concrete bed. A wall of cement lay flat on either side of the stream, like two strange concrete shores. The water had no choice but to follow the man-made bed. Then Josie said, "I just love the countryside, don't you?"

I know that feeling superior to people is not polite, but how could anybody think a funny little culvert just outside the city was real countryside? Obviously, Josie didn't know a river from a hole in the ground. I felt mad at her for being so dense, and a teeny bit of contempt, too, because she hadn't guessed I was a girl. Then, the next thing I knew, Josie was slapping her chest and shrieking at me about a bee getting caught in her blouse. And all of a sudden she was lying flat on her back in some bushes, and I knew something was going to happen that I didn't like.

"It's inside my brassiere, Nick. Get it out, please!"

I bent down and started to peer under her blouse, and she kicked me impatiently.

"Hurry, it's stinging! Ouch! Oh, it's mad as can be." She grabbed my hand and made it yank down the cups of her bra, and then she was spilling out everywhere—lying like a crazy fool in the bushes, her tubby legs spread and her poor pillow-sized breasts bare for all the world to see.

She'd stopped moaning and just lay there without moving. I thought she'd died. And then she said my name in a whispery little voice, and I knew she wasn't hurt and maybe there hadn't even been a bee at all. And what's worse, I understood that this was the moment Kong was waiting for, and I've never felt so frightened in all my life. Josie looked not just fat but big—bigger than me by a hundred times. Bigger than the ski mountain in Madoc's Landing. And I thought with a little shock, this is how you'd look, too,

Mouse, if you were lying there waiting for a boy's hands to love you. I'd be scared—maybe more scared than the boy. And not knowing that I was a mountain to be scaled.

"Nick, sit down like a good boy." She patted the ground beside her, and I did what she said, but I kept on my cap to hide my long hair, and even Lewis's sunglasses, because I was afraid she would see I had girls' eyes and not boys' eyes, although, as it turned out, she kept her own eyes half-shut, as if she didn't want to see what was dead obvious to anybody who cared to look.

I lit a fag to stall for time and thought what a shame it was I had to act tough when my ideal man was John Kennedy. The least I could do was behave like a gentleman and not stare at her breasts. If John Kennedy had been in my position, I know he would have kept his eyes averted. Besides, Josie had embarrassing breasts, and I was sure somebody with breasts like that wouldn't want anyone looking at them too closely. Funny little white lines ran off from the edges of her nipples, as if her breasts were starting to crack open like a window some kid had broken with a stone. I knew those funny-looking lines were stretch marks, because I'd seen them on Sal's cousin Ginny, whose body fell to pieces, Sal said, after Ginny had five kids.

Meanwhile, Josie started squeezing me all over and giggling and whispering in my ear about how hard my legs were when they weren't hard at all. She inched her fingers up toward my crotch and asked me in that fake whispery voice if I had a rubber. I didn't have a clue what she meant, and she started to laugh again, and just when I thought I couldn't stand her laughing at me anymore, she kissed me with a wide-open mouth. And I kissed her back, my sunglasses still on. I knew that's what she wanted me to do, and I did it not just to be polite but because I was curious, too. And she opened her mouth even wider, and all of a sudden I had the stupidest idea that she was like a house with too many open windows. I wanted to warn her to board herself up, because any robber could crawl into a house like that. And then she snatched my hand and placed it on her breast, and for no good reason I let my hand rest on her soft cool skin—as cool as Plasticine. And then she suggested that I take off my shirt, too, because she wanted to see my breasts.

"Not on your life," I said, forgetting I wasn't supposed to speak English, and that's when I realized that Josie had never believed I couldn't speak English in the first place. And she'd never believed I was a boy, either.

"You don't like me because I'm fat," she said, and started to cry, as if I'd been manhandling her.

"That's not true," I said weakly.

"Liar," she said, sobbing, as she tucked herself back into her bra.

Then she ran off, weeping, and I stood for a long time smoking while Sal's shaming voice rang and rang in my head. It said all the usual things and a few new bits about how disgusting it was for one girl to touch another, but mostly it kept at me about getting what I deserved for being deceitful, and I had to grant the voice it had a point on that count. When I told Lewis about it, I left out the part about Josie knowing I was a girl, and I wondered if Lewis knew. I said Josie got mad when I touched her, and all Lewis replied was, "You can't be a real boy, Mouse, until you stop getting sucked in by what girls say. They always want to make everything your fault."

This wasn't exactly true, but for the life of me I didn't know how to argue with him.

27

November 9, 1963

Dear Mr. Kennedy,

It's high time I told you about the tests. I've promised Paulie I won't say a word to the other girls, and a Mouse always keeps her promises. That's me to a T—I mean an M. I'm a promise keeper.

Today is a pretty weird day for me. I have to do something that Paulie dreamed up to show my mastery over nature. I'm a little nervous. I feel like Roy Orbison in his song "Runnin' Scared." You know that song, Mr. President? I'm sure you've heard it, but you probably prefer old-fashioned stuff like "The Shrimp Boats Are Coming." Well, I'm running scared all the time, too, hoping things will turn out all right in the end.

Right now, I'm in a shed with a pigeon. I'm supposed to kill it to prove I'm a man. Well, not a man—*you're* a man. To prove I'm manly. I don't want to do it, and yet I know I have to. Paulie says men have to do things to prove they are men. And they kill the thing they love—like Oscar Wilde said. That's too much to ask of anybody, but I guess men can't protect women and children unless they learn to be bad. There's no way around it. As Paulie says, women are good only for having babies, and men are in charge of death, which is a very, very tough job. If you want to be as good as a man, you have to learn to administer death, too.

Not that I want to be mean to the pigeon, or think it deserves to die. Sure, it pecked my foot a few minutes ago, but I don't hold that against it. Actually, it looks a little sick. It'd really be putting it out of its misery by killing it. That happens in war, doesn't it? Your best buddy asks you to do him in because he's so far gone he knows he's not going to live. A poet here named Earle Birney wrote a long poem about two men climbing a mountain. One of them got pretty smashed up during a fall on the rocks. So he asked his buddy to roll him off the cliff, and—can you guess the rest? His buddy didn't want to do it. But David begged and pleaded, and finally his friend rolled him over like a log into empty space.

I hope you don't think I'm showing off, but I read about how you said poetry kept you from getting conceited. You said it's easy when somebody is running the country for them to get too big for their britches and forget about important things. (Like the northern lights on evenings in August and being nice to daughters—the top of my list, Mr. President.) I guess this pigeon is my David, and I have to put it out of its misery. It's just that I don't think I can kill a pigeon, Mr. President—even a sick one. But Paulie will be here any moment, and that's what I have to do. Correction: that's what I *will* do.

Your pal,
Mouse

November 13, 1963

Dear Mr. Kennedy,

I have great news about Morley! (My father, in case you've forgotten.) He came to see me! And I was lucky enough to get him to myself for an hour and twelve minutes. Without Sal. Can you believe that, Mr. President? I was coming out of Mrs. Peddie's class at 3:30 when I saw a tall figure in a fedora standing in the front hall. I'd know that fedora anywhere. It's black, and Sal turns the brim up because she says it will balance the sag of Morley's big, sloping shoulders.

For a second or two, I thought Morley looked a little sad standing there by himself, like Dr. Kildare on the wrong TV set, staring with his nice, big eyes at the packs of girls in green tunics swarming past him, their arms full of books. (By the way, I am proud to say I have Morley's eyes, which are prone to showing circles of fatigue.) Then Morley spotted me, and the next thing I knew he was cuffing me on the cheek and handing me a food package that Sal had made up (ten packages of yellow Chiclets, my fav, and five Oh! Henrys, my second-fav.) I will give the Chiclets to Paulie and keep the candy bars for myself. I'm glad I don't have to diet like the other girls even though food and mail are the only things I have to live for. (Not that I get many letters.) So I thanked my father, and I would have kissed him, too, except that Morley and I don't have that kind of relationship.

Then we went for a walk around the hedge, which is where all the girls go with their visitors. Morley shuffled along in his big tan wing tips, not noticing the gorgeous waxy brown leaves still on the oak trees in the ravine or the older girls playing field hockey on the pitch below us. And not—I'm afraid to say—noticing me. You see, Morley always acts like he is asleep or dead, Mr. President. That's because he works too hard. Like you, he's very busy. Everybody wants him.

I hoped he would say the wonderful things he's always wanted to tell me. You know the kind of fatherly remarks I mean. He doesn't normally say them, because he doesn't like to make Sal jealous. Well, maybe he's afraid I would tell her, because that afternoon Morley didn't talk much. Once, just once, when I was telling him about having our tunics inspected by the matrons, he stopped and said, "You're all right, aren't you, Mouser?" I almost told him then about the pigeon, but when he looked at me with his worn-out, old eyes, I just couldn't bring myself to say how much I hated Bath Ladies College. I didn't want to cause trouble between him and Sal. So I said, "I'm fine, Morley." Then we sat in his Olds, and finally he made my cheek sting with his big hand. "Morley's love taps," my stepmother says when he pats her good-bye like that. If only you knew how much I hated myself for not being able to talk to him the way I can talk to you! I think it's because you understand the dark side of things. I know you do, because I read about you giving a talk at Amherst College and how you quoted Robert Frost's line, "I have been one acquainted with the night." I have been acquainted with the night, too, Mr. President. In fact, inside this dump it always feels like night.

I don't mean that Morley doesn't know about pain, because he does, and he also has the kindest eyes of anybody you ever saw. Your eyes, Mr. President, are more frank and glad than Morley's. You always look expectant, as if somebody we can't see is about to give you a very nice surprise. Morley's eyes look like he is expecting nothing except problems. Maybe Morley sees just a little too much pain for any decent person to handle. Well, sayonara, Mr. President. It's been a ball talking to you.

Your buddy,
Mouse Bradford

P.S. By the way, the pigeon died. (Not at my hands.) I thought it should have a sporting chance, so I took it out to the hill behind the school. I set it down and let it stagger around, hoping it would have the sense to fly away. And just at that terrible moment when it didn't fly off and I knew I had to get out Paulie's bowie knife, and I felt like Abraham after God asked him to sacrifice Isaac—just then Spruce, Sergeant's corgi, came tearing down the hill and grabbed the pigeon and ran off shaking it by its neck. Well, I ran after the dog, hitting it with a stick to make it drop the bird. But it was too late—the dastardly deed was done. Spruce chewed the head off the poor thing. I bawled my eyes out, and then Paulie got mad and said I was a disgrace to the male sex. I don't like being a man that much, Mr. President. I don't know how you do it.

November 15, 1963

Dear Mr. President,

Today is a red-letter day because you wrote me. I can't believe it. I have your note taped over my bed beside my Kennedy half-dollar. I especially liked the part *"Regards, John F. Kennedy,"* but I also did appreciate your advice, "Being a child has many difficulties, and parents are not perfect, but we must each give each other the best we have to offer." Thanks a million, Mr. President. I don't mean to sound sentimental, but you are the greatest friend I have ever had.

All my love,
M.B.

P.S. What do you think of a father who cuffs you on the cheek with the back of his hand when he says good-bye? Would you do that to Caroline? Just wondering.

— Mouse?

— What?

— He really wrote you, didn't he?

— He really did. But I didn't send my last three letters. I was afraid he wouldn't approve of the tests, either.

28

One night, when Ismay had gone with the school to the Royal Winter Fair, a pigeon tumbled onto the windowsill of our room and fell with a soft thud onto the floor. I yelled, and Paulie jumped almost ten feet. We both crept closer to see—Paulie purposeful, me cowering, my hands near my face in case the pigeon flew straight for my head in the flukey way that birds and bats do. What if it was the mate of the pigeon I'd tried to kill coming for revenge?

"This is your last chance, Bradford."

"Somebody will come in," I stammered. At the sound of my voice, the bird's pale eyelids slid apart, and two moist pink balls peeked sorrowfully up at me over the ridge of its beak. Then the gauzy lids slowly shut again. It knew—the way animals always do—what I'd tried to do to its wife or brother.

"Not if you're fast," Paulie said. "Do you want me to show you how?" Paulie held her pillow over the bird, which sat without moving—a puffed-up mass of beak and dirty feathers as round as a football.

"Don't be weird!" I shouted. "This pigeon still has a chance to live. Leave it alone!"

"What do you mean, I'm weird, Bradford?" Paulie handed me her pillow and I stood like a dope holding it over the bird's wilted head. Honest to God, I don't know what I would have done if I hadn't heard footsteps in the corridor. Paulie and I stared at each other. There was no mistaking who it was. The door swung open, and there she stood, a study in toneless greys. Her bloodhound eyes flicked left and right. Then she saw the bird. "Don't tell me that's another sick pigeon. Why do people poison dumb creatures?" the Virgin said irritably.

"Well, they're not very smart," Paulie said.

The Virgin stared at her.

"I mean, they aren't any smarter than turkeys. I don't see that it's any big deal."

"Is that so? Take this bird to the infirmary, will you, Tilly?" The Virgin waved her hand, and Miss Phillips, who had been waiting outside in the corridor, walked in and carried off the frightened bird in Paulie's towel. I was very relieved to see it being taken out of Paulie's clutches. I sat down on my bed and waited. The Virgin didn't just drop by for nothing.

"I know you must be wondering why I'm here." The Virgin chuckled and waited for us to chuckle, too, but neither of us made a sound. "Well, Paulie knows, don't you, Paulie?"

Paulie sat down on her bed and turned her back to us. She didn't answer.

The Virgin walked over to look at the photographs of President Kennedy I'd pinned up on my bulletin board. "He's a literary man, isn't he?" the Virgin said. "You must like that. Have you read his *Profiles in Courage*?"

"Yes, Miss Vaughan." I stared down at the floor. In front of me rested the pair of snub-nosed pumps we all dreaded to hear in the hall. And the powerful legs that drove the gunboats. These legs were encased in support hose that squashed down the unshaved hair that grew in thick and lush just above her ankles. How gross! But at least the Virgin's gunboats had more verve than Miss Phillips's plain lace-up boots.

"I see you have asked permission to go out with your aunt and uncle this weekend. Are they going to take you to the Visitor's

Luncheon at Kings College? You must be looking forward to seeing Victoria there."

"Wait—wait! What about me?" Paulie asked. "Can I go?"

"Excuse me, Pauline. I was talking to Mary Beatrice. But since you've joined in, I have a question for you. Why haven't you been keeping your promise to me about your visits to Dr. Torval?"

Paulie turned her back to us again and didn't reply.

"Now, Pauline, listen to me. I'm asking you to give Dr. Torval a chance even if you don't think he's a suitable choice. Don't you think she should go, Mary Beatrice?"

"Go where?" I asked.

"He's a shrink, Mouse." Paulie suddenly jumped up and addressed me as if we were alone in the room. "And he stinks! His B.O. makes me want to puke."

"Pauline! Would you please show more maturity! You're almost a grown woman."

"I am not. I am not a woman!" Paulie cried.

"Is being a woman so bad, Pauline?"

"Yes, it is, and you know it." Paulie paused. "And so does Mrs. Peddie." I couldn't believe my ears. I knew Paulie was referring to the incident we'd read about in their letters to each other.

For once, the Virgin had nothing to say. I wasn't sure if the Virgin was silent because she realized Paulie knew more than she should about her personal life, or if she had just run out of patience. To this day I'm not sure, but I've often wondered why the Virgin didn't keep a tighter check on Paulie than she did. Maybe she was trying to be "progressive" or maybe she didn't want to upset Paulie in case Paulie spilled the beans about her lesbian love affair.

"Very well, Pauline. You may have your way on this matter. But if I don't see a change in your behaviour, you won't be able to room with Tory next term."

"You promised you wouldn't do that!" Paulie cried.

"If you break your promise, how can you expect me to keep mine?" The Virgin walked out, her left cheek twitching.

I timidly put my hand on Paulie's arm.

"Why don't you go and see this doctor," I said. "And get her off your back."

"That's just what she wanted you to say. Why do you always let her trick you?" Paulie shrugged away my hand and walked out, slamming the door.

I watched her go sadly and began to pack my bag. The Virgin had given me special permission to stay with my uncle, Reverend Holmes, at the Park Plaza the following night. I should have been excited about getting out of school, but I dreaded having to spend my precious "out" weekend with my uncle.

29

The Trouble with My Uncle

I know I ought to tell you about my life with my guardian and Uncle Rev Winnie Holmes, or the Rev, as his parishioners call him. Then you could understand how Paulie's crime affected me. But there isn't a lot to say about things in Point Edward, except that my uncle's guest bedroom has a view of the St. Clair River, where, at night, the lake boats float out like lighted Christmas trees into the black water of Lake Huron.

1. He has an embarrassing name—Winston Churchill Frederick Holmes (Winnie for short).

2. He talks too much. And always boringly, on subjects that sound like homework assignments. Take, for instance, the six Humours. That's his description of the six geographical parts of Canada, which he's matched up with human characteristics—i.e., Newfoundland is synonymous with devotion, because, he says, one hundred percent belong to a church. (He always has his own statistics, which nobody else has ever heard about.) Quebec, with its large number of religious and educational institutions, represents scholarly aptitude. And Ontario, with its financial center on Bay Street, stands for avarice. (He says sermons on the last point are well received in the other provinces.)

3. He makes up embarrassing poems. I.e., "It's the Rev here,

to sing you cheer, to tell you what you need to know, and ask, God willing, for some dough."

4. He puts on a father act.

5. He feels sorry for himself because Morley made more money than he does. (That's the worst and scariest part, because I feel sorry for myself, too, on account of Morley, and I don't want to be like my uncle in even the smallest way.)

6. He calls me Old Mouser and smiles like a cat swallowing a canary when he says it.

7. He likes me and spends time with me and he isn't Morley.

The Moral of the Fuller's Teasel

Alice was bothering me the morning of the Visitor's Luncheon at Kings College. She was making my chest tight and my breathing hurt, and I sat in the back seat of my uncle's jalopy gulping aspirins and pretending I was made of see-through plastic. That's a trick I do when I don't want to be where I am. For one thing, I slow down and almost stop my breathing, which makes Alice happy. And for another, I concentrate on feeling weightless, which is the next best thing to being invisible. Sad to say, my trick wasn't working because in the rear-view mirror I saw my uncle watching me as if he were trying to figure out what was wrong. So I stared out the window with a nice fakey smile. I didn't want that blowhard to notice how dread was filling me from the tips of my dumb Mouse feet to the top of my old Mouse head. I'd never been to a mixed party before, and I didn't think the boys would like Alice or me. Plus I was a boarder, which was a strike against me as far as the day girls were concerned. I knew Tory didn't think this, and I longed to see her, but I couldn't exactly spend the whole time talking to her.

In the rear-view mirror, my uncle quivered his chins at me.

"Old Mouser, what do you want to do when you grow up?" he asked.

I didn't answer. A rushing stream of buses and cars flowed up and down the hill around us as we climbed north, heading for the tall stone gates of Kings College, which sat at the top of the busy avenue like pharaoh's monument.

"Now, Winnie. Mary Beatrice doesn't want to hear the story of the fuller's teasel today."

"It will only take a minute, Margaret." His chins acknowledged the pale green spire of the school's clock tower. "She may meet an important young man up there today. Isn't that right, Old Mouser?"

"I guess so." I bent down so he couldn't see me and sneaked another aspirin. My upper back felt like one single jammed muscle, and I wished I could shake it out the way Sal shook the sand out of Morley's beach towel.

"Now, you just hold your horses and listen." My uncle's double chins quaked. "Because to see the fuller's teasel, you'd think it was good for nothing. Its flowers are covered with bristles, but it's these useless-looking bristles that can be used to raise the nap on blankets."

To my relief, my uncle stopped talking as he drove through the gates and past a small guardhouse near a row of boarded-up hockey rinks. Like me, he was gawking at the buildings and the vast, grassy field beyond us, where boys in bulgy blue sweaters hurled themselves at one another with the assurance of the professional football players Morley liked to watch on TV. I stopped breathing totally now. Behind us the noise of city traffic faded, and I could hear birds chirping in the trees lining the long drive. My uncle stopped directly in front of the main building; up close, its six-story clock tower looked as grand and costly as the Peace Tower in Ottawa. A stream of girls in raccoon and camel's-hair coats were staggering up the wide stone steps between two chubby Grecian columns. They walked slightly knock-kneed, the way girls walk when they wear high heels for the first time. Even with their stupid walk, they looked glamorous and better dressed than me. I had on the navy dress I wore for church and plain black shoes with low wedge heels. Only day girls knew that "dress casual" meant high heels.

"Aren't they a little young to be wearing shoes like that?" my uncle asked. My aunt smiled. "You'll have to keep up with the times, Winnie. They all wear high heels now." I stared down fearfully at my feet. The shoe salesman had stuck in two extra soles in my right wedgie for support, but there was no way around it: I still walked favouring one side for every damn boy to see.

"As I was saying, Old Mouser, nothing else has ever been invented that can raise the nap on cloth this well."

I groaned, and my aunt said impatiently, "Winnie, for heaven's sake. Let the girl go."

"Directly, Margaret. Only let me finish this first. You see, Mary Beatrice, if you start to think that there's nothing you're qualified to do, just remember the fuller's teasel and ask, 'What do I have that is special?' Your aunt, for instance, used to ask this as a girl. Now she knows that taking care of me is what she does best."

"That's enough, dear. Have fun, Mary Beatrice." My aunt opened the door for me, and I slid out. Several of the day girls turned to look, and I hoped they wouldn't see who I'd come with, but my aunt and uncle both lumbered out of the car and walked me over to the school. My aunt wore a heavy brown coat with felt trim that matched her felt hat, and, in her low heels, she placed one foot after the other as if she expected the Kings College grounds to give way under her like thin spring ice. My uncle wore no coat, only a fedora, like Morley, and his black vest puckered in dimplelike creases over his stomach. I mumbled good-bye and slowly trudged up the steps after the day girls and into a large marble hall on whose walls I saw silver swords with maple leafs and pieces of faded material commemorating the school's role in suppressing old rebellions in Upper Canada.

Just inside the entrance, I passed a full-length portrait of Queen

Elizabeth and her husband, the duke. They called him the Visitor, and the luncheon was in his honour, even though he was back in England doing whatever it is dukes do. He wasn't as cute as President Kennedy, but in his nice dark suit he looked a lot more fun than the queen, who held her hands in a finky way in front of her silver gown as if she had a broken finger. I followed the stream of girls into a sitting room that was almost as big as our school's gym. Its walls were lined with stiff wing chairs that looked as if nobody ever sat in them and shiny mahogany sideboards and lamp tables. Right away, I looked for the first thing on my mind: food. I spotted the starched white linen on the sideboards, where silver trays sat full of devilled eggs, jellied salad, and my favourite— chicken à la king in pastry shells. We got that at school, too. It wasn't bad, even though the hot chicken had a habit of melting the jellied salad.

As I shuffled over, I snapped down another aspirin and noticed several Kings College boys in grey flannel pants and zigzaggy blue-and-white ties staring at me. I just knew they were looking at my shoulder, and when they whispered among themselves my stupid old Mouse heart stopped, as if somebody had pulled the plug. Now, Alice, don't take it personally, I thought; those snobby boys aren't worth the nail on your baby finger. But I could tell she didn't believe me. I was about to pick up one of the porcelain plates when a stout woman in a white uniform like a nurse asked me to wait until I was invited. Mortified, I slouched past a group of boys and girls waiting to shake the hand of a man with a face like a skull. He stood at the end of a line of masters and wives, and I realized he must be the lieutenant governor, the old queen's stand-in when the duke couldn't make it. A lot of the girls wore white gloves and actually curtsied when he shook their hand. Then somebody called my name, and there was Ismay sitting with a group of boarders from Bath Ladies College on a long green leather sofa next to a cavernous fake fireplace. They had come on

Sergeant's bus. I hurried, lightheaded with relief to see Ismay, of all things, and sat near my poor old fellow boarders in one of the enormous wing chairs. We huddled together like lost souls, mumbling among ourselves and staring enviously at the day girls, who strolled through the crowded hall with the confidence of adult women in stockings and high heels and knee-length tea dresses or tight wool suits.

And then the skinny woman I'd seen the day Tory hurt herself—the woman who looked like a gorgeous blond fish—waved at our little group. She wore a Chanel suit with braided trim and an enormous pair of sunglasses in the shape of butterflies. We all stood up awkwardly.

"Oh, my darling girl. How super! To meet you at last!"

I looked at the other boarders to see who she meant; then her pink minnow mouth tickled my cheek.

"You have no idea how grateful I am to you for helping Tory the day of her accident. She's my favourite child, you know. Even if I can't get her to stick to a diet!"

"A diet?" I said stupidly.

"Oh, yes, you darling girl! You can't be too rich or too thin, you know. Now, where is the silly child? Oh, yoo-hoo! Over here, you two!" Canon Quinn was walking toward us with a very tall boy whose pale, bespectacled face made me think of the giant pandas Morley and Sal and I had seen at the Detroit zoo. I'd got into an argument with Sal that day because she said the pandas were mean. Mrs. Quinn immediately threw her arms around the tall boy. "This is Jack O'Malley, the school projectionist," she said. "We couldn't do without him, could we, Bruno?"

"Do you ever show the movie *King Kong*?" I asked.

I don't know how I had the nerve to ask him about Paulie's and my favourite movie, but he seemed very pleased as he shook my hand with a funny, formal little jerk of his head and said he'd just shown it the week before. As far as he was concerned, it was the greatest monster flick of all time—way better than *Godzilla*. And I said I'd never believed in *Godzilla* for a minute, even though the Japanese were wizards at special effects. And then I realized I was tendrilling right under the noses of Tory's parents, and I shut up like a clam.

Tory's mother giggled. "Well, well," she said, and hugged me into her Chanel suit. She smelled comforting, the way I imagined a real mother would smell, of face powder and lily of the valley.

"You mustn't be too free in front of the girls, Panny," Canon Quinn said. He rested his hand on his wife's shoulder in a possessive gesture that was totally unlike the way Morley touched Sal or me. "They like to think we're old nincompoops."

"Speak for yourself, my pet," Mrs. Quinn said. She handed him a paper and motioned for the room to be quiet. Then she announced that the boarders from both schools who had blind dates arranged by the teachers should line up on either side of the rotunda. A long straggling line of us marched back out into the large hall. We stood on one side, next to a glass case that displayed a tiny silver woman on her knees reaching up imploringly to a tiny silver soldier on a horse. And the boys stood on the other side of the crowded room, next to a large doorway that led to the classrooms.

If there's one thing I hate, it's having to go through with something you know isn't going to work in the first place. People do it all the time, of course. Look at Sal and Morley. Sal goes to her bridge lessons every Thursday and comes back mad as a wet hen, because she hates Charles Van Goren's rules for bidding. She doesn't like to play cards by the book, she says. As for Morley, his whole life is something he doesn't want to do, and does, over and over. So why should I mind when I have to put up with getting a blind date? I ask you. Why should I care if some finky boy likes me or hates me?

Still, I couldn't see a way to avoid what was going to happen next without dropping dead on the spot, so I trooped over to join the girls, and that is when I saw *him* standing outside in the courtyard by the statue of an old war hero whose sword was lifted to the heavens. I should say "her," but Paulie looked so much like a boy in Lewis's clothes that only the masculine pronoun will do. He was dressed in his hunting cap and navy windbreaker—the same clothes he'd worn on our outing to the Old Mill. He was smoking, of course, and shuffling through the leaves. As I watched, he stopped and stared at the school, as if he wished he were inside with us, and the next thing I knew I'd stopped breathing again. Not on account of Alice, but because of the longing I saw on Lewis's face.

In the center of the rotunda, Canon Quinn was reading out a list of names, and, one by one, nervous-looking boys in navy blazers walked across the long hall and stood waiting with the principal for one of our boarders to join them. The boy and girl then shook hands while everybody stared at them. The teachers hadn't attempted to pair them off according to height, and the boys' line snickered every time a couple looked mismatched. I wanted to reassure Alice that we'd do okay, but I didn't have the energy right then, so I closed my eyes and pretended I was back in Madoc's Landing cutting onions for Sal because she didn't like it when onions made her cry and I loved to bawl my eyes out when I could get away with it.

And then I heard my name. I opened my eyes, but I couldn't make my feet move. Somebody in the boys' line laughed and said, "You got a no-show, Perce!" Canon Quinn called my name again, and this time I walked slowly to the center of the room. I could feel the boys and girls looking at me, but I kept my eyes on my new wedgies. I felt a firm tap on my shoulder—the non-Alice shoulder.

"Shake hands with Percy Longfellow, Mary Beatrice!" Canon Quinn said.

From the boys' line, I heard somebody whisper, "Perce struck out!" And another boy whispered back, "Longfellow's got a hunchback." I looked down. Percy Longfellow was three inches shorter than me and covered with zits. Blushing, he shook my hand. It was even wetter than mine.

We silently made our way over to the group of boys and girls now matched into pairs. Beside me, Percy Longfellow swayed strangely and shuffled his feet. He had a headache, he whispered. "Here, take this," I whispered back, and gave him an aspirin from the bottle in my purse. But he only shook his head, and I knew the worst had happened, the way it always does, and I felt a flat, sad feeling all mixed up with relief, because the worst is what I know how to manage best.

I looked back out the window again. Lewis had changed his position. He stood now on the tall base of the military statue, looping a roll of toilet paper around its head and shoulders. Below, a girl in a raccoon coat stood, watching. It was Tory. I didn't recognize her out of uniform. She looked foreign—like a day girl. Then Lewis jumped down, and the two of them walked slowly out of the quad, Lewis waiting as Tory took little hobbling hops on her crutches. I mean, they just looked totally happy and absorbed—the way Lady looks when she begs for date squares. Behind them, the threads of toilet paper on the statue blew backwards in the slight wind. I felt so moved by the sight of them together, with Lewis looking so patient and kind, that I didn't notice the girls and boys around me banging on the window. One of the boys was swearing, and then one of the masters rushed out of the room, and another boy ran after him, and now I saw Lewis and Tory looking our way with startled faces, and then Tory put her hand on Lewis's cheek, and Lewis kissed it very tenderly and then ran off as fast as he could through the quad, while Tory just stood on her crutches watching him go. I knew just how Tory felt, because it's how I feel after Morley pats me on the cheek and drives off in Blinky. And that's when something happened that made all of us forget Lewis. Down the hall I heard a radio, and a woman cry out, "Oh my God! Who would do such a thing?" Canon Quinn opened the tall wooden door of the reception room, his batwing brows flaring. Mrs. Quinn stood in the doorway, looking sad.

"Somebody has shot the president of the United States!" she said. "A madman has shot him!"

"President Kennedy has been shot?" one of the masters asked.

I forgot all about Percy Longfellow's headache and cried, "It's a mistake! I don't believe it!" Canon Quinn only nodded, very gravely, and boys and girls around me started to say they didn't believe it, either. And you know the rest. Except for this: I'd seen the world of men, and nobody there was as nice as John F. Kennedy. And he was dead.

30

November 25, 1963

Dear Mr. Kennedy,

I can't believe you're dead. None of us can. After Mrs. Quinn broke the news, Canon Quinn cancelled the dance, and we all went into the Quinns' library and watched the American news on television. A man called Dan told us you had been shot three times. I couldn't help wishing Governor Connally had been sitting up just a little higher in your bubble-top convertible. (No offence intended to the governor.)

What I don't understand, Mr. President, is why couldn't somebody save you? There was time. Well, a second or so between the second and third shots. Why didn't Jackie pull you down into her lap then? That's what Mrs. Connally did for her husband. I know Jackie climbed across the trunk of the limousine. I guess she was going for help, but it looked to me like a stupid thing to do. Like she was running away. And exposing herself to getting shot, too.

I like to think that if I'd been there, Mr. President, I could have done something for you. I would have stood up in my bulletproof vest and deflected the bullets. I'm just Mouse Bradford, and it wouldn't have mattered so much to the world if I'd got hit. Except that I don't think bulletproof vests cover your neck, do they? Which is where you got it. And in the back of your beautiful head.

I'm trying not to sniffle as I write this, Mr. Kennedy. I want to take it on the chin like you would. But the world doesn't feel safe anymore without you. You made it a nicer place, because you always acted as if everybody had good intentions—or at least started out with good intentions, no matter what they did after. Nobody else I know does that. Sure, I've got Morley and Sal at home, but I told you the problems with them. Particularly Morley. He hasn't written me since I've been here. You managed to send me one letter, and a very good letter it was, too.

I'm writing this in study. The Virgin is patrolling the halls. I hear the rat-a-tat-tat of her gunboats on the floor of the corridor. None of us have been able to study since it happened.

The night Oswald shot you, my aunt and uncle let me stay up to hear the late-night news on the CBC. Mr. Pearson (he is our nice prime minister—the one with the bow tie) said we all have to have a deeper resolve to be better ourselves, because a young and good man has gone from the face of the planet. It made me and my aunt Margaret cry a little, Mr. President, and even my stupid old uncle looked pretty sad.

Then we switched to CBS, the American channel, for man-on-the-street interviews.

I can't remember what anybody said, but the mouths in the shuffling crowd opened and uttered one single despairing moan, as if somebody had hit all their heads at the same time with a big block of wood.

I'm trying my best, Mr. President, to get on with life. For instance, I have a physics test on Monday. But I feel like I'm not being loyal to you, having to think about other things.

In a few minutes study will be over, and I will practise my role in *How to Succeed in Business without Really Trying*. I play the office dandy who doesn't do anything except fawn over his superiors. Ismay the Terrible plays one of the secretaries. Everybody giggles like crazy when Ismay has to say her line in the song about not being an Erector set. It's just a ball to hear somebody like Ismay say something dirty. I have to (groan) hold her hand when we take our bows. Well, time to go. I can't believe you're dead, Mr. President. I hope I'll wake up tomorrow and find that the events of November 22 were a terrible, terrible, terrible mistake.

Yours forever,
Mouse Bradford

31

A few weeks before the end of term, Paulie and I ducked out of games and hid near the ravine fence. Not far from us the janitors were digging a pit to bury the mysteriously poisoned pigeons, whose corpses now sat in the little cart attached to Willy's tractor. And down on the empty basketball courts, a few day girls were hitting a tennis ball back and forth. You had to hand it to them— I'd never have had the energy to exert myself like that. I didn't even have the energy to keep up with the boarders, huddled into little groups, walking around the hedge, their heads down against the wind. Basically, you understand, it was my unfav time of year—late November—and the leaves were off most of the ravine trees, blown into the school hedges, where they clung like tufts of badly matted brown hair. I was sitting next to Paulie in Virginia Woolf's hiding place, although old Virginia would have wanted to do herself in then and there if she'd seen how desolate it looked now. One glance at the dead asters and withered grass all silver from the frost and she'd have waded as fast as anything out into the river Ouse with her stone-packed pockets. Poor Virginia. I like to think she might have picked out a stone as smooth and pancake-flat as a Lake Huron skipping stone and zinged it across the surface of the water, *zip-zip-zip*, before she did her Ophelia number. I was feeling pretty low that afternoon, because Sal had written with disappointing news about my Christmas holidays.

November 24, 1963

Dear Mouse,

Isn't it awful about President Kennedy? I know you were a big fan of his, so I'm sending you some clippings from the *Bulletin*. As Lester Pearson said, he was a special friend to us up here in Canada, and we feel almost as bad as the Americans do. Our neighbours to the south may be ignorant showoffs, but they had a half-decent president, I grant them that.

Love,
Sal

P.S. I expect your Uncle Winnie told you the news about Christmas. I've arranged for you to stay with him in Point Edward for the holidays. I've already told Miss Vaughan you will be well chaperoned. Don't get blue, now, Mouse. You know you have a tendency to be overly serious about things. Morley and I will come to visit you in the city before we leave. I promise.

I was angry with Sal for going away at Christmas, so her feelings about our mutual hero felt like a phony gesture. Maybe I was growing up. Maybe Sal had always been like that—good at confidences, so you thought you were thick as a pack of dogs (to use one of her sayings). And then, just when you least expected it, she'd do something that showed you didn't mean a thing to her. Like sending you off to school when you didn't want to go. Or leaving you behind on a holiday she'd promised was partly yours. Sal's confidence didn't say anything about her feelings for you. Her secrets just meant she liked telling secrets.

The Only Good Thing

The only good thing in my life was Jack O'Malley, the boy I'd met at the Kings College luncheon. He'd written me a letter, too.

November 29, 1963

Dear Mary,

How the h--- (pardon my French) are you? I have a record player in our dorm, and we play rock-and-roll like crazy. Last night we had a huge dancing session with broomsticks, and Bo Johnson and myself got caned for making too much noise. Did the boy's backside hurt or what! Well, we had to do something after the memorial service in the Great Hall for President Kennedy. You could have heard a pin drop when old Cannonballs quoted from Kennedy's inauguration speech: "Let us never negotiate out of fear. But let us never fear to negotiate." All kidding aside, it will be a long time before a man like that crosses our paths, Mary. By the way, I hope the food at your school is edible. We had toad-in-the-hole yesterday again. That's twice in one week. The suffering we boarders go through in the name of education! Say, I was just wondering if you are getting out on the weekend of Dec. 2 to see *It's a Mad Mad Mad Mad World*? If you could get out, I would love to take you.

Regards,
Jack

P.S. Tory said you are from Madoc's Landing. How's that for a small world? I'm from Orillia, birthplace of Stephen Leacock, the funniest dead Canadian! Har-de-har-har, as Jackie Gleason would say. And guess what? I'm showing *Godzilla* to the boys next Saturday. After the hockey game.

Two days after his letter arrived Jack called me up. He sounded all out-of-breath and nervous on the phone. To my surprise, I felt pleased and calm when I said I'd go with him, as if I could afford to be confident, although I'd never been out with a boy before and didn't know what to expect. Would he try to feel me up, like Paulie got me to do with the girl from St. Mary's? The idea of kissing him was like kissing a star or the top of a pine tree. Not that I was interested in going all the way or anything. Sal liked to say that sex came in two forms, hamburgers and lobster dinners, and if you had a choice between great seafood or ground chuck, why go for cheap food when you could have it deluxe? The only problem with Sal's analogy was that if sex was like food, then wasn't it better to have a hamburger instead of starving yourself? Why wait until a lobster dinner came along? Naturally, I didn't want to discuss these problems with Paulie, who was sitting beside me, scowling at the janitors as if she hated their guts.

The digging of the pigeons' grave looked like a tough job. The earth had already hardened from the cold, and Sergeant and Willy had to jab their spades into the ground as if they were attacking a layer of permafrost. Then, just after the pit was dug and the pigeons dumped into it, Sergeant suddenly lifted up his dog, Spruce, who was wrapped in a Glengarry plaid blanket. Poor little Spruce didn't move. He must have eaten one of the dead birds and died from poison himself. Sergeant stood there cradling Spruce, tears running down his cheeks. Then Willy touched his shoulder, and Sergeant laid Spruce down beside the birds. I watched sadly as Willy shovelled dirt over Sergeant's little dog and then did the same for the pigeons. The birds, their small heads as wobbly as Jell-O, made me think of the mass human graves the Allies had uncovered at Auschwitz. Then they were done. Sergeant heaved himself into the little car behind Willy's tractor, and Willy drove off talking loudly in Czech, as if he were trying to console Sergeant.

"A man shouldn't break down like that," Paulie said. "Not that you can call those assholes men." Personally, I didn't agree. Men were always breaking down, as far as I could tell. Look at the way Morley acted at hockey games, smashing the fedora of the man next to him (as if he was somebody Sal and I didn't know at all) and climbing the wire-mesh fence behind the goalie when the referee made a wrong call on Dave Keon.

"Everybody cries sometimes," I said. My own eyes were a little wet, so I tried to think of something funny, like Miss Phillips in her curlers, to stop me from imagining how uncomfortable the poison must have made Spruce feel.

Paulie lit up a cigarette and passed it to me. I hesitated.

"Go on," Paulie said. "Nobody can see us here."

"I'm in uniform," I said.

"Be a scaredy-cat, then." Beside me, Paulie spat one of her expert loads at my shoe, missing me by a fraction of an inch.

I sighed and held out two fingers. "Okay," I said, hating myself for being afraid. "Give me one."

"That's more like it." Paulie grinned and lit me a cigarette. "Listen, Bradford. I have something important to tell you. We have to finish the test today. Kong's orders."

"You mean there are more tests?" I asked, trying to exhale through my nostrils like Paulie.

"We have to cane each other, remember?" Paulie picked up an old blackboard pointer that was lying near the fence. It was just about in splinters.

"I stole this from the physics lab," Paulie said. "We'll flip to see who goes first."

32

Paulie took off her tunic and pulled down her school bloomers. She was wearing a pair of boy's boxer shorts underneath. She turned around and pulled down the boxers; then she bent over and touched her toes. "This is how they do it at Kings College, Mouse," she said. "But the boys keep their trousers on. We're going one better."

I stood with the shabby pointer in my hand, staring at her small bare bum. I had no idea what to do.

"Okay, Bradford," Paulie said. "Let me have it."

I swung the pointer slowly, as if I were practising a baseball swing for old Hammerhead, and the tip lightly stroked Paulie's bum. "Christ, Mouse! I can't feel a thing!" she called. "Hit me harder!" I swung again but drew back at the last minute, afraid I'd hurt her. "Paulie, I can't do this." I put the pointer down and, honest to God, I started to giggle. I felt the same way I did when I used to tease Lady, covering her up with sofa cushions and then lying on her for the fun of hearing her growl.

"So you think this is funny, do you?" Paulie whirled around and grabbed the pointer out of my hand. Her boxers were still around her ankles, and I couldn't help staring at the feathery blur of her pubic hair. I inhaled deep and hard. I guess I believed in Paulie so much, I was expecting to see a penis, for God's sake.

"Keep your eyes to yourself," Paulie snarled. "Bend over. I'm going to show you how it's done."

Now it was my turn. I took off my tunic and yanked down my bloomers and my cotton underpants. Then I leaned over, and Paulie pushed my head down, because I couldn't bend over very far on account of Alice. Nothing happened, and I was sure she was going to stop and tell me it was a dopey idea. And then I heard a whooshy sound, and something long and skinny sliced deep into the tops of my thighs, like hundreds of stinging horseflies. My whole body jerked back toward Paulie, and Alice jerked, too, and I gasped. "Paulie, stop!" I yelled, and the next thing I knew the tops of my thighs felt raw and hot. I began to sob; pee was running down my legs.

"Shut up, Bradford!" Paulie yelled. "Show some guts for once!" She put her muscular hand back on my neck and tried to push my head down again, but I wouldn't bend over, so she whacked Alice hard, and I screamed and toppled, weeping, to my knees. I heard another whistling whoosh behind my head, and this time the pointer cut me across my buttocks, spitefully on target. I shrieked and crawled off on all fours as fast as I could, but Paulie grabbed my hair. *Schwaaak!* She whacked my bum with all her might.

"Paulie! Stop it!" I cried. "Stop it!" I wrapped my hand around my bum to protect myself, and the pointer burned across my knuckles. *Schwaaaaaak!*

"It's for your own good!" Paulie's screeching voice sounded high and shrill, and I knew now she wasn't talking to me but to herself, and the hatred I felt rushing out of her was coming from her phantoms, and those spooks had nothing to do with me.

"Liar!" I screamed. "It is not! It is not for my own good!"

"Kong lives! Long live Kong! Kong lives! Long live Kong!" Paulie pushed the side of my face into the ground, grabbed my hair, and yanked my head each time I tried to jerk away. *Schwaaaaaak! Schwwwaaaak!* The pointer cut into my bum and thighs, which were all stingy wet with pee. And then I stopped feeling the fiery pain, even though I could still hear the awful whistling sounds the pointer made in the air. I curled into a ball and wept noisily into the hard ground, which tasted of minerals and mud, cold and dark and earthwormy. Oh, Mouse, poor Mouse, a small scared voice in my head said from a long way off, nobody can help you now. And then Sal's shaming voice added cruelly, And you deserve this, Mouse Bradford, you aren't good enough to get our love. And then the pointer snapped. Paulie raised the broken-off stick to give me another whack, and I caught her eye, and we stared at each other without saying anything. Still glaring at me, she let her arm drop.

"Crybaby," she said finally, and walked off cursing and smacking what was left of the pointer on every tree she passed. I watched her go in surprise, my cheeks still wet with tears. My backside throbbed, and my legs were stained with pee and blood. But the oddest thing had happened: the more she hit me, the more wicked she became, and the more innocent I was—of everything. Of looking ungainly, of not winning Morley's love, of my lack of friends.

33

Why did I go along with Paulie when the tests got more serious? Why did I keep doing what she asked me? It wasn't just my need for approval that made me do what Paulie said. I was enthralled by her imagination—which the court tried to deny. Especially Miss Whitlaw's chief defense witness, Dr. Torval. But the Crown had to prove Paulie was *not* insane before she could be found guilty. The old Juvenile Delinquent Act defined a child as somebody under the age of sixteen. So Paulie, who was almost seventeen at the time of the crime, was tried as an adult. That meant the crazier Miss Whitlaw's defense witnesses could make Paulie look, the better chance Paulie had of avoiding a criminal conviction. I don't think Miss Whitlaw or the judge liked Dr. Torval any better than I did.

HIS LORDSHIP: Dr. Torval, let us get back to the defendant for a minute. You have told us, I believe, that she was a victim of a gender disorder.

DR. TORVAL: Well, not exactly, my lord. She is psychologically unusual. This is what I was trying to explain. . . .

HIS LORDSHIP: Yes, I have noticed your efforts in that regard. But could you now address the question of the defendant's sanity? Was she responsible for her actions?

DR. TORVAL: Let me put it this way, my lord: she was and she wasn't.

HIS LORDSHIP: Excuse me, Dr. Torval, but I don't think you have responded to my question. Can you tell us whether Miss Sykes was responsible for her actions or not?

DR. TORVAL: That's exactly what I'm trying to do, my lord. You see, we can measure schizophrenia through the proverb test. Now, the proverb test doesn't measure intelligence but rather the ability to abstract. A clever and stable person will be able to interpret the proverbs. Can I read out the proverbs I gave Pauline Sykes, my lord? It won't take long.

HIS LORDSHIP: Could you just get on with it, Dr. Torval?

DR. TORVAL: Sorry, yes. And if you can't interpret these proverbs, my lord, don't worry. To the proverb "Like carrying coals to Newcastle," Pauline Sykes answered—

HIS LORDSHIP: I think you need to speak a little more slowly.

DR. TORVAL: I am sorry. To the proverb "Like carrying coals to Newcastle," the defendant replied, "Coal makes fires burn." To the proverb "Pride goes before a fall," the defendant replied, "If you don't watch where you're going." To the proverb "No man is an island," the defendant replied, "An island is hard to get to."

HIS LORDSHIP: I'm puzzled, Dr. Torval. Are you suggesting the defendant is sick? Her responses sound intelligent enough.

DR. TORVAL: If I may continue, I believe this will become clear, my lord.

HIS LORDSHIP: Let us hope so, Dr. Torval.

DR. TORVAL: To the proverb "Wisdom is better than rubies," the defendant replied, "Rubies look nice." And to the proverb "Any port in a storm," the defendant made no answer.

HIS LORDSHIP: Thank you, Dr. Torval. Did you give her any other tests?

DR. TORVAL: No. Because, you see, from the proverb test, my lord, it was obvious the defendant is not capable of abstract thinking. She sees things in black and white and is not able to make any of the leaps in her mind that even the most ordinary person is capable of doing.

Paulie not capable of abstract thought? Or an act of the imagination? What else, I ask you, was her strange and frightening act if not that?

34

"Miss Vaughan wants to see you after the show," Ismay the Terrible said as we ran out to take our places in the school play. She didn't give me a chance to ask why.

We performed in the gym, which the junior school had decorated for our Christmas party. Ugly crepe Christmas trees on sand-coloured crepe trunks snaked up the wall between the stained-glass windows, and across the huge double doors at the entrance the junior school had hung tennis nets decorated with little snow-covered houses made of construction paper and cotton batting. On one end of the fleecy mural sat a big grey house with a spire—Bath Ladies College. A replica of the Kings College clock tower had been pasted on the opposite side of the mural. In the middle dangled cutout replicas of the baby Jesus, Mary, and Joseph.

I could feel my hands sweating as I held Ismay's arm to take our bows. The girls clapped and called out "Encore, encore," which is what they imagined audiences said in the real world. But the Virgin didn't move a muscle. Instead, she eyed me and whispered to Mrs. Peddie. What had I done this time? It was true I'd put on nail polish in study again, but I'd made sure nobody saw me. And I'd perfected the old-girls' trick of stealing Oreos—stuffing them, in one scoop, into the sleeve of my dressing gown. These misdemeanours were too small to make the Virgin look at me so strangely. Maybe she knew about Lewis and Nick.

All the Really Horrible, Inconvenient Feelings

The Virgin rose from her seat the moment I exited. In the dressing room, I sat waiting before the mirror. Behind me, Ismay struggled out of her ugly nylons with the black seams that ran up the backs of her thighs like highway dividers. I wanted to signal to Paulie, who was one of the stagehands putting away the props, but I hadn't spoken to her since the beatings. Still, if I was about to get expelled, why did the Virgin look so sad? Maybe she had a heart after all. But how dumb! I already knew she did—and so did Mrs. Peddie, because I had seen it in their letters. My own eyes had read the words that said the two biddies were capable of the most embarrassing emotions: love and anger and humiliation—all the really horrible, inconvenient feelings you could hope for swarmed in their matronly bosoms.

The Virgin walked in first; then Mrs. Peddie entered three paces behind, like Prince Philip following Queen Elizabeth. Neither of them spoke. The Virgin held out her hand. It wasn't a gesture that asked for me to hold out mine in return.

"Mary, there's been some bad news," the Virgin said. "Could you come to my office, please."

Ismay hurried away, not daring to look at me, and Mrs. Peddie and I followed the Virgin's bearlike form down the shadowy corridor behind the stage leading to her office. We passed the secret cubby hole where Miss Vaughan let Clare, the boarder captain, go to cry when helping the matrons run the boarding school became too much for her. Maybe Clare was crouched there now, crying like a fool.

At the door, Mrs. Peddie stepped aside, smiling guiltily, as if to say, I'm sorry, Mary Beatrice, I can't go any farther with you: each of us must travel solo into the sulphurous bowels of hell. The Virgin banged the door shut on Mrs. Peddie's concerned face and waved me to a chair. She sat down and put her elbows on the desk in front of her. She sighed heavily. It's all over, Mouse, I thought.

"Mary Beatrice, your father's dead," the Virgin said finally. "We don't know the details, but your stepmother wants you to phone her."

For one embarrassing second, I didn't react. Then I nodded—twice, in case Miss Vaughan hadn't understood the first time. I didn't see why she should be upset. Everybody said Morley worked too hard. So I knew Morley would kick the bucket one of these days; that's why I'd written Norman Vincent Peale. But nobody had listened to me. Now I wouldn't be going out on my date with Jack O'Malley.

The Virgin stared at me and then turned her back and dialled the phone. A moment later, she handed me the receiver. I heard Sal's voice at the other end. It was like a weird echo of Sal, not the Sal I knew. Her voice was muffled by sobs, so I had to concentrate hard to hear her.

"He's left us, Mouse," she said. There was a long silence. I didn't say anything. Then she sobbed again. "Mouse? Are you there?"

"Yes," I said finally.

"He died on his way to Barry Island. A woman was having her baby there, and none of the other doctors would go." Sal began to weep so hard I could barely hear her. "Isn't that just typical?"

I didn't say anything. Barry Island was an Indian reserve near Madoc's Landing. I handed the phone back to the Virgin. I didn't want to talk long-distance anymore. I watched the Virgin talk to Sal. The Virgin said, "Oh, yes, very upset. Too upset to talk to you right now, Mrs. Bradford." Then the Virgin said how terribly sorry she was and uttered phrases like, "Car got stuck in the slush, did it?" and, "Oh I see. He went for help, did he? And then a heart attack. Yes. The cold. Ah—too much for him. Yes. Wait. She's asking me something." I'd stood up. "Lady?" I said. "Our dog?"

"Lost, I'm afraid," the Virgin said to me. And then: "No, not now. Let me get her trip up to Madoc's Landing organized."

The Virgin put down the phone. "I'm terribly sorry, Mary Beatrice," she said.

I stood up and walked out the door without waiting for her permission.

Part Two

35

Down the icy hill, through an archway of snow-covered branches, I saw the doctor's house. That's what people in Madoc's Landing called our large, gabled home. It was the only house on the block with a wreath on the door. At first I thought it was a Christmas decoration, and then I realized it was too early—only the first of December. The wreath was for Morley.

Our house was of new red brick with gingerbread trim over the windows and large brick chimneys that sprouted from the roof in unlikely places. The old bay window I liked on the first floor was hidden behind a new addition with a garish California picture window that Sal had made Morley build. The other homes had been built over a hundred and fifty years before for British naval officers who came to Madoc's Landing to stop the Americans from invading Canada. Now these three-story clapboard houses belonged to schoolteachers and shopkeepers in the Landing.

To the east of our house, behind a grove of spruce, crouched the asylum. It was a huge brick mausoleum eight or ten times the size of our house with a screened veranda and twin cupolas. It had been built the same year. Our house had once belonged to the head of the nuthouse (Sal's word for it), but now the staff of the asylum lived in concrete quarters built farther down the hill, toward the bay. They drove shiny new Buicks because they made so much money from overtime, and people in the Landing said they used tear gas and German shepherd dogs on the prisoners, just like guards did in real prisons. Morley said these rumours were garbage. He used to play tennis with the inmates, and he was sometimes called the nuthouse doctor because he used to visit the mental patients for free. He put up paintings in our living room by his favourite patient, an older woman who thought she was a tennis pro. These paintings—small, brooding scenes of ice-locked lakes and cars abandoned on old roads—were done with thick brushstrokes, as if she were imitating Van Gogh. I often thought that if I looked at these paintings hard enough, I would find she had left me a terrible message.

The taxi crept up our drive, spinning its wheels on the slippery pavement. The snow was already high—almost up to the sill of the picture window. I paid the driver with the money the Virgin had given me and then walked slowly up the steps and knocked on my own front door. It swung open and I saw an expansive, high-ceilinged room with blazing fires. I felt as if it were the home of somebody I didn't know and then Sal was throwing her arms around me. Behind her, two shadowy figures moved slowly toward us—Uncle Winnie and Aunt Margaret. I walked in and stood in front of the fire, warming my hands, and my uncle came over, smiling chummily.

"There are many things I could say, Old Mouser. I think you know what they are, so there's no point saying them now."

He looked at me as if he'd done me a favour. But this was a time I wanted him to talk. I needed him to make me feel better about Morley—to say something about what a good man he was. Sal seemed to be waiting, too; she stood beside me weeping and smelling of Listerine—a bad sign.

"Why don't you say a prayer, Winnie?" my aunt said.

"Oh, God, give us the spiritual courage to continue day after day without our dearly beloved father and brother-in-law, Morley Bradford." My uncle paused to resettle his hands on his stomach.

"And give to this young girl among us grace and fortitude in her new life with Margaret and myself."

I started to say something, but the floor wobbled beneath me. When I opened my eyes, I found myself with Sal in the guest room, where she put Morley or me if we were sick. She said I shouldn't take my uncle's offer seriously. He said he wanted to be my guardian, but he was only doing what he thought was expected of him. His heart wasn't in it, Sal said. I listened suspiciously and sighed my old Mouse sigh when she crawled into bed beside me and began to sob again. "Oh, Mouse," she whispered. "I loved him the moment he walked through the hospital door and said, Sal, you're a sight for sore eyes. He always liked me to take care of him, but I couldn't cure him of his bad heart, could I, Mouse?"

"It wasn't your fault, Sal," I said. "It wasn't your fault he worked so hard." I stared at the ceiling. Sal was drunk, so I couldn't tell her how much I needed her not to talk about Morley's love for her. There just wasn't enough Morley love to go around, and I hadn't got my share.

36

Ahead of our car, the hearse skidded down the narrow road into the cemetery of St. Patrick's banging its grille into the high, stiff banks of snow that rose on either side of us like walls of frozen shaving cream. The snow came earlier in Madoc's Landing than it did in Toronto, and my hometown had already been through two thaws and two freeze-overs. We all held our breath and then the hearse bounced back again onto the road. My uncle breathed out in relief, his fingers still tight on the wheel. He was in charge of driving Blinky, and one of the funeral directors sat in the front beside him—a tall, red-haired man with a moustache that Sal said you saw only on Fuller Brush salesmen.

Sal sat beside me in the back seat. My aunt was on the other side, rubbing at the frosted windows in order to make a peephole. It was below zero.

I felt safe in Blinky. The car made me think Morley was with us, and I knew how put off he'd be by the way my uncle was braking his car on the slippery country road. If you grow up in northern Ontario, you know you have to pump the brake over ice so you don't skid.

Good-bye to Morley

The funeral director helped my aunt out first. Then he took Sal's hand, and I saw his eyes dart sideways when she staggered a little. I stumbled out as quickly as I could, grabbing her elbow in case she slipped. It was as if Morley were watching me now from the back of the hearse—smiling at me in his planting suit, as Sal said the undertaker had called the striped worsted suit he'd put on my father. I hated the word "planting." It was a farmer's word, and Sal had repeated it as a joke, because that's what her people called the clothes they put on a corpse.

Most of the people from Madoc's Landing had come to Morley's funeral, and now they were getting out of their cars behind us—farmers still in thigh-high rubber boots, the shop owners and their wives muffled up in winter clothes like the cartoon ad of Mr. Bib, the Michelin tire man. I noticed the other doctors and nurses from the General, and some of my old schoolmates, who looked at me sympathetically from under the pompommed peaks of wool toques. I didn't want their pity, and I resented Morley for dying and putting us in a vulnerable position in front of the town. It felt as if his death had left me without my skin, only easy-to-bruise blood and guts.

I looked over the mourners' heads at the little lake at the bottom of the cemetery. It, too, lay covered with snow; skating there would be difficult. I'd only skated on the lake once, with Sal, and I'd wobbled over on my ankles until I couldn't stop crying, and Sal had made me give it up. But I knew I had to act grown-up from now on. I had to do things that made people say Mouse Bradford has common sense, so Morley would finally be proud of me.

We began to gather in a long line behind my uncle. He was ignoring what the funeral director said to him and was waving at small groups of people to come closer. He had draped a fringed

ecclesiastical scarf outside his winter coat so there was no mistaking
who he was. Sal had given him one of Morley's Homburg hats and
Morley's fine beige kid gloves. He looked like a funhouse carica-
ture of my father. He was half Morley's height, with a face swollen
up like a boil from overeating. I wondered what Kong would think
of him and how he would do with Paulie's tests. Men had all the
luck: they got to be men by an accident of birth. My uncle
frowned, as if he'd heard me and staggered ahead of the funeral
director in his unzipped sheepskin-lined galoshes, whose sides
flapped open right to his toes. He stopped and waved at something, and I saw Morley's grave. About twenty feet away a cast-iron
wood stove smoked in a half-dug rectangular hole. Beside it, two
men whacked the frozen earth with pickaxes. My uncle waved
again, and the two men scrambled up and faded into the crowd like
a pair of crows. The snow near the grave was churned up into an
ugly red slush. I stared at the room in the ground where Morley's
body was to go and looked away. And then—to my shock— who
did I see staring at me across that strange, half-finished trench but
the Virgin. The December wind was tugging at her white hair,
which was smashed flat under a navy cloche hat. I smiled gratefully.
I couldn't believe she had come all the way to Madoc's Landing
for my father's funeral. She smiled back at me across the space and
pointed to somebody. Paulie, also in the school's navy church-
going hat and coat. Chewing gum and staring down into Morley's
grave, as if she were looking at the grave Sergeant and Willy had
dug for the pigeons.

In her shapeless clothes, the Virgin looked like what the boys in
Madoc's Landing call a dud—somebody you won't take out unless
you can put a bag over her head. And Paulie, whose sinewy,
masculine body was hidden in our Sunday uniform—Paulie just
looked shorter than I remembered and immature.

It began to snow again on the way back to our house. My uncle
said Morley's body would be stored in the stone chapel at the front

of the cemetery until the men could unthaw the earth with the stove and dig a proper grave. The delay comforted me; I couldn't bear to think of Morley under the snowy earth. If it had been me, I'd have liked to stay in the chapel for good.

As my uncle turned right at the cemetery gate, my aunt handed me a package of letters from the girls at the school. "That very tall, distinguished-looking woman gave these to me for you." My aunt stared at Sal's head on my shoulder. I said Sal was worn out from the ordeal of the funeral and my aunt smiled at me. She was the kind of woman who wanted to believe the best of people, so if you could come up with an excuse—anything that sounded halfway acceptable—she took you at your word. This meant I had insurance against my uncle's disapproving code. One member of that family would be what Sal called biddable—somebody who would try to see something in my terms.

In the car, I skimmed the perfunctory letters from class presidents on white notepaper sprinkled with embossed silver ferns asking me to let them know if there was anything they could do for me. I thought it was a stupid thing to offer. How could they do something for me when I was in Madoc's Landing? And even if I were back at school, what could they do? I felt embarrassed for them, as if I were looking at letters sent to somebody else and I was just an intermediary in a ritual.

There was one letter I did read—from Tory.

December 13, 1963

Dear Mouse,

We are all dreadfully sorry to hear about your father. The Virgin told us the news in prayers and looked quite sad for you. Even Old Phillips seemed affected!! As you may have guessed, I am back at the dungeon. My legs are almost healed, and I whiz around like anything on my trusty crutches. By the way, I am sleeping in your bed. Don't worry, Mouse! I won't take your place! I can't wait until next term, when we will all be together again!!! Ismay and Paulie hate each other's guts, and it's all I can do to keep the peace around here. After Christmas, Miss Vaughan is putting Ismay back in a single room. The worst thing is, Paulie's taken to thinking I like Ismay better than her. All because Ismay brought me homework in November!! But you know how hard it is to talk Paulie out of something once she's made her mind up. I guess that's why we love her, huh?

Meanwhile, the girl who took your part in the play forgets her lines and doesn't look like an office boy at all. It was pretty upsetting to see everybody take their bows without you. We are all thinking of you and pulling for you.

Love,
Tory

P.S. I started to sign this "puddles of purple passion" and then thought better of it. You're not supposed to write stuff like that on these notes, are you?

Dear old Tory. She always managed to break through a convention that got in her way. If she wanted to, she could rule the world. I stuffed her letter into the pocket of my horrible old tweed coat and thought about how I was going to get Sal through the reception ahead.

37

Sal and I stood beside the fireplace. Morley's first wife, my mother, had filled it with mirrors—mirrors over the fireplace and along the west wall. It made everything grander, bigger. And that day, it made the old house look as if all of Madoc's Landing were in our two front parlours. Our next-door neighbour, Mrs. Florie Buck, was telling the other women where to put the tuna-fish casseroles on the dining-room table along with the cheese and pickles and hard-boiled eggs and angel-food cakes. There was to be liquor at the reception. This worried me. I didn't know how long she'd last with the cups of coffee Mrs. Buck kept bringing her. Sal smiled at each new person as they came in, her weepy eyes on the brown bags under our guests' arms. It was only a matter of time. And then my uncle would see her at her worst. He'd have no trouble proving she was an unfit guardian.

I began taking the packages of liquor into the pantry. I knew Sal wouldn't start drinking right away, so I had time to empty and refill her mickeys with water without her catching me. I was quick at it; I'd done it before.

A Hopeless Case

In one of Morley's mirrors, I saw a hopeless case with a protruding head and lopsided shoulders. I checked to make sure the polka-dot blouse wasn't sticking out at the back above its vile shiny black satin skirt. I was wearing Sal's things because I didn't have anything appropriate. Sal said you didn't need to be draped in black from head to toe like the Victorians anymore. As long as you had on one or two dark things. Something sober, so everyone would know you were taking it the way you were meant to.

And then behind me in the mirror I saw Paulie walk in with the Virgin. Her head was down as if she were embarrassed, and no wonder. People here would think they were related. I'd never really thought seriously before about what it meant for Paulie not to have a mother. At least I had Sal, even if I wasn't at the top of her list of things to look after. But Paulie had only her sick grandfather and the Virgin, and it was hard to tell if the Virgin actually liked her or if she helped out because she felt it was her duty. How could I stay mad at Paulie when she didn't have a real family? I signalled for her to join me and she signalled back and began to make her way through the crowd of Morley's female patients, who surrounded Sal, making fools of themselves.

"Dr. Bradford was like a father to me. He'd say, Hello, Mrs. Tierney, I'm going to make you well. And he was so big, I believed him," the woman sobbed to Sal, and Sal sobbed back, "That was Morley all over." Good old Morley and his Morley worshippers.

In the pantry, Paulie blew smoke at me through the fine holes of her navy veil. "Kong sent you these," she said, and handed me a package. "He said you'd need them up here."

Under the brown paper wrapping I found Nick's things. It was odd to see the cap and dark glasses in the pantry where Sal put her strawberry jam to cool when she was sober enough to do preserves. Madoc's Landing business mixing with the business of Bath Ladies College? The two weren't on the same planet. And I had to live in both places, like a spy who didn't belong anywhere. When I'd put on Nick's clothes, it didn't matter. But now I knew I'd never want to be Nick again—not for Paulie or for me. I was done with Kong and his silly tests.

I began quickly to empty the bottles of gin and refill them with water. Paulie helped for a bit and then stopped and blew smoke ominously through both her nostrils. Then she said in a low voice: "Remember Tory's brother? The blond boy we fought by the river?"

"Rick?" I lowered my voice, too.

"Yeah," Paulie said. "He's been trying to turn Tory against me."

"So what?" I said, a little distracted by the two remaining gin bottles.

"Tory worships him—that's so what, Bradford." Paulie took off her hat, and for the first time I noticed her swollen eyes.

"Sssh, Paulie." I pointed over her shoulder. "My stepmother's coming."

I finished filling the last gin bottle with water and turned around quickly. Sal was smiling queerly. She must have had a few shots in the washroom. She patted Paulie on the shoulder, as if she thought Paulie needed comforting; she didn't touch me. She said we needed more liquor in the living room. She sounded pleased with herself. I could see Paulie looking at her, sensing that something wasn't quite right. And then the kitchen door swung open and the Virgin was standing there staring at the smoke curling up behind Paulie's back. She jerked her head impatiently, and Paulie put her cigarette out, scowling. Now the Virgin's insolent black eyes fixed on Sal with the inquisitor's stare that made us all tremble in our oxymorons. But Sal was too tipsy to be frightened. She stared back as bold as you please and offered the Virgin my services. It was an old habit of Sal's, which I didn't like, but I had no idea how to say so.

The Virgin seemed to know this. She said she'd get the water herself. She walked over to the sink and turned on the tap. Then she leaned back against the counter. She must have been waiting for Sal to get it through her thick noggin that she was supposed to be scared of her, but Sal only helped herself to some gin, taking it from the bottle I'd just refilled with water. Then she shrugged her shoulders and walked off into the living room without saying anything. I loaded the tray with the watered bottles, and Paulie took them into the living room.

And then I was alone with the Virgin.

"Mary Beatrice, there are so many things I'd like to say to you," she said. I wondered if she was going to give me the same little speech as my uncle.

"Feeling as I do about my mother's death, I can imagine something of what you're going through."

She put her hand out as if she wanted to touch me. I shuddered a little. Only the most fragile of barriers made us different: my age and my secret Mouse will.

I asked her if she wanted a cup of tea. "What a good hostess you are!" she said, and smiled. "But no thank you." Her lips trembled, and her eyes became fixed in a far-off expression that I used to notice on Morley. There it was: the family resemblance. A melancholic strain in both of them. I'd never thought of Morley having genuinely sad feelings—well, sad feelings of some sort, but not deep down blue feelings like mine. The Virgin turned toward the window so I could no longer see her face. She seemed very vulnerable.

"You found some documents that belong to me and someone who is very important to me," the Virgin said. "Miss Phillips brought them to me. Can I ask you to keep to yourself what you read in them?"

"Yes," I said.

"You must be a great comfort to your stepmother, Mary Beatrice," she said, and went back into the living room.

38

Florie Buck's husband, Lyall, had discovered the water in the gin bottles and accused Florie in a low voice of diluting his drink. Soon after, everybody left, muttering to each other about water in the drinks. Nobody figured out that I'd been the one to do it, and I smiled when my uncle said he'd like to shake the hand of that smart aleck, whoever he was, for knowing what was best for people.

I saw Sal watching me after she'd caught that smile, but she didn't say anything. She'd managed to find a reserve bottle of Gilbey's and gone to bed with it, leaving me with my uncle and my aunt to clean up. When it was done, I said I was going to visit a school friend and went into the garage and changed quickly into Nick's clothes. I knew it would be the last time I wore them. I took a pair of long underwear and extra sweaters, because it was going to be hard being Nick in Madoc's Landing when the temperature that night was ten below.

Good-bye to Nick

I walked the streets, looking into the houses of some of the guests who'd come to Morley's funeral. I saw Lyall Buck sitting in a sulk in his living room. Two houses up, I saw Mrs. Tierney, who had told Sal that Morley was like a father to her. She lived by herself, and she was standing in her kitchen in her slip, drinking beer and watching the hockey game.

In her underwear, she looked younger than she had at the wake, and I wondered if Morley had found her attractive. Maybe she had even been his mistress.

It bothered me to think of old Morley lumbering into her kitchen with his black cowhide doctor's bag—a handy prop, it occurred to me, if you were going to visit somebody on the sly. Did he pinch her on the cheek or cuff her with the back of his hand like he did me? Or maybe I was wrong. Poor old Morley was probably too tired to do anything that strenuous. She'd only wished something of the sort had gone on. Morley was so—big.

I walked down Pelster Avenue. It was named after a German baron—a real baron, who made a fortune in lumber. Snow was still falling. I lit a cigarette and looked boldly into Morley's study. My uncle was already comfortably stretched out on Morley's sofa. My aunt sat in a wing chair, knitting. They were both watching the hockey game. A coal fire flickered in the grate. Once or twice my uncle looked my way, but he didn't seem to notice me. I hung back in the shadows so my icy breath wouldn't steam the window. I walked back up the street and threw a snowball at the Bucks' window. I saw old Lyall peer out and shake his fist at me. Then I walked up to the divorced woman's house and knocked over her garbage can. And then I went home.

39

Two days after New Year's, Billy Bugle brought us empty cartons from the grocer. Billy Bugle was the town tramp, a drifter who'd stayed on after the Depression. He put the cartons in Morley's office, looking around sadly on his way out. Even he had loved Morley. Sal had already taken down Morley's calendar with the curious bug-eyed people called dingbats. They had knobs at the end of their antennae as big as golf balls. I liked the dingbats. I felt they were connected to me, not Morley, and it surprised me that he enjoyed their goofiness. Sal had also taken down a plaque that said, *"But then at last when recompense is asked, he* [Morley's patient] *passeth me in dread. For lo! To him I stand a devil horned from out the lowest depths."* Sal said she had no use now for gifts from Morley's patients. She was going to turn our home into a rooming house. She sat on a chair drinking from a cup she'd laced with gin, telling me which things to put in which boxes.

I stood on Morley's examining stool and began to take his unwanted books out of a glass cabinet. I put in the first box a novel by Morton Thompson, *Not As a Stranger.* Its cover showed a fierce-eyed doctor peering out at me over a face mask. And then a book about the Kon Tiki expedition by Thor Heyerdahl and the novel *Tontine* by Thomas B. Costain.

"He was always going to read those." Sal's voice was in "B" mode, half-phony and half-real. "And he never did. He never had time, did he, Mouse?"

I didn't answer. I continued putting Morley's things in the boxes. In went the German textbook Morley used to read so he could understand what the German immigrants were saying when they described their symptoms to him. I put in his old geometry text (Morley used to do the exercises in it for fun) and a plaque from the minister of national defence for the Canadian navy appointing Morley to the position of Sea Cadet Surgeon Lieutenant. I had never known he was a sea cadet.

Sal looked up from the ad she was composing for the *Medical Post*. She was going to sell Morley's practice. "Lovely small town on Great Lake. Does that sound nice, Mouse?"

"I wouldn't use the word 'lovely' myself," I replied.

I stopped to look at one of Morley's old autopsy reports, scribbled onto his prescription notepaper. He sometimes did autopsies when the local coroner was caught in a pinch, i.e., when he had too many bodies after a boating accident or a family suicide pact. This man had been shot deer hunting, so Morley said he had made a coronal mastoid incision in the scalp to cut out the slug.

"Mouse, you're not paying attention. I want the ad to say that the new doctor will make piles of money, the way Morley did."

"Active, lucrative professional practice," I said. Now Morley was describing the way he had carved up the chest in a Y instead of a slit from head to toe. He favoured this as a technique, Morley said, because it was easier to sew the bodies up again for viewing by the relatives.

"Lovely small town on Great Lake. Active, lucrative practice. Mouse, that sounds like it'll hook our customer, don't it?"

"Doesn't it." I felt like I was going to faint as I put Morley's report in my pocket.

Meanwhile, Sal was starting to take down photographs. She left up the studio portrait of Morley in his twenties with a full head of heavily oiled black hair that rolled away from his forehead in waves. He was holding a pipe at a distance from his mouth and smiling fondly at it, as if it were somebody he knew and loved.

Quickly, she took down the matching set of portraits showing Morley and Alice, my mother, in their graduation robes. In the photograph, Morley's eyes looked left, as if he knew my mother's portrait was right beside him. My mother didn't look his way, though. In her portrait, she stared right out at you, a little sullenly, as if she were annoyed with having to sit so long under blazing-hot studio lights. Her hair was white-blond and soft as cotton batting, and her mouth was slightly parted, as if she were about to say something. She looked crushable, like the sort of timid person who would do anything rather than hurt your feelings.

Sal said she didn't have enough backbone to be a doctor's wife. She wasn't cut out for it. She was just a scared college girl who'd had a hard time getting to know people in Madoc's Landing. You had to be a special breed, like Sal, to put up with the loneliness that went with being the wife of the great Morley Bradford. Sal called Alice, my dead mother, "Morley's blond beauty," as if she were his palomino horse. I knew Sal didn't like having my mother's photograph in the hall. She didn't like Morley's eyes drifting toward my mother from his photograph, either. In its place, Sal put a photograph of Morley and herself taken thirty years later. He was staring right into the camera, his hair and eyes the way I remembered him. He and Sal were sitting with a couple they'd met at a hotel in the Bahamas. Morley had on a short-sleeved polo shirt that he'd done up too tightly around his neck. I realized with a start how deteriorated he looked. The circles of fatigue were shiny and black under his nice, kind eyes, as if somebody had punched him there, and his teeth looked long and yellow—uncared-for, even. Why, Morley was dying on us, I thought. Dying on us by inches as Sal and I watched. We'd been helpless to do anything about it. Morley had kept up his working schedule of twelve-hour days with an hour off for each meal, and he and Sal had gone on a trip south and posed for photographs like this one, and everybody had smiled into the camera and pretended they didn't notice Morley was going downhill.

I picked up a pathology textbook, not thinking, just aimlessly flipping over the pages until something caught my eye. I stopped at a photograph of a baby whose pudgy cheeks were covered with burns the size of quarters. Its mother had taken bromides. The baby looked up at me angrily, as if it were about to wail. This was Morley's world—the world of kidneys, stopped larynxes, and squalling burnt-up children with sores on their skins as crusty as lava pits. A subterranean world of strange, disfigured patients shyly displaying their diseases, which the textbooks classified as acute, subacute, or chronic, so that doctors like Morley would know which ones to take seriously. Morley was at home here. He could plunge into the realm of malformed bodies and hunt down the symptoms with that little lamp he wore on top of his head like a miner's light. He could put his huge surgeon's hands on the squalling brat and wrap its sores with gauze, doing it carefully so it wouldn't pull the skin off afterwards. And he'd take the bandage off tenderly—not unflinching and insensitive, like the father in the Nick Adams stories who cut up pregnant Indian ladies and didn't care how loudly they screamed or if their screams made their husbands commit suicide in the bunk bed above them.

Morley was nicer. And more hopeless. Morley was too resigned. He practised his art like he was half-dead himself. A slow-moving cadaver caring for the sick and leaking life from himself at every turn. He could walk down that dark corridor of disease and pain and silently place the stethoscope on an ailing heart just because it had to be done and he knew how to do it and it made him feel good. All those things. And I couldn't follow him there. I couldn't go where he walked on his slow, dying feet. Not me. Not Mouse Bradford. I couldn't be like him or save him from himself.

I Began to Retch

Morley was sawing something and doing a poor job of it because he wasn't using his Stryker electric bone saw or his new cast cutter which can split open the toughest plaster in seconds. He was using an old-fashioned handsaw. He threw down the saw and pried at the thing he had been sawing with his bare hands. It was a head; folds of peeled-back scalp covered its face. I heard a liquid sucking sound, and Morley stepped back, cradling the top of a skull in those long fingers that can tie a bow in a matchbox with a piece of string. There was a little splash as he plopped it in a pail by his feet.

Now I could see the body on his operating table: Viola Higgs. He bent over and made a Y-like incision on her chest, starting from her shoulders and ending below her belly button. I hid my face in my hands so I didn't have to see what he'd do next—hack out her breastbone so he could get at the innards. Using her tongue as his handle, Morley'd pull out the whole kit and caboodle in one piece.

A minute passed. Morley called me over in his rumbly voice and ordered me to look. I began to retch. The corpse's jaw had sagged open and I was looking into the hole of her gutted throat. And then, before Morley could grab me, I was plunging head over heels, tumbling free-fall down her empty windpipe into the dark.

40

Sal's Shrine

I have my shrine to Morley, the father, and Sal has her shrine to
Morley and Sal, the couple. In the front hall, where my mother's
photograph used to hang, she's put up one of herself in her nurse's
uniform. This shows a younger, thinner Sal with a nurse's cap stuck
on her dark head like a scoop of vanilla ice cream. She gave me my
mother's portrait and the only snapshot I have of my mother
laughing. My mother is wearing a long flannel skirt, and she's
standing on the lawn in front of my grandmother's house holding
me by the hand. She looks carefree and happy. And I look bald,
with luminous, deep-set eyes—Morley's eyes. And a pair of fan-
shaped ears. Mouse Bradford. I had my mouseness even before the
polio. Then there's another picture of me with my mother, after
the polio. I'm sitting on a tall white wall. My shoulders are as high
as my ears; one leg is stuck awkwardly forward. I'm in a white
pinafore, and my mother has her hand on my shoulder, looking
into the camera over my head. She looks sad.

And Mine

Let Sal have her shrine; I'd got what I wanted. I'd sneaked it when
Sal had gone out to stop Billy Bugle from burning down our

garage with trash from the incinerator. Morley's doctor's bag. I was keeping it so that Morley could come back and claim it, just in case he decided to get himself resurrected. His bag was as big as a lady's purse, with neat leather compartments designed to hold bottles and narrow instruments like a pair of surgical scissors and Liston's single-edged amputating knife—a seven-and-a-half-inch blade as elegant as a cheese knife. I kept everything I found inside the bag. I needed it all—even the nasty-looking scalpels and dissecting scissors. Not that I intended to use them. I simply wanted everything of Morley I could jam into his doctor's bag. The stomach and intestinal clamps, the Clay Adams utility forceps—which looked like the tongs Sal used for extracting hot dogs from boiling water—and, of course, the stethoscope. I wanted the Stryker electric bone saw, but I couldn't fit the foot switch into the bag, so I left it on the examining couch. A puzzle for Sal to brood over.

41

Sal was verging on her "C" mood the morning I left for school, but she made me my favourite breakfast, anyway—boiled eggs with only the yolk. And she didn't ask me to finish my milk. I hate milk. It's too white—like bones. I don't like egg white, either—too much like skin. Sal says I have these food preferences to annoy her. She says everybody likes milk and egg white. That morning, she didn't say anything like that, so I figured it was safe to ask her a few questions.

Q: Why didn't Morley spend time with me?

SAL'S ANSWER: Why would he do something for you that he didn't do for me? We were members of a doctor's family. We had to accept that we were second-best.

Q: Is it right for a father not to have conversations with his daughter?

SAL'S ANSWER: How could you expect a man bushed from standing on his feet all day to come home and chatter away with you? When he was about to drop on the spot? Why not expect him to play canasta, too?

Q: Was it my fault Morley didn't pay more attention to me?

SAL'S ANSWER: Mouse, you're too much of a worrier. I never heard Morley say he wished you were a boy, even if you didn't play baseball or know how to throw a football. Be sensible. With your shoulder, how could you be good at sports?

I didn't ask Sal any more questions. I let her drive me to the Greyhound stop on the main street in Madoc's Landing. I didn't kiss her good-bye. Instead, I turned and said: "I guess you wish you'd given Morley a son. That way, he might have stayed home with us more."

Sal just sat behind the wheel of Blinky, her mouth open, and I knew I'd put my finger on an old nerve. I climbed into the bus with my suitcase, not looking around once.

Part Three

42

The Beatles song "She Loves You" was playing on the radio the afternoon the taxi drove me through the school gates.

It surprised me that there was no snow. The leaves were off the trees, and the ravine looked ragged and unwelcoming as we climbed toward the school, which now rose clearly visible through the stripped camperdown elms—as much a prison as ever. No pigeons flew up from its mock turrets as the driver opened my door. I wondered if the mysterious poisoner had finished them off. Behind the hockey pitch I saw a huge mound of dirt and rubble. It was the excavation for the new wing, which everybody said the Virgin was building to accommodate male boarders when Bath Ladies College merged with Kings College. Its dark lump made me think of Morley's grave. I wondered if the earth had thawed enough so he could be buried. I looked around, startled that I lived in such an old-fashioned place. Bath Ladies College would make a perfect creepola subject for one of Mrs. Peddie's assignments asking you to use specific description to create a menacing atmosphere. I thought of the essay I'd written for her on *Wuthering Heights*. "Stormy weather and the powerful north wind had slanted the few stunted firs at the end of the house, and the range of gaunt thorns all stretched their limbs in one direction." Not bad. What would I say about our school? "The cold winter rains from the lake had stained its chiselled fieldstone with ominous

brooding shapes that no sunshine would ever turn white again."
It sounded like old Charles Dickens. I preferred Brontë.

The scent of fresh paste wax hit me the second I walked in. Now
Tory personally loved that smell; she called it words like "heady"
and "full-bodied" and said it spoke to her of new beginnings. Not
me. I've never been able to smell cleaning fluids of any kind since
then without getting pretty depressed.

For once, I was one of the last girls there. Miss Cockshutt sat
in her cubicle unplugging and plugging small rubber hoses into the
switchboard panel and angrily answering a question from a student
I didn't know. Slowly I walked up the circular stairs dragging my
suitcase. The staircase looked just as I'd remembered it, the red
paint worn off in the middle of each step, where thousands of girls
had tread before me. I noticed my legs were stronger, and this
made me think of Tory, and I wondered whether she'd be back.

In my room, I saw a fourth bed. And a new girl with dark
hair—coiled as tightly as a poodle's—reading on a chair. Then I
saw the wide-open windows. I sighed. Ismay the Terrible. She'd
had a perm.

"Guess who's been kicked out of the room?" Ismay said. She
was reading *Reach for the Sky*.

I guessed. "Paulie?"

"Well done, Bradford, old girl. And we've got a new roommate,
Asa Abrams. Apparently, Asa asked if she could room with you and
Victoria." I shrugged and turned my back to her.

"We're all dreadfully sorry about your father, of course," she
added. To my surprise, I heard real sympathy in her voice.

Then the door opened, and Tory hobbled in ahead of Asa and
thrust a Gideon bible into my hand. Tory was no longer on
crutches, but she looked thinner and older, and a little distracted,
as if she had something sad on her mind. I thought immediately
of Paulie and of what she'd told me at Morley's funeral about Rick,
and I wondered if this had anything to do with the new bewildered
expression I saw on Tory's face. I wanted to put my arms around

her and hug her, but I was too shy. So I just stood there, smiling a little and feeling the same old grateful feeling I always felt when I saw her: just thrilled to pieces that somebody as nice and gentle as Tory would have time for me. I opened the bible to the frontis-piece, where she'd inscribed the words, "To Mary Beatrice Brad-ford, who is true blue—This is Peter Marshall's prayer for a time of bereavement." It was such a Tory thing to do—to give me a modern version of the New Testament with a nice prayer. I read the first two lines: "Thou hast promised to wipe away all tears from our eyes. I ask thee to fulfill that promise now."

I sat down heavily on my bed and tried to think of something distracting, like Jack O'Malley, so I wouldn't cry. And the next thing I knew, our room was full of girls unloading the pockets of their dressing gowns with my all-time fav, peppermint Oreos. They stood single-file in front of my bed as if they were lining up for prayers and, one by one, deposited the cookies on my pillow. I felt touched, and surprised; I couldn't even manage a Mouse nibble to show them I appreciated their concern.

Excusing myself, I picked up my pyjamas and went off to the washroom to undress. I heard Tory whisper as I went out, "Poor Mouse. She's going off to cry."

The small, cramped washroom felt clammy from the black stockings and purple bloomers that had been hung up to dry. It was very still, and I sensed the girls listening from my room. I didn't want to cry and get people worked up for nothing but I couldn't seem to help myself.

I bent my head and began to sob in short bursts like hiccups. Sob and wait. Sob and wait so the noise wouldn't bring Miss Phillips. I could feel the sympathy from Tory and the other girls back in my room, and this made me bawl even more. And then I heard Tory making excuses for me to the matron. One good thing about Morley's death: I'd get special privileges—for a day or so, anyway.

43

"Pssst, Bradford. In here," I heard somebody call. The voice was coming from Asa Abrams's old cubicle. I recognized the plaque on the door. It was a quote by Frances Ridley Havergal. "Why did God promise us a new heart?" the Anglican hymn maker had written. "Because our old hearts are so evil that they cannot be made any better; so nothing will do any good but giving us quite a new heart." I peeked in. A radio was playing "Big Girls Don't Cry" by the Four Seasons, and Paulie was mouthing the words as she stood on her bed, her head stuck out the high, skinny little opening that passed for a window in most of the tower rooms. The room reeked of hairspray. Paulie turned slowly around and blew a smoke ring at me. She didn't say anything and for a second, I thought she didn't know who I was. Her eyes looked mean and little. I wondered why I hadn't noticed that before. Or maybe it was the weird blue light. Paulie had put a blue bulb in her study lamp, turning King Kong in the poster above her bed blue as well.

"Did you see her?"

"Who?"

"Tory, you nitwit." Paulie threw me a fag and grinned then like her old self, and I felt better. "I heard her telling you how sorry she was about your old man. Did you like the bible she gave you? She bought it with me last weekend." Paulie reached outside the window and brought in a bottle of Old Vienna. "Come on up. I've been cooling the suds for your return."

I hoisted myself up carefully. I'd promised myself I wouldn't act like her flunkey this term, and here I was sliding right back into it. Of course, it wasn't just my weak Mouse will. I was curious, too.

"C'mon. Let's see you do it in one go." Paulie clapped my good shoulder, just the way Morley used to greet my uncle Winnie. "Chugalug it like a man."

I thanked her meekly. I knew the beer was a sign she felt sorry for me, only I didn't want somebody to clap me on the back and hand me a beer. For once, I wished Paulie would act like the other girls.

But I sipped a little of the beer to be polite, and we leaned out her window, passing it back and forth between us while Paulie told me the reason for the change in rooms. She'd picked a fight with Tory's brother over the holidays and cut Rick with her bowie knife. The Virgin had taken away the knife and told Paulie she had "no other choice" (the Virgin's very words) but to isolate Paulie from Tory and the rest of her schoolmates until she proved she was capable of getting along with people.

"You knifed her brother!" I said. "That's horrible. Tory must be mad at you."

"I only nicked his hand. I could have done worse."

Paulie gestured to her throat and then flipped her lit cigarette so it stood straight up from her bottom lip like it was stuck on with glue. A new trick. I made a little gasping sound.

"Okay. Tory was a little upset, all right? But she'll get over it. Because he got off easy this time. Nobody calls me a punk and gets away with it."

"What do you mean, this time?"

Paulie grinned. "Nothing. I was only kidding. You aren't mad at me, are you, Bradford?"

I couldn't believe my ears. Paulie worried about me being mad at her? Looking back, I understand. Paulie was afraid of losing me. She'd lost her place as Tory's roommate, and she couldn't afford to get on the wrong side of me. She sensed what had started with Morley's death. Despite myself, I was moving away from her. One day at a time, I was leaving Paulie for good.

44

— Mouse, did you hear the one about the woman on an airplane? It's really my worst penis joke.

— Leave me alone. It's time to re-create the night of the murder.

— A man sat down beside a woman on an airplane and asked her what she was reading. She said, I'm reading a book about penises, and he said, and what are you finding out? And she said, this book says black men have long, thin penises and Jewish men have short, thick ones. What's your name? she said. And he said, Benjy Goldstein.

— That *is* your worst penis joke.

— You're getting tired of me, aren't you?

— It's just that a part of me is still there—always will be. For ever and ever. Some things don't end.

— I want to hear you say it out loud. You're sick of me.

— Of you, Alice? Never.

— Yes, you are. I can tell.

— All right. You said it, not me. Oh, Alice, who would think the male organ could be lopped off and reapplied so easily?

— I know what you mean. As if the penis is a Groucho Marx nose girls can put on when they feel like it.

— Exactly. Only it wasn't that easy. Not when you know what really happened.

In January, the Virgin announced the merger with Kings College and everybody got depressed, and then in February an underground rebellion began. Mysterious announcements were posted in long corridors demanding nondenominational prayers in morning chapel and denouncing the system of compulsory games. I tried to imagine the faces of the rebels in the older girls who passed me each morning in the corridors, their tunics swinging, their arms full of books. Who had written the exciting sentences—"We demand student-run clubs without staff control! School spirit is irrelevant! We want political analysis and action—down with bourgeois attitudes! " I couldn't believe these words lurked behind the cheerful faces I saw. I didn't think these girls had it in them.

To relieve the atmosphere, the Virgin announced that our usual school dance would be held early, immediately after exams. Soon nobody cared about the manifestoes anymore. The Virgin was clever. She was one step ahead of her "wards," as she called us—to my chagrin. It was a word that always made me think of orphans.

I lay on my bed in my housecoat, listening to the day girls chattering with some boarders down the tower corridor. The day girls were allowed to visit the boarding school before the dance, although none of them had come into our room. They didn't like Ismay, and Tory had gone home to her parents to help her mother prepare the breakfast party. Asa was in the bathroom washing out the horrible hairdo she'd got at Crescendo's, and Ismay was standing in her merry widow bleaching her arm hairs with peroxide. For aesthetic reasons, of course. None of the girls liked black hair on their arms or legs. It looked too hairy. At the window, our formals spun and twirled from the curtain rod, like bodies in plastic cleaner bags.

I was waiting for my chance in the bathroom and flipping through Morley's copy of *Gray's Anatomy*. I often looked at my father's books when I felt nervous because it reminded me of Morley.

"Mary Beatrice, are you listening to me?" Ismay had finished with her arms and was dabbing at the faint moustache above her lips. "Paulie's been stealing things, you know. That bloody girl wants to be here in my place."

"Oh, you're exaggerating," I said. I skipped through a thousand pages or so (who would think the body could take up so much space!), and now I was staring at the diagram of the female organs of generation. What I saw gave me the willies: a head with wild, wavy hair spreading like flames around its face. And this face had no features except for two small open wailing mouths calling out in distress. As if this weren't bad enough, two flattened cylindrical flaps lay like pea-pod ears on either side of the tiny mouths. For the life of me, I couldn't see what a boy would find to like in something so weird. Not that a boy's penis would take the prize at a poultry show. I thought of Jack then and turned with an embarrassing fluttery feeling to the section on male organs.

"Somebody's taken all my musical scores, and last night I found a horrible little stick drawing over my bed."

"A stick drawing?"

"Yes, made with a penknife or something." Now Ismay was swabbing the black stubble of her shaved armpit. She said the dark stubble looked gross. "Paulie's dangerous, that's what I think. She doesn't have a normal background, you know. Her mother's dead."

"I don't have a normal background, either," I said, still looking for the section on the penis. Somebody had torn it out. I closed the book, puzzled. I considered asking Paulie about it and then thought better of it. Maybe Morley had taken it out for some reason. Maybe, I smiled to myself, he was worried I'd read his book someday and didn't want me to see that part.

"Mouse! Pay attention! I need your help."

I put the medical text down. Ismay had stopped the bleach job, and her upper lip was erupting into a blotchy mess as we watched.

"I must be allergic to hydrogen peroxide," she sobbed, and pushed past me, making a terrible racket, to find Miss Phillips. I quickly walked over to Ismay's bed. On the wall above the headboard somebody had carved a strange little drawing of a boy and a girl. The girl consisted of three circles—one for the head and two grotesque balloons for her breasts. The boy had equally large and grotesque genitals. Underneath I read the words, "I.T. sucks cock."

"What's wrong with that suck now?" Paulie had walked in without my noticing. She closed the window Ismay had opened so wide and lay down on Ismay's bed, her hands behind her head. Her braid rested across one breast. She looked almost pretty, except she had on boys' boxers and a short-sleeved undershirt, so I could see her arm muscles and her large hands.

"She peroxided her armpits. She's having a reaction."

Paulie began to laugh. "Was she telling you nasty things about me before it happened?"

"Yeah. She said you stole her music scores."

"Would you be upset if I had?"

"I guess so."

Paulie smiled. "Well, I haven't. She's just making stuff up to get my goat."

45

I could see the top of my head in the rear-view mirror of the school bus, which Sergeant had loaned us for the evening. Paulie—I mean Lewis—was driving. Slowly, I raised my eyes to check myself out. Under my navy Sunday coat I was wearing a short strapless taffeta formal that had looked better on the store rack than it did on me. The nurse had gone with me to help pick it out and she'd persuaded me to buy it because the boxy taffeta jacket that went with it would hide Alice. I'd also sprinkled glitter in my dark hair, which had been pulled straight back from my forehead and tied in a bump at the top. At least the pompadour hairdo made me look older and aggressively stylish. What does Jack O'Malley think of girls wearing their hair up? I wondered.

The bus screeched around the parking lot into the front drive of Kings College. And there he stood on the steps in front of the boarding school, a corsage box in his hand. He wore an old army duffle coat, which made him look even taller. When he saw us, he waved and strode over, stiffly swinging his shoulders as if a curtain rod ran from one side of his long body to the other, holding him up.

Lewis opened the door, and Jack bent his head and stepped in. He hardly looked at Lewis, who had on an old top hat and one of Willy's old suits. Jack sat down, and the motion of his bum hitting the seat made me bounce. Then he smiled anxiously and put his arm along the back of my seat, almost touching Alice. "You look nice," he said, and I moved a little so his hand wouldn't touch her by mistake. I knew he'd noticed Alice at the Visitor's Luncheon, but he didn't seem to hold her against me. But then neither did Tory or Paulie so why should he? Still, I didn't want to press my luck so I just sat there, glad he'd come and afraid to say anything in case I did something to drive him away. To my surprise, he smelled wonderful. English Leather, maybe. Morley had used it on special occasions, too. Then Jack handed me the box. I knew I was expected to open it, but I was too shy. I let Lewis do the talking for me as we careened down a lane toward Tory's house.

"Is anything wrong?" Jack asked as Lewis gunned the old bus past the bushes of Canon Quinn's hedges.

"Bradford—uh, Mary—doesn't talk much," Lewis called over his shoulder. "You know how some girls are."

"I guess you high-school boys have lots of experience," Jack said solemnly.

I looked at him to see if he was joking, and he stared down at his shoes. He wore oxblood wing tips, like my father. Here's somebody as backward as you are, Mouse, I thought. Who is not a snob.

Lewis hadn't heard Jack's remark, but I doubt if it would have impressed him the way it had me. Anyway, he was too busy trying to drive the dilapidated old bus. We jiggled up and down over a rut in the lane and I sat looking straight ahead, my ankles crossed and my hands folded in my lap. Perfect deportment. The Virgin would be pleased.

The bus jerked and stopped in front of Tory's house. Lewis leapt out, and Jack and I found ourselves alone. He smiled at me again and let his long arm drop down on the back of my seat. I shifted uncomfortably. I knew I should smile up at him as if I were used to accepting a boy's attentions—as if they were a homage I took for granted. Now his hand moved toward my good shoulder.

It rested there for a moment, warm. Jack talked nervously to me about the condition of the roads that night. There was a storm warning, and the temperature was expected to drop.

It was already snowing lightly, and the clock tower of Kings College said a quarter to eight. I couldn't think of anything intelligent to say about snow so I didn't answer, and finally he sighed heavily and we both sat without talking, looking at Tory's house. The Grecian portico overlooking the playing field was well lit by two tall coach lamps, so it was easy to see the front steps, where Canon Quinn and Mrs. Quinn stood with Tory and her brother, Rick, talking to Lewis. I didn't recognize Tory in her mother's full-length mink coat. As I watched, Tory turned and buried her face in her mother's shoulder, and Canon Quinn placed his hand with the evil worm fingers on Tory's head and stroked her hair, and Mrs. Quinn put her arm around Tory, and then the pair followed Canon Quinn inside. Through the falling snow I saw Rick give Lewis a little shove, as if he were pushing him off their property, and Lewis pushed him back.

And then Lewis jumped back in the bus and slammed the door, but he was so angry, he couldn't make it shut. He swore and slammed it again and then jammed the key as he tried to start it up.

"Isn't your date coming?" Jack asked.

"What does it fucking look like, Mr. Kings College?" Lewis said. "Do you see her with me?"

Jack stared at me from behind his new glasses. I think he'd bought them especially for the dance. They were black-rimmed like Buddy Holly's. I shrugged. I didn't know what had happened and I was afraid to guess.

46

Nobody talked on our way back to the dance. Lewis stared out the windshield like a zombie. Several times we skidded on the road, and Lewis cursed the slippery pavement. It was snowing harder now. When Lewis laid rubber by the Old Mill, Jack mumbled something about wanting to get out and walk. He kept staring at me, as if he were waiting for me to do something.

As we pulled up to Bath Ladies College, I whispered that I wanted to speak to Lewis in private. Jack nodded, but at the door of the school he turned around to look at me suspiciously, and I was afraid he wished he hadn't come. Maybe he wanted to ditch me on the spot, or maybe he thought I wanted to ditch him for Lewis, who sat beside me now smoking a fag and waving him on.

"Yeah, keep going, you jerk. Get out of my sight, Mr. Fucking Kings College cocksucker. Nobody fucking asks your date to show his dick, do they, Mouse? It's his own private business."

"What are you talking about?" I kept my eye on Jack as he disappeared into the school.

Lewis spat and tossed his cigarette out the window. "But, oh, no. They ask me. Tory's brother, that fuckface. What right does he have to ask me about my dick? I bet his is the size of a pencil."

"He wants you to show him your penis?"

"No shit, Bradford. He wants to see my p-e-n-i-s."

"What are you going to do?"

"What the fuck do you think I'm going to do? Maybe we should ask your finky boyfriend what to do. He's a real man, isn't he?"

"Oh, God. I'm sorry."And I was sorry too, and a little ashamed of myself for being so concerned with Jack.

"Yeah, sure you are." Lewis—I mean Paulie banged her head down on the steering wheel. Her back shook and she sobbed like a little girl, not like the Paulie I knew. You see, her game was up and Paulie knew it only she wouldn't say so. I put my hand on her shoulder. I was always afraid to touch Paulie—in case she took it the wrong way. In case she interpreted it as me thinking she was soft. But I couldn't help myself. I wanted to comfort her because I'd never seen her so sad and lost.

It did seem unfair that Paulie needed a penis to be a man. John Wayne would still be John Wayne if he had a vagina, wouldn't he? I didn't say anything like this to Paulie, but I hated Canon Quinn and Tory's brother, Rick, for not letting her see Tory. It wasn't as if Paulie were doing anything wrong, exactly. If the world didn't give boys so many advantages, Paulie wouldn't want to be one. At least, that's how I saw it then. Paulie saw it differently, because as far as she was concerned, she was a boy, period.

I heard a rap on my window. The Virgin was standing at the curb, waving at us to move the bus so that other cars could pull up. She was wearing a baggy old purple dress that wasn't even full-length and a muskrat coat and she'd smeared two idiotic clownlike dots of rouge on her cheeks. Why didn't she learn to put on makeup right? "The Virgin," I hissed, and Paulie sat up, her head turned so the Virgin couldn't tell that Paulie had been crying. The Virgin peered angrily at us through my window, and Paulie started up the old vehicle and we lurched forward, creaking off toward the parking lot. I didn't hear the Quinns' version of what they said to Paulie until the trial. All I knew was what Paulie had told me that night.

47

HIS LORDSHIP: Now, you took statements from both Richard
Quinn and Victoria Quinn as to their relationships with Pauline
Sykes over this period of time. Is that correct?

INSPECTOR GEORGE: Yes, my lord. I also interviewed their father,
Canon Bruno Quinn.

HIS LORDSHIP: Would you read the statement you obtained from
Canon Quinn?

INSPECTOR GEORGE: Yes. This is the statement of Canon Bruno
Quinn:

"I am fifty-three years of age, married with two children, a
boy of nineteen and a girl who will be eighteen this month. I am
employed by Kings College, which recently acquired Bath Ladies
College—"

HIS LORDSHIP: You can spare us the details of the school history.

INSPECTOR GEORGE: Yes, my lord.

"About eight months ago, I learned that my daughter, Victoria, had a boyfriend. His name was Lewis. I first saw Lewis in
the autumn of 1963. He came to visit my daughter one afternoon for tea. I subsequently saw him at the girls' school, Bath
Ladies College, where he was employed as a gardener.

"As I told the other policeman, I was not entirely happy with
their relationship. I felt she would have more in common with
somebody from Kings College, but my daughter is very head-
strong. She said those boys hadn't the life experience of somebody like Lewis. I believe I understood what she meant and
thought it best that she find her own way through this.

"I sometimes chatted with Lewis when he went about his work on the grounds. He seemed devoted to my daughter and concerned that I should approve of their relationship.

"I never had any reason to doubt that Lewis was anything other than a boy. He conducted himself in all ways like a young man. I must say, I have been teaching at a boys' school for the past twenty years, and I was entirely deceived by the situation. I believe my daughter was deceived, too, but she will not talk to me. She is still very loyal to Lewis and has visited her several times in jail.

"In any case, on the day of my daughter's school dance, an officer from the Richmond Hill division visited me at my office and told me he had taken in the boy Lewis Sykes for questioning. Lewis and my son had had a fight over the Christmas holidays, but Richard had not told me about it because he knew I strongly disapprove of violent behaviour. I had, of course, known beforehand that he was not in favour of Victoria seeing Lewis. Richard believed Lewis was not good enough for his sister. I had always seen this as typical brotherly protectiveness.

"The officer said he had deliberated for a few weeks before coming in to see me. Then the officer said he had something to tell me that would shock me. He said that they had searched the boy at the station and discovered that Lewis was not a boy but rather a girl. I couldn't believe my ears—Lewis a female? It was—it was unthinkable. I asked my daughter about it, and she insisted Lewis was a boy. The problem caused quite an upset in our family, I can tell you. Victoria's welfare is very precious to my wife and myself. Finally, we decided the safest course of action was to prevent Victoria from seeing Lewis until I had got to the bottom of this matter."

HIS LORDSHIP: And this, I presume, is when all the problems started.

INSPECTOR GEORGE: I'm afraid so, my lord.

48

Jack was waiting for me in the stone foyer when I came in after talking to Paulie. I didn't want to explain to him what was going on because he was a boy, and a boy, even if he was nice enough not to mention Alice, couldn't understand. So I made up some dumb excuse about Lewis having a fight with his girlfriend, but I'm a lousy liar, and I could tell he didn't believe me. He kept cracking jokes and talking about what a bust *Godzilla* was, and every so often he disappeared to the washroom and came back smelling of gin and nicotine. I recognized the booze on account of Sal. He no longer smelled wonderful, and his bad breath made me wonder if my breath smelt bad, too.

"Do you like me?" Jack whispered as we sat together on one of Sir Jonathon's old benches. He bent his big head down and said it to my corsage, so it took a moment to realize he was talking to me. I squinted down at my corsage as if it would give me the answer. It was an orchid. I leaned back and uncrossed my ankles.

"A little," I whispered.

"Well, that's a start," he sighed, and then kissed me on the ear. I put my hand there, pleased but a little scared that the Virgin might have seen. She was coming our way with Mrs. Peddie, who was wearing a tight lace blouse and a black taffeta skirt you wouldn't dress a dog in. The sight of the two of them walking together in what they thought were proper evening clothes was enough to make you die from shame. Even worse, the Virgin had placed one hand on Mrs. Peddie's shoulder and I was afraid they were going to do something crazy like hold hands in front of us. I was sure Jack found their clothes embarrassing too and was looking down on them, and on me by association. Yes, I knew how Jack must see me and every other girl and woman at my school because we were all Wives of Bath—from the teachers who terrorized us with their bells and gatings to the overfed boarders and snobby day girls, to Paulie and me who tried to play by our own set of rules. But no matter how hard any of us struggled, we still looked dumb in the eyes of somebody like Jack because Bath Ladies College was only a fiefdom in the kingdom of men.

I felt so disappointed it was all I could do to introduce the Virgin to Jack. She eyed him suspiciously. She doesn't like boys, I reminded myself. He jumped to his feet and then sat back down so she couldn't smell his breath, his lanky legs set wide apart. For a moment, I expected her to tell him to cross his ankles and put his hands in his lap. But nobody tells boys stuff like that.

"Have you seen Sergeant?" the Virgin asked me. "He promised to give us a little demonstration of the sport of the three-wheeler."

"If he ever gets his surprise ready in time," Mrs. Peddie said, smiling in that way she had.

"Maybe it's a good thing Sergeant isn't here." The Virgin pointed to the foyer crowded with girls and pimple-faced boys lining up to have their photographs taken by the door to the library. Most of the boys had on Kings College blazers. "He'd consider this an invasion by Kings, wouldn't he, Mary?" The Virgin winked at me, and I blushed.

I felt glad when Ismay and a Kings College boy rescued us from the Virgin, and we all escaped outside, where the snow was filling the crotches of the school elms with white powder. Ismay and her date got into the back of Sergeant's bus to neck, and I held the tails of Jack's jacket while he threw up in the snow. Then I forgot about

Paulie, because I sipped some of Jack's gin and we started fooling around for the longest time standing up. I don't know what Jack thought of the whole business, but I found it a little exhausting. Basically, I had to make sure I stood with my good shoulder closest to him so he wouldn't feel Alice, and he kept pressing his crotch against me, but he was so tall his pelvis brushed my waist, and I thought I would need an operation before the big poker I felt against my body could fit inside me. Does this mean we are engaged now? I thought as I stared up at his pale panda face. He had taken his glasses off to kiss me, and I realized he had a second, nicer face underneath that only a lucky few got to see. Fortunately, Jack seemed to like me too, i.e., he acted more grateful than Sal ever had when I did what she wanted, and that made me feel relieved. Here's somebody who appreciates the helper that lives inside you, Mouse, I told myself.

Goners the Moment You Breathe on Them

I still have our photograph from the dance. We face the camera like exhausted soldiers under a huge school crest made of Bristol board. The name "Bath Ladies College" has been stencilled in between green laurel leaves that run up the side of the crest like the footprints of a rabbit. Asa is unrecognizable in an Empire-style black sheath with a pink satin sash, and the voluptuous Ismay is smirking at her date. All our faces are red and overheated from dancing, and Ismay's stiff beehive and my pompadour have fallen in sticky strands around our heads. Jack and I stand like Mutt and Jeff, smiling at some point over the photographer's head. A pair of identical diamond-shaped stars glow in our eyes—the afterimage of the camera flash—and Jack's big hand is hanging off my waist. My corsage is wilted. It's pinned to my shoulder strap, a rubbery-looking thing tied with a purple ribbon. I don't know why men give women orchids: they die as soon as you breathe on them.

49

I walked into the tower bathroom, and there she was in her pyjamas, yanking down the other girls' clothes from the washing lines. Piles of damp underthings lay on the floor: pale white undershirts, purple bloomers, black stockings, middies, and white cotton panties, all with nametapes—one of the school rules. The bathroom mirror was smashed, and I noticed sanitary napkins floating in the toilet bowl in the cubicle nearest me.

Paulie spun around as if she were going to sock me, but when she saw who it was she put down her fists. She had hacked off her braid and cut three horrible zigzaggy slashes in the skin of her left cheek, and she had pasted over the slashes with tiny pieces of toilet paper, which were now soaked through with blood. Her other cheek was covered with foam, as if she hadn't got around to it yet. And then I remembered seeing Lewis on my first day at school, when I'd surprised him in the washroom, and I knew she'd been shaving in the hope that her facial hair would grow in.

"Well, look who's here," Paulie said. "Has your creepy boyfriend left you and gone home?"

"Paulie, are you okay?" I asked. I could hardly breathe. I'd just noticed the bloody razor in the sink.

"Do I fucking look like I'm okay, Bradford? Do I?"

"You—you cut yourself."

"No. The razor just walked over and did it all by itself," Paulie said. "Just like the washing on the floor. It fucking decided all by itself to fall off the clothesline." Paulie sneered. "If you think this is a mess, wait till you see the staff room tomorrow."

"Paulie, you're upset. Let's go have a smoke," I said.

" 'Paulie, you're upset,' " she mimicked. " ' Let's go have a smoke.' "

"I know what happened is awful, but maybe you should—well, maybe you should give up on Tory."

"Just give up? Is that your answer, Bradford? What about me? Does anybody care about how I feel? All they want to do is interrogate me or keep me locked up in this fucking school. It's too late. I'll lose everything if I just fucking give up now."

Neither of us had given a thought to Miss Phillips or the other matrons who were still downstairs cleaning up or seeing off the girls, now going to the breakfast parties at day girls' houses. So when we heard a voice, we nearly jumped out of our skins. Somebody was coming our way, cursing and puffing like an out-of-shape athlete. We both turned to look. For a second I thought I was dreaming. Viola Higgs was pedalling toward us down the corridor, her shoulders hunched in a racing crouch, her long yellowy-white braid hanging down the back of her dark shoulders like a young girl's. The sight of her powdered face straining with determined energy made my hands and feet go cold. Paulie and I hid behind the door and watched.

The ghost seemed to be having trouble managing her old bike, and she cursed again as she stood up and heaved her unwieldy machine around the curve in the tower corridor. Then she started down the south hall, and immediately she began picking up speed, as if she were getting used to the tricycle, whose ridiculous headlight flickered against the wall just the way I had seen it in my first dream about her. Now she was no longer pedalling but standing up and coasting—a flying virago whose shadow billowed on the wall behind us like a bat's, taking the breath out of our lungs and leaving us awed and terrified, like the children we were trying not to be. Then the squeak of wheels died out and she was gone.

Paulie whistled. "Don't stand there like a dope," she hissed. "Let's go after her."

She pointed down a corridor. I should take that one, she said, and she'd take the other. I did as she told me but walked slowly, shuffling my feet, not wanting to be alone but afraid to disobey her.

No sooner had Paulie rounded the corner than I heard a creepy snapping noise. I tiptoed down the small flight of steps to the fifth-floor landing. The junior school was just below me. Outside, the blizzard was so thick now, I couldn't see the clock of Kings College or the roofs of the houses just outside the school grounds. I listened again for the noise and then giggled. It was the Union Jack on the roof cracking in the wind. I went back to find Paulie, but now she, too, had disappeared. I checked her room; it was empty. I called her name, but she didn't answer. For once at old Before Christ I had privacy. And then I saw Paulie's keys on the dresser—the clump with her master key to all the rooms in the boarding school and the key to her trunk. I didn't think about it; I just did it. I opened Paulie's steamer trunk. Inside, I found Ismay's missing musical scores and the torn-out pages of Morley's *Gray's Anatomy.* It was the section on the penis.

At the bottom of the page, next to a paragraph subtitled "Surgical Anatomy," Paulie had written in big block letters, "VERY IMPORTANT." The section read: "The penis occasionally requires removal for malignant disease. . . . Sometimes it is requisite to remove the whole organ from its attachment to the rami of the ossa pubis and ischia. The former operation is performed by cutting off the whole of the anterior part of the penis with one sweep of the knife." The sentence had been underlined with a long wavy line.

I stared at the pages uneasily. I wondered if she'd taken other things of Morley's that I hadn't noticed were missing. That was the moment when I should have put two and two together, but I did no such thing. Worn-out and slightly tipsy from Jack's gin, I headed off to my room and went to bed.

50

When I awoke, there wasn't a sound in the tower except for Ismay snoring and the wind moving through the creaking elms outside. It had stopped blizzarding. It was very cold—colder than usual. I crept out of my bedroom past the cubicles of sleeping girls, their bedrooms littered with crinolines and long white gloves, and here and there a ruined pair of dyed cloth high heels, streaked with water stains from walking through the snow. Paulie's bed was empty. Where was she? Down in the heating tunnel? The door to Mrs. Peddie's room was unlocked. I peered in. Her bed was empty. I remembered she was going off duty after the dance. I walked around the Heintzman and stood in front of the door to the tunnel. I listened for the noise of the heating pipes. Maybe the Virgin had switched off the plant for the night. That would be just like her—cutting costs. And then I heard the familiar banging clatter of the heat rushing down the pipes. I whispered anxiously, "Paulie! Paulie! Are you in there?"

I heard somebody panting. Panting hard. Mouse, sharpen up. It's you, I scolded myself. And only you who is making that sound. I called Paulie's name again. No answer. The atmosphere felt strange. As if I weren't alone in Mrs. Peddie's room. As if something waited for me behind that corniced door. I couldn't say for sure just what. But something.

In my mind, I heard Paulie's voice: Oh, Mouse, you're just a scaredy-cat. Open the door and go down. I turned the knob, hoping the door was locked. If I opened it, would I see Viola's ghost again? Or was something more truly horrible than even I could imagine waiting for me at the mouth of the tunnel? Shaking, I descended the stairs slowly. I had to cover my nose so I wouldn't choke on the dusty air. I was getting good at sneaking around. Once, twice, I stopped and called Paulie, and the sound of my voice reverberated in the gloomy tunnel like the school's bell ringing underwater.

The mouth of a new tunnel. A gust of cold blew right into my face. Sharp February wind. I shivered fiercely. Where was it coming from? This tunnel sloped downward and became more zigzaggy, and darker and narrower. It was stacked with extra chairs for the auditorium, so I couldn't even squeeze up against the wall if I wanted a place to hide. I heard Sal's voice advocating caution, scolding me for my foolishness. But my own Mouse voice was telling me to go on.

Up ahead, a beam of light no bigger than a yellow eye was shining on the rusty old pipes hanging above me like tubby worms. I stopped, panting again in fear. And then I noticed Viola's custom-made tricycle upended on the ground. The light beam streamed up from the antique headlamp on the handlebars. Strewn on the ground around the bike were the contents of the old headmistress's cycling trunk—mudguards, steering rods, trumpet-shaped horns, and tire glue.

Paulie was on her knees in the middle of the mess of tools and old bicycle parts. She was holding a box in her hands. When she saw me, she pushed the box back into the shadows.

"Bradford, is that you?"

Paulie came over to me and shook my arm. "Something terrible has happened." Her voice sounded unnaturally earnest, and I felt a little chill.

"Did you hurt yourself?"

"It's not me, it's Sergeant. He fell against one of the heating pipes."

"Sergeant?" I noticed I was gasping.

"You've got to save him—the way you did Tory."

"What are you talking about?"

"Mouth-to-mouth. You know." Paulie was yanking my arm so hard, she was hurting me. "First-aid."

"Where is he?"

"Farther down the tunnel. Oh, Bradford, hurry. Maybe he's not dead yet."

I clomped down the old passageway, trying my best to keep up with Paulie, who was taking giant strides.

51

Sergeant's body was about four hundred yards farther down the tunnel. He lay spread-eagled across a broken flow pipe, still made up as Viola Higgs in a funny black dress with a lace bib. He wasn't wearing the wig he'd had on when Paulie and I had first seen him up in the tower. It was a little hard to see how hurt he was, because it was very hot and misty in the tunnel and the noise of escaping steam made me feel like I was standing inside a boiling kettle. Light seemed to shoot off in all directions from his small body, and there was an odour I'd never smelt before. I didn't want to think about where it was coming from, because I knew it was coming from him.

"Oh, my God! Oh, my God, Paulie!" I moaned. I bent down over him, trying to be self-assured like Morley, and lifted one of his little hands to feel for his pulse. His arm had been lying across the scalding pipe, and the upper layer of skin came off in my fingers like greasy paper. I dropped his hand and my shoulders heaved, but nothing came out of my mouth. The dwarf's mouth was open and slightly twisted, as if he were disapproving of something. Both his eyes were open, and his right eye, I noticed, was purplish black and swollen, as if somebody had punched him there.

"Yeah," Paulie said. "Ding-dong, pussy's in the well."

"Don't talk like that! It's horrible." I was suddenly shouting. "We've got to go and tell somebody!"

"If we tell, they'll think we did it."

"Are you crazy, Paulie? We've got to tell Miss Vaughan. This is a dead man!"

"So you go and tell," Paulie said.

"You don't seem very upset."

Paulie didn't answer. I grabbed one of his legs. "Let's move him off the pipe so he doesn't get more burnt." Paulie sucked her teeth as if I'd done something unfair, but she picked up his other leg to help. We tried to drag him, but he slid awkwardly out of our hands, as if we were struggling to pull a mattress off a bed. We each grabbed an arm, and this gave us more leverage; we dragged him away from the flow pipe, and his bandy legs trailed easily along behind him. His head rolled on his neck like a heavy cabbage. We laid him down behind the cycling trunk, and I started to cry again as I covered him with a blanket to keep the stray steam from falling on him.

Paulie pointed toward the far end of the tunnel. "Go get Willy," she said. "He's in the garage. I'll wait here." And I ran as fast as my shaking legs would carry me off down the tunnel. I found Willy asleep in the room he shared with Sergeant above the garage. He came without arguing, bringing along a shovel, as if he were going to bury Sergeant on the spot or ward off an attacker—I'm not sure which. When we got back, Paulie was gone. I called her name again and again, and then I knew. Slowly, I lifted Sergeant's skirt.

Before I felt the nausea, I felt something like awe. Willy, beside me, said something in Czech and crossed himself.

Between Sergeant's legs was a gash as long as an appendicitis scar. Inside the gash I could see the walls of fatty red muscle, and I faintly smelled the horrible odour again. The left side of his pelvis was a light-blueberry colour. Postmortem staining, the forensic specialist said in court. But there was almost no blood on his groin and his thighs. Dead men don't bleed. I learned that in court, too. Bleeding is a vital reaction. The coroner said there was no chance

I could have saved him. The first blows with the field-hockey stick had been fatal. By the time I went down the stairs into the tunnel, he was already dead.

For a few minutes, Willy and I stood by Sergeant's corpse, like strangers loitering. I felt sick to my stomach again and confused about what to do. Finally, Willy took me to see the Virgin, who was in her housecoat making early-morning tea in her apartment. She seemed annoyed at first, as if she didn't want to be interrupted, and then she smiled when she saw who it was. And I felt complicit, the way I always felt when I noticed her affection for me. I knew I no longer had to be loyal to Paulie, but the words took a long time to come out.

52

During her trial, Paulie sat beside Miss Whitlaw, her lawyer—an older woman whose gravel-pit voice would have put the Virgin's to shame. She seemed to like Paulie, and I was glad. Sometimes Paulie smiled when the courtroom reporter passed her my notes, but she never read them—not that I could tell. Only crumpled them up and laid them on the bench beside her. And not once did she turn around to look at me. Not once. As far as she was concerned, I was a traitor even though what I told the police helped convince the jury that she was mentally unbalanced and shouldn't be found guilty of murder. Because I was only thirteen at the time, the school made a deal with the Crown, so I didn't have to testify. But the court read my statement. I sat three rows behind Paulie every day, staring at the back of her head. She'd cut her hair short now in a Prince Valiant style. It suited her. On the second-to-last day of the trial, the inspector read my statement.

HIS LORDSHIP: Am I correct in assuming that the accused female before the court, Pauline Lee Sykes, was sixteen years of age at the time of her arrest?

MR. JOCELYN: Yes, my lord.

HIS LORDSHIP: And for a number of years Pauline Sykes has wanted to be a boy and has used the name Lewis Sykes.

MR. JOCELYN: That is correct, my lord.

His Lordship: And that she became friendly with a girl whose name is Victoria Quinn, also sixteen years of age.

Mr. Jocelyn: Yes, my lord. They went steady for about a year, and all during their relationship Paulie led Victoria to believe she was a boy named Lewis Sykes.

His Lordship: Did no one else know of this special relationship?

Mr. Jocelyn: Only one other, my lord: a student at the school who roomed with the accused.

His Lordship: You don't mean to tell me that the accused was able to get away with being a boy from the inside of a girls' dormitory? [Noises in the courtroom]

Mr. Jocelyn: Yes, my lord.

His Lordship: And you have the statement of the student who knew about the relationship of the accused with Victoria Quinn?

Mr. Jocelyn: Yes, my lord. This is the statement of Mary Beatrice Bradford:

"In the fall of 1963, I roomed with Pauline Sykes. I had no reason to consider her insane—"

Miss Whitlaw: Objection, my lord. The stress that he puts on that line is inappropriate, since the statement by Miss Bradford concludes with the remark that the accused was, and I quote, "often out of her head."

His Lordship: Thank you, Miss Whitlaw. Go on, Mr. Jocelyn.

Mr. Jocelyn: "It was Pauline Sykes who tutored me in masculine behaviour—"

Miss Whitlaw: Objection, my lord. In what Pauline Sykes believed was expected of boys.

His Lordship: Thank you, Miss Whitlaw. Please continue, Mr. Jocelyn.

Mr. Jocelyn: "On the instructions of Pauline Sykes, I performed a series of tests. These included whipping the accused and letting Pauline Sykes whip me; walking along the ramparts of the school tower blindfolded—"

His Lordship: These young girls actually whipped each other?

Mr. Jocelyn: Yes, my lord. They also tormented animals together.

His Lordship: Bed-wetting, cat-getting, fire-setting—aren't these the early symptoms of a disordered mind?

Mr. Jocelyn: That is the Macdonald triad, my lord, used to predict violence in young males. Only the student, Mary Beatrice Bradford, appeared to have feelings of remorse for what they did, while the accused did not.

His Lordship: The accused had considerable influence over the Bradford girl, then?

Mr. Jocelyn: Oh, considerable, my lord. She said, and I am quoting from her statement now, "It was necessary for me to win the approval of Paulie—ah, Pauline Sykes because I wasn't well-liked at school."

His Lordship: I see. She has a physical handicap, this girl?

Mr. Jocelyn: A slightly hunched shoulder, my lord. I believe her condition has been improving under the medical care initiated by the school nurse.

His Lordship: Now, Inspector George, will you read us the statement of the person you met in the ravine near Wilbury Hollow on the night of February 23, 1964.

Inspector George: Yes, my lord. I asked, "Where do you live?" She replied, "Bath Ladies College." I then asked, "What is your telephone number?" She replied, "Six-nine-two, one-one-one-one." I asked, "What do you do there?" She replied, "I am a gardener." I then said, "Pauline, I must warn you that you are arrested on a charge of murder. Do you wish to say anything in answer to the charge? You are not obliged to say anything unless you wish to do so, but whatever you say may be taken down in writing and used in evidence against you. Do you understand?" She said yes. She then asked me what was going to happen to her, and I said I was taking her to the station and we could talk there.

His Lordship: Can you summarize some of this, Inspector?

Inspector George: Of course, my lord. At the station, Constable Jocelyn asked her if she knew what she'd done. She said, "I killed a guy, he was a homo." She smiled in a pleased way and finished eating a bag of potato chips.

HIS LORDSHIP: We are not interested in her diet at this point, Inspector.

INSPECTOR GEORGE: Yes, my lord. We asked her why she did it. And she replied that her girlfriend's family had found out she wasn't a boy, so she killed a man to get his penis, my lord.

HIS LORDSHIP: Can you read us the brother's statement, Sergeant?

INSPECTOR GEORGE: Yes, my lord. Begging your pardon, my lord. This is the statement of Richard Quinn, the brother of Victoria Quinn.

HIS LORDSHIP: Inspector George, I assume the defendant knew this boy?

INSPECTOR GEORGE: Yes, my lord. He disapproved of her relationship with his sister and challenged the defendant to prove she was a male, so she killed the school janitor to get his genitals.

HIS LORDSHIP: And when did she remove his genitals?

INSPECTOR GEORGE: After his death, my lord. Before she enlisted the help of Mary Bradford. Should I read his statement now?

HIS LORDSHIP: By all means.

INSPECTOR GEORGE: "As soon as it was light, I heard a knock on my bedroom door. It was my sister, Victoria. She said her friend Lewis wanted to prove to me he was a boy. We agreed to leave my father out of this, and I took them to the gym at Kings College. It was early Saturday morning, so nobody was there. Then I said, all right, this is what I want you to do. I dropped my pants and showed my penis. Lewis said okay, and then he dropped his pants only partway. I got angry and asked him if he knew the trouble he'd caused my sister. I said his embarrassment was nothing compared with what he'd put Victoria through.

"Then I said he had to pull his pants all the way down. He had no choice, I said, if he wanted to see Victoria again. I pulled my pants down again and told him to do it right this time. But Lewis said he'd had enough of my test. He said what he'd done should have satisfied me, and he left the gym.

"I told Victoria that I needed more proof. So my sister went after him and begged him to show all of himself to me. I could hear her crying and so on, and finally Lewis walked back and said he was willing to do what I wanted. He dropped his pants to his knees and showed himself to me. He had stuck something on him that didn't look like a real penis. It looked pale, synthetic— like rubber or something. So I said, God damn you, that's fake. You're a girl.

"Lewis got really mad then. He started to yell, 'I'm a boy, I'm a boy.' And I walked over and lifted his privates up and said I could see he was a girl underneath. And he just kept yelling, 'I'm not a girl, I'm a boy.' "

HIS LORDSHIP: Thank you, Inspector George. The genitals were found somewhat later in a doctor's bag back at the girls' school.

INSPECTOR GEORGE: That's correct, my lord. In a doctor's bag in the school's hockey shed. The genitals were smeared with glue, my lord.

HIS LORDSHIP: Glue?

INSPECTOR GEORGE: She used tire glue to stick on the genitals, my lord. I believe it was a type of cement paste.

What Happened After

I went back to Madoc's Landing a year after the court ruled that a disease of the mind had made Paulie unable to know that her act was wrong. Sal had realized she couldn't cope without me, and I think she'd begun to understand that what had happened had had nothing to do with me. It had to do with Paulie, who the psychiatrists said was incapable of abstract reasoning. Paulie was found insane under Section 16-2(b) of the old version of the Canadian Criminal Code.

Although none of the psychiatrists could agree on what Paulie's disease of the mind was, there was a consensus that one existed. And this disorder they couldn't identify had affected her ability on the night of February 23, 1964, to understand the consequences of her action.

Did Paulie feel any remorse for Sergeant and his unfinished life? I'm not certain. What I do know is this:

Paulie couldn't bear to lose Tory, so she cut off Sergeant's genitals and pasted them on with glue. Paulie did what she did for love. And Paulie wasn't a penis cutter because she envied men. It was because she didn't respect women.

As for Sergeant, I can guess what he felt. He visited me in a dream the night after his memorial service at Bath Ladies College, where the Virgin praised him for performing valuable tasks that everybody took for granted, like making sure our school clock kept the proper time.

This is what Sergeant said to me in my dream—or what I imagine Sergeant said, if you want to be strict, like Sal, about the facts:

Listen well, Mouse Bradford, he whispered, as he coasted up and down over my bed. *We have to be fair about this. Being fair is what builds character. And you have all the story now except the voice of the victim telling you what it was like to be murdered by the likes of Paulie Sykes, who surprised me in the heating tunnel and killed me dead. I never expected to be hurt by a girl, I can tell you that. Even though I'm on the small side.*

So when that lass sprang out of the shadows at me waving her field-hockey stick, I just laughed out loud and whistled a tune or two to show her how ridiculous she looked—the foolish child, trying to scare me like that. Didn't she know she was dealing with an old lake-boat hand—a sailor who was as lionhearted as his captain? "Pipe down," I said. "Do you think I'm going to quiver and quake because a girl is waving a stick at me?" And I turned my back to spite her. I was still on my bike, you see, and that's when she clubbed me for the first time. Well, I jumped off the bike, and made a grab for the stick, and she hit me again on the left side of my head, just above the eye, and I felt it snap shut and swell up all in a matter of seconds, and I couldn't see out of it. And then she struck me again and again, swearing at me as if I was a stranger and not somebody she saw every day of her life. "You fucking homo," she screamed at me. "You'll never see daylight again."

"Paulie Sykes," I said. "I'm no faggot. Can't you understand? I put on this fool costume to play a trick on the boarding school." But she didn't listen, not her. She'd gone loony, Mouse; some girls do. They can't stand the regimentation. It's like the army, you know. They strip you of your identity. That's how they control you. Oh, I've seen it many times, the way those women stamp the spirit out of the girls who come in as wild as racehorses.

Well, sir, I backed up in a hurry, but it was the wrong thing to do, because I was backing into the crawl space behind the pipes, and she followed me there, swearing and hitting everything that got in her way. And what do you know if she didn't hit one of the cast-iron fittings on the flow pipe (the bracket had rusted, you see), and the bloody pipe burst so there was steam everywhere, and I was hotter than a furnace myself in the old principal's clothes.

The heat made me reckless, so I crawled a little piece out, and didn't she charge me through the steam, whacking the pipes to the left and right. Her second blow by my eye had broke off something inside my head, and the pain was very bad. Somehow I managed to heave myself to my feet, and that's when I fell backwards, right into the old piping system.

"Help me! Oh, help me, somebody!" I called, but nobody did. And by and by, I knew there was nothing to do except close the other eye and hope it wouldn't take long. You may as well go here as anywhere else, I told myself, even if some of the lasses don't appreciate the work you do for them because they think they're from a better class.

I'm glad Paulie wasn't dressed as Lewis when she killed Sergeant with Tory's hockey stick. At least he didn't feel that he was betrayed by somebody he had treated as a friend. And I'm glad Morley couldn't read about Paulie and me in the press, although the newspapers, for their own reasons, buried the story.

Perhaps the nature of Paulie's crime was too scandalous.

Not long after Paulie's trial, my stepmother, Sal, married the ambulance driver in Madoc's Landing. Sal visits me sometimes here in Point Edward, where I live with my aunt and uncle, Margaret and the Padre Winnie Holmes. What else? Ismay Thom dropped out of school and is training to be a stockbroker. And Victoria Quinn was sent to a girls' school on the west coast of Canada. I never heard from Tory after the trial. Asa Abrams told me in a letter that everybody's saying Tory was a lesbian but I'm not so sure about that. I believe Tory was just being Tory. Maybe she knew Lewis was Paulie and pretended she didn't as part of a game they played together. And maybe not. Most of us had crushes on girls at school only the two of them just took things one step farther.

Then there's Kong. I still see him in the late-night movies and wonder what he'd say if he knew he'd inspired a two-girl fan club in the days before President Kennedy died. That leaves Paulie, who was sent to an institution near Kingston. I heard from her last month. She wrote me that her treatment at St. Agnes' Hospital was going well and said that she'd gone to a dance the other week and let a man lead. Her letter didn't sound like Paulie.

As for me, I try not to talk to Alice anymore. I'm sixteen now and mostly grown-up and although being a girl is the most difficult thing on God's green earth, it's not half-bad once you get the hang of it. My shoulder looks almost passable on account of the padded jackets and custom-built shoes my aunt Margaret likes to buy for me. These shoes are more stylish than the old orthopedic ones they made me wear at school. And the chiropractic treatment has re-duced the angle of spinal curvature because the nurse had me start it before I'd finished my full growth. I owe the school thanks for that, at least.

One more thing. Because of the murder, the merger with Kings College was put off indefinitely. And the Virgin and Mrs. Peddie moved in together when the Virgin's father died and left his house to her. It must be nice for them finally to be together. I know this sounds weird coming from me, but in their own way, the two of them were actually pretty grand. They managed to run their lives on their own terms—which is what Paulie tried to do before she went too far.

One way or another, they inspired me to be Mouse Bradford. And that's how I intend to live, as myself and nobody else, for now and always, inside the great heart of the world. But I beg your pardon. Back to the root, as Sal would say. I've told you all I know about what Paulie did to the best of my ability and there is no more tendrilling to be done—at least, as far as I can tell for now. M.B.

Acknowledgments

My first thanks go to my three editors, who have tended and fussed over the creation of Mouse Bradford with the devotion of fairy godmothers. I will always be in their debt. They are: Louise Dennys, Knopf Canada; Jenny McPhee, Knopf, New York; and *Granta* editor Catherine Eccles in England. I am also grateful to my agents Kim Witherspoon and Janet Irving; and to writer Donya Peroff, a witty and incurable storyteller, who coined the word "tendrilling"; to my daughter, Samantha Haywood (a modern young woman who is an inspiration to me always); to Jack Press at the Coroner's Office in Toronto; to the Gender Clinic at the Clarke Institute of Psychiatry, and to Elise Chenier for her research into lesbian history in Toronto. And finally, thank you to the many others whose insights and support helped me on my way: Bill Edgar, Nina Ogaard, Emily and Jane Urquhart, Dr. John Shewfelt, Clayton Ruby, Mary Ann Evans, Mary Canary, Linda Blank, Vasilis Argyros, Mary Susanne Lamont, Richard Hawley, John Irving, Nancy Willard, Robert Pack, Eve Drobot, Alberto Manguel, and Gillian Morton. I would also like to thank the Ontario Arts Council, the Canada Council, and the Bread Loaf Writers' Conference in Vermont.

A Note About the Author

Susan Swan's last novel, *The Wives of Bath*, was recently listed in the McFarland Readers' Guide (U.S.) as one of the best novels of the nineties. It was a finalist for the United Kingdom's *Guardian* Fiction Award and Ontario's Trillium Book Award. *Lost and Delirious*, a film based on this novel, was featured as a Premiere Selection at the 2001 Sundance Film Festival and was also screened at the Berlin International Film Festival. Susan Swan's fiction has been published internationally, her stories have appeared in *Granta* and *Ms.* magazine, and her novel *The Biggest Modern Woman of the World* was a Finalist for the Governor General's Award. Susan Swan is an associate professor of Humanities at York University, Ontario, Canada, and was chosen as the Robarts Millennial Scholar for 1999–2000. She lives in Toronto.

A Note on the Type

This book was set in ITC Galliard, a typeface drawn by Matthew Carter for the Mergenthaler Linotype Company in 1978.

Carter, one of the foremost type designers of the twentieth century, studied and worked with historic hand-cut punches before designing typefaces for Linotype, film and digital composition. He based his Galliard design on sixteenth-century types by Robert Granjon. Galliard has the classic look of the old Granjon types, as well as a vibrant, dashing quality which gives it a contemporary feel.

Composed by ComCom,
a division of Haddon Craftsmen,
Allentown, Pennsylvania

Designed by Cassandra J. Pappas